Berkeley's Telephone

and other fictions

For Deirdre

Berkeley's Telephone

and other fictions

Harry Clifton

THE LILLIPUT PRESS
DUBLIN

First published 2000 by
THE LILLIPUT PRESS LTD
62–63 Sitric Road, Arbour Hill,
Dublin 7, Ireland
www.lilliputpress.ie

A CIP record for this title is available from
The British Library.

1 3 5 7 9 10 8 6 4 2

ISBN 1 901866 50 5

Acknowledgment is due to the editors of
Phoenix Irish Short Stories 1996 and 2000, the *Irish Times*
and the *Irish Press* 'New Irish Writing',
where earlier versions of some of these texts first appeared.

*The Lilliput Press receives financial assistance
from An Chomhairle Ealaíon / The Arts Council of Ireland.*

Set in 10.5 on 15 Adobe Caslon
Printed in England by MPG Books, Bodmin, Cornwall

Contents

Moonlighting

When I first knew him, Xavier kept telling me about the docks. I had an epic vision of the docks – forever poised at the end of a lost era of foghorns, derricks and emigrants vanishing, never to return. Their warehouses and transit sheds, rank with the ghosts of men and cattle for export, were the antechambers to huge pasts and futures. Xavier, the way he spoke of them, only added to the myth. He was literary himself. He had worked for years on the docks, as a watchman.

We had met through my friend Eugene. All of us, that autumn, were fresh from the lecture halls of universities. Superfluous men, with little to recommend us to the world. Xavier had broken with his girlfriend, and the docks suited him as a hideaway, on the pretext of literary scholarship. I was reading Schelling's *Transcendental Idealism* and dreaming up a long poem about Dublin. Eugene, like his colleagues Noonan and Fogarty, was still a professional student. Only his girlfriend Nuala, who worked on restoring the Irish names to places, had a stake in the country.

'Xavier is passing through', said Eugene, 'on his way to better things.'

On a cold grey day at the end of October, we got together in a coffee-house on Middle Abbey Street. He was between shifts, crossing the city, on his way out to the docks.

'I was an undergraduate,' he told me, 'hungry, lonely, up from the country. Someone took me to Blytheman at Safety First. He's put half of Dublin through university. You move about at first, and then get a regular spot. You settle in with your mattress and books. You put up your course prospectus and boil yourself tea. Who else gets paid for reading and sleeping anyway?'

I decided to join. One wet November night we crossed the centre of Dublin to the office of Safety First, in an attic over-looking Parnell Square. Crowds of office workers and shop assis-tants hurried home through the darkness. Blytheman, tall and white-haired, was waiting for his wife to collect him, warming his hands at an electric fire and staring out into the night. Rumours of traffic rose from the streets. Buses stopped and started in the rain. As we came in, he swivelled round and playfully aimed an ancient Civil War revolver at us.

'Xavier, good man! Terrible about the bombings in the North. Would this be any use to them, do you think?'

'Tom,' said Xavier, 'this is Charlie. He was thinking of join-ing us.'

'Charlie, good man! We pay a fiver a shift, Charlie, night or day. A nice rate, I'd say, for a nice bunch of fellows. Plenty of time for the higher stuff, the study and books …'

He broke off a moment, rapt at the perfection of life as a night-watchman. Then he began to pore through the yellowing sheets of a duty chart.

'Where could we put you? Kilmainham perhaps, the heart of

Irish history. Or Tallaght, where the hard men go. You could get the bus from the city centre (never be late there, Dinnie Hoban gets aggressive if he's not released on time). Beautiful view of the mountains, behind the factory roofs. Coolock, on the north side, would be awkward for you to get at. Xavier, you're doing Burke's Works tonight. Would that be Alexandra Road or the South Wall?'

'Alexandra Road, Tom.'

'Take Charlie down there this evening. And get him a uniform from the boxroom, would you?'

That night, on the long walk out, I took in the cold beauty of the docklands. The North Wall and Spencer Dock on one side. On the other, half-hidden by transit sheds and depots, the icy sheen of the Liffey. At Alexandra Road there was a checkpoint, and beyond, an electric wilderness of wet, gusty streets through which Harbour Police cars roamed all night, their sirens moaning. Somewhere in this wilderness, Xavier unlocked a door in a huge wall.

'This', he said, 'is Burke's Works. Never take the South Wall branch. The rats and fleas would keep you awake all night.'

We were standing in a concrete yard just large enough for a single lorry to turn in. Seagulls clung along the top of the iron gate, their feathers ruffled by the breeze off the Irish Sea. Xavier switched on the light in the blockhouse and two mice, feeding on milk thrown out by the last watchman, vanished into the darkness.

'At each of thirteen points', he said, showing me round the factory floor, 'you turn a key in a clock, to prove you were there at that time. Do it once an hour till midnight, then knock off until five in the morning.'

Except for a couple of dim security bulbs, the works were in darkness. We walked through a forest of still machinery, pits and hoists, chains rotting like creepers above our heads. On the upper levels, catwalks of rotted wood and broken windowpanes rattled in the wind. Outside was the red glare of river and docklands, the all-night droning of ships and machinery.

'This place will be phased out by next summer,' said Xavier. 'It's all being bought by the Port and Docks. The workers have been given redundancy notice. They don't care how carefully you watch the place now. No new orders. They're just finishing the work in hand.'

We stripped seating material from the half-assembled cars on the ramps and carried it back to the blockhouse for bedding. Xavier cooked soup on the grilles of the electric heater. The windows steamed up. A stink of tobacco, smoked by generations of night-watchmen, came off the brownish walls. The telephone rang and I picked it up.

'Hello?'

I made out, through a silence at the other end, the sounds of a household. Xavier took the receiver, listened, and put it down with a sneer.

'McGrath,' he said. 'The works manager, checking up. I recognize the bedlam of his kids.'

We finished the soup. I took out the poem I was working on and read bits of it to Xavier. In this city of ours, I explained, there were only the forces of commerce and religion, both exhausted, both weighing the same, like feathers and iron, on the scale of doubting intellect.

> *The dealer in feathers*
> *Has bolted an iron gate*
> *On his merchandise, and pays a policeman to stay there,*
> *And all his other business there can wait,*

I suppose, until Monday.
I walk through afternoon streets
In the centre of Dublin. It is still only Sunday,
Only the religions compete.

Xavier listened and noted the rhymes. I liked him. He was good for my self-esteem. He sat at my feet, or pretended to. Naturally, he had his own agenda. Burke and his Works had put him through college, but he would not be here forever. The ticking minutes, the grim industrial past, would be ancient Irish history. He was digging himself out of a hole. That night, he read from manuscripts by living playwrights. He had uncollected poems of Kavanagh's, and part of an unpublished novel. And in brown paper bags, the typescripts of our own slight work – Eugene's, my own, some poems by Fogarty.

We slept until five the next morning and put the carseats back in place before the daywatchman wheeled his bicycle in. He settled down, immemorially, with sandwiches and transistor, an early edition of the *Irish Independent*.

Morning was breaking, grey and wintry. Factory hands were drifting into the docklands, in twos and threes, from all across the city. We were walking against the tide – they on their way to work, we to our own nocturnal world. Middle Abbey Street, when we reached it, was still almost empty. The daily papers lay in bundles at the porches of newsagents. Shopkeepers were rolling up their metal frontages. Xavier was catching an early bus to Tallaght, for a stint of daywatching, and we split up. I sat at the counter of a coffee-house, watching the secretaries and clerks, the trim executives, swallow a hasty breakfast. The life of the city was about to go ahead without me. I felt myself dissolving into eyes and ears, a nose for poetry.

Berkeley's Telephone and other fictions

In the grey marketplace
Of Smithfield I draw breath, sit down by the weighhouse
Nobody uses
At weekends. Brown workhorses drowse
By a wholesale office – gypsies, delayed all day
From continuing, till the horsefeed stores
Throw open their doors …

Xavier I didn't see again for weeks, and then only on O'Connell bridge where our paths crossed in the morning or evening, on our way to different parts of the city. Over Christmas, Eugene joined. Noonan stopped work on his history thesis, rose up from the old newspapers in the National Library and joined. Fogarty threw in his schoolteaching and joined. For a while, it was like a conspiracy.

Over Christmas, I continued my reading of *Transcendental Idealism* in the icy glare of the docks at night, earning double time. Blytheman, however, thought I was worthy of higher things and called me in for a pep-talk.

'With your education', he said, 'we need you in one of Ireland's more forward-looking establishments. We're putting you in Future Finance. We'll leave Burke's to an undergraduate.'

I entered the future of Ireland, so to speak, through the emergency door. I was there to see without being seen. The after-hours scatter of papers on desks, the half-finished bottles of wine on the canteen tables, the cards from everywhere, pinned above hooded machines in the typing pool, stood frozen in time at two in the morning, in a Pompeian silence broken only by the gate-crashing of a drunken executive after closing time, on his way upstairs with his girlfriend.

'Would you believe it,' said O'Kelly, who looked after the day shift. 'They get paid for building Lego models all day.'

I had seen the Lego models. Red and white plastic, structure upon geometric structure, the cities of the mind that would one day shine in glass and steel and shiver in the wind off the Irish Sea on the very sites I had moonlighted on only yesterday, in a smell of engine-oil and cattle excrement. For better or worse, the country was mucking out, cleaning its own stables.

'I wouldn't lower myself to that bunch,' O'Kelly spat, going up on the balls of his feet to strengthen his point. 'O'Kelly of the Irish Army has better things on his mind.'

As winter became spring, I got used to the special silence of Future Finance at night. An ozone of power and abstraction, feeding itself endlessly through extractor fans, and the sleepless chatter of a telex machine in the small hours. The days dawned, the street outside was frozen and empty. There was an absolute silence, before the first human of the day appeared. Wild cats nuzzled against the plateglass doors. Crows and magpies hopped about fearlessly in the middle of the road. This was how it would end, in Ireland and everywhere else, the business energy spent.

Then, suddenly, Xavier moved, and I was sent to replace him in Tallaght. As a golden handshake, Blytheman had given him a wooden hut in the shadow of Grattan's parliament, opposite Trinity College, with access to cinemas, bookshops and university night-life. There he presided, in his final phase, over small-hours seminars for the disenchanted from across the road, one of them the Canadian who is now his wife. Eugene was up in Coolock, with weekend stints in Burke's. Noonan, meanwhile, was getting history at first hand in Kilmainham.

I didn't last long in Tallaght. A works manager caught me asleep on an air-bed, Schelling's *Transcendental Idealism* spread like a bible across my chest, and that was the end. I decided to retire, for a while, from moonlighting, and went to Parnell Square to collect my wages.

I had come to know Parnell Square in all its seasons: autumn drizzle, winter frost and spring bloom in the Garden of Remembrance where Blytheman walked among the flowers, escaping his creditors. He refused to recognize me in the Garden of Remembrance – only in his attic, where the unreality was mutual

'They're nice spots, aren't they Charlie? Pleasant, scenic? Ideal for the books, the reading. Of course, you won't be here forever. Dinnie Hoban went abroad too, and fought for us in Katanga. A great old soldier. He's still holding the fort in Tallaght and foaming at the mouth.'

He tittered to himself, a silver-haired schoolboy enjoying a joke at the nation's expense. While he rummaged in his jute sack full of grubby fivers, I thought of Dinnie and the others in Tallaght, whispering at night to each other down the lines, a lost republic of voices gone underground. The revolver, a relic of the Civil War, sat on Blytheman's desk as he counted out my sweaty notes. Behind us, a draught tinkled the hangers in the boxroom. Skeletons in a cupboard. Empty uniforms, through which had trooped an army of Irish ghosts

I had not been near Safety First for two months when Eugene rang to tell me he had been fired for having a woman down the docks on night shift. The woman was Nuala, on a break from Irish Placenames. It was the end of the line, he said, he was getting apprenticed to a solicitor. Xavier too had left, and was preparing for Canada with his girlfriend. Meanwhile, I still believed in my poem. I felt another stretch under Blytheman might see me from the fiftieth line to the end.

Sabbatical, the silence of God undoes
What six days industry did. In the smashed gold

Moonlighting

Of high distillery windows
Pigeons roost – John Jameson's ruined freehold,

Building land, a plot already rank
With sighing weeds. Where did his enterprise fail?
Whenever I try to think
Of the truth of sad religion, the sad truth of commerce prevails.

'Charlie, good man! How about doing Burke's for us? As nice a spot as you could find in this weather.'

It was the hottest summer for decades in Dublin. Day after day, the sky dawned cloudless and blue, and the city roasted through to darkness after eleven. In the fanlights, pigeons died of suffocation. Schools of mullet swam daily above the sluice-gates of Spencer Dock. Children leapt into the green water of the deep-water quays, for sheer relief.

That summer, the Port and Docks were demolishing the heart of the old docklands. Brickdust hung in the air with the sounds and smells of demolition, and the blue of Dublin bay showed through half-smashed buildings. Burke's too was marked for destruction – its flyblown ramps and transit shed full of gloom and unused machinery, its mouse-eaten management floors, its clock still buzzing for the workers long since laid off.

From the walls of his office, Senan Burke's round face stared out at me, the pride of a lost Ireland – the young sportsman, the sodality member, the Old IRA associate. I rummaged through his abandoned desk but found nothing with which I might reconstruct his life. I was alone at the heart of a century that was quietly falling to pieces. I was seeing into it from a strange angle, in solitude and peace.

Berkeley's Telephone and other fictions

What it must be
To be purely commercial! Sea containers to wait
Without impatience, links in a chain of pure necessity,
Consignments of haulage, huge like freight

From deepest Europe
Lying around in Smithfield, protected by the laws of
*   its own weight*
From ever being stolen.
Goods in transit, timed to disintegrate,

To return, perhaps from a limbo of disuse,
Unable ever to fail,
Knowing no other judgement, metallic and precise,
Than a weighing scale.

That the poem was a failure went without saying. But finishing it, I turned a key for the last time in the depths of Burke's Works, and left a memory-trace. I was free to move on.

Xavier came down, and the pair of us wandered around the docks on those calm summer nights. Ships were in from all over the world. Across the dark blue water their decklights blazed, and the noise of foreign music came from the cabins – Greece and Turkey, Russia and Nigeria. Sailors fished with handlines for crabs. Others passed us in the shadows, under the huge cranes, shouting in their own argot, on their way to the city centre. When we got back, there were notes in the pages of my Schelling.

Called around but you were not on duty. Why? This cannot be tolerated. I will have to ring your boss about it. I will be around later.
J. McGrath (Works Manager)

By now, there was nothing left in Burke's Works worth stealing. Anyway, like Xavier, I going away at the end of summer. At first I didn't know where, but one hot morning, crossing O'Connell bridge from the night shift, I met Noonan and a friend. The friend was wearing dark glasses. He looked bronzed, faraway. I saw myself reflected in his glasses.

'Why not come to Africa?'

'Africa?'

'Do what I'm doing and retire at thirty-five. No, make that twenty-eight.'

I never saw him again. But I did go to Africa. A hot moonlit night, the electric chirring of insects. Another page turned in *Transcendental Idealism.* And the vastness of the docklands shrinking now to a kind of innocence, as the vastness and solitude of these moonlit nights will do in time, when I move elsewhere.

Independence

Roughly on schedule, his flight droned south through the small hours. Rome to Kano, five night hours. The Mediterranean was a moonlit glitter fifteen thousand feet below. Then the landmass of Africa, the vastness of desert and mountain, blacked out visibility. Chinnakone stopped reading then, and tried to sleep in the airless heat of Economy Class, with the snorings of a man in white djellaba in the seat beside him, and chickens in cages squawking under the seat.

It was September. The flight from London was heavily booked. British expatriates, returning from home leave. Such few of them as had not, long since, been replaced by Asians like himself. At Rome, the Asians joined the flight. Crowds of them, pushing and shoving, bribing their way aboard the remaining places. Agitated fathers with large mute families, waving their paper degrees at the airline officials, getting down on their knees, protesting their penniless condition, demanding to know how they might survive in Rome until the following midnight. From

Bombay they had come, from Karachi, Colombo and Manila, lured by the chance of a living. The black officials watched them with pity, and the beginnings of contempt. You need Africa, their gaze seemed to say, but Africa can do without you.

Chinnakone was tired, after changing planes from Colombo. Tired and anxious. His loose front tooth flicked up and down when he was anxious. He of all people, an old hand at the immigration game. But he had seen the attitudes harden, over the last ten years. Nothing was easy now.

He checked his watch: they were flying due south, no need to change from European time. Dawn broke, a reddish glow, as they descended to the treeless plain of northern Nigeria, the landing-lights of Kano. The plane taxied to the terminal, a converted colonial building. Confusion began, a struggle with belongings. Chinnakone picked up his briefcase, his portable radio. He looked with pity at the obvious first-timers, their mute wives and tired crying children. For them, the shock of immigration was entering its first day.

'Nationality?'

'Ceylonese … Sri Lankan.'

A black boy about fourteen years old, in a ragged shift, fingered his passport at the immigration counter.

'Occupation?'

'Engineer.'

'Bring documents.'

'They're in my baggage …'

'No good. Can't let you into the country.'

The black boy sniffed, looking nowhere in particular. Outside, the plane took off into the dawn, on the last leg of its flight to Lagos. Chinnakone felt the heat, already at this hour, and the pressure of so many anxieties in the queue behind him. His front tooth rattled.

'How much?' he whispered.

'Five naira.'

'I'll see you outside.'

'No problem.'

The baggage arrived, to be chalked and inspected. Soldiers were everywhere, bristling with weaponry. The air was heavy with tension. Yellow bunting, pictures of Obasanjo, posters for renegades wanted dead or alive reminded him that tomorrow was Independence Day. Bad luck! He decided that this was not a time for standing on his rights. He was getting on in years, too old for clashes with the black administration.

'How much?' he whispered.

'Twenty naira.'

'I … don't have twenty naira.'

'How much you go give me?'

'Ten?'

'Bring your money.'

The soldier chalked his bags and he passed through to the transit lounge. Ten naira, twenty naira, he wasn't complaining. Compared to the thousands he had smuggled out in the last ten years – in his socks, in the underwear of his women friends, in their children's African dolls – this was nothing. His objectives were narrow and pure.

First, get every cent his contract entitled him to.

Second, get as much of it out of this godforsaken hole as possible.

Third, retire and die in his own homeland.

Looking back, he saw the earlier stages of his own fate in the

Filipinos, Pakistanis and Indians coming through. Immigrants, forced upon the world, hardened with the same will to survive.

From eight until twelve noon, he sweated on a bench in the transit lounge, waiting for his flight to the interior. In his hands, a volume of Madame Blavatsky's writings on theosophy, or world religion, lay unread. Lately, a craving for spiritual unity had begun to assert itself in him, the desire to feel he had been right all along in his conclusions about this world. And how could he be wrong, travelling as he had, and concluding that all beliefs were one belief? Sometimes, though, this neat solution seemed a political and social convenience rather than a passionate conviction maintained in the teeth of real suffering. If he believed in everything, he believed in nothing. If he had learned to blend in to every situation, might it not mean that he himself, Chinnakone, was no one in the first place?

Starving pilgrims, in their Moslem rags, slept on the airport floors and counters. It was the season of the Haj, and these, the truly poor people of the earth, were passing through to Mecca. Yet they belonged, they had dignity of place in a huge brotherhood, even as beggars. It ate into him, that disquiet, while he sat still and an old fan bandied the flies to and fro above his head.

Black-marketeers approached him.

Boys passed, balancing boxes of warm Seven-Up on their heads.

A beggar with no legs crawled up to him.

A white missioner, introducing himself as Jim Crouch, gave him a Christian address to look up.

As the hours passed, the crowd of immigrants in the transit lounge thinned out. Flights were called for Sokoto and Maiduguri in the north, for Kaduna in the west. Families of Indians and Filipinos boarded the planes, disappeared into a wilderness of heat and dust, not to reappear for years, when their leave became due, if politics allowed it.

At twelve-thirty, his own flight was finally called – to the Jos plateau, high and cool, in the centre of the country. The unpressurized Fokker bucked a little as they crossed the escarpment, feeling the onset of squalls, the dropping temperatures. They landed, at two in the afternoon, on an airstrip in the high, wild grasses of the plateau, under the biggest, loneliest skies he had ever known.

Twelve years ago, he had first taken the airport road into town. Then, it had been a red laterite track, churned into mud by the Rains. There had been no town either, outside the colonial quarter. Certainly not this sea of shining roofs, the zinc of the shanties that caught his eye on the drive in now. Then, the country hardly belonged to itself. The metals mined from the plateau went overseas, and the money lay coffered in Switzerland, under the names of European companies. Everywhere, the broken remains of sluices and cranes interrupted the skyline, where sites had been worked out and abandoned. Engineers' houses stood roofless, laid waste by the winds at four thousand feet. Among its mineral hills Jos sprawled. Independence had upstaged the colonial dream. It had become a state capital.

That first time, an old taxi had bumped him along the dirt track to a yellow tenement in the town centre. There, the Ministry of Works had set up temporary quarters. He remembered the corridors – stone-floored, urinous, cheerful, crowded with secretaries braiding each other's hair or bargaining through the windows with street traders. Relaxed, easy days, those early days of Independence. The country was rearranging itself internally, like the pieces of a jigsaw that wouldn't fit into place. With each coup, the sign outside the ministry building had been changed. He remembered himself, callow and hysterical, bursting into the Staff Officer's room that first afternoon, demanding to know why he hadn't been met on arrival, and the Staff Officer, without raising his head from the desk where he had been sleeping, ringing a bell for his driver Obekpa, and drawling out a single instruction: 'Scipio Africanus Hotel.'

Wordlessly, Obekpa had picked up his bags and carried them to a ministry car. They had bumped over potholed streets at nightfall to a two-storey house on a shanty street. Black children played naked outside it, squirting ditchwater at each other through used syringes. Inside, they had sat at a table, sharing beer and roast corn-on-the-cob while the bags were carried upstairs.

'You want a woman?' Obekpa had asked him out of politeness. 'Ten naira for a short time …'

'No.'

He remembered Obekpa's laughter, full of healthy amusement, and the tall African women hovering in the background. When Obekpa had gone, he had climbed to his room, disoriented, his head swimming, an immigrant in a raw country. That was twelve years ago and it still came back to him, the room where his first night in Africa had passed. The bare wooden table with an empty whiskey bottle on it, and his hot sleeplessness, trying to shut out the voice of one of the women through the flimsy walls.

'Don' shout … don' shout,' she was saying gently to a man who was moaning. 'See? I keep you inside me after you finish …'

Since then, he had learned the immigrant's code of survival. The first law was: remember names and addresses. Today, for instance, there had been this man Jim Crouch. He found himself directing the taxi-driver to the address he had been given, a Christian mission in the good part of town.

'We put pretty flowers on the table', the hostess was lecturing her steward when he walked in, 'because they make people happy, isn't that right?'

The steward nodded and went on arranging the flowers while she searched in the kitchen for a key to one of the empty rooms that gave onto the compound. Chinnakone sat at the table and finished the cakes left by the missioners from their afternoon tea.

The room he was given was cool and dark, with many religious objects. He had slept in places like this before, in towns and bush villages all over the country. They were spotless, and the mosquitoes never got beyond the screens stretched across the window creating a permanent green gloom, even in the brightest hours. Stewards left buckets of hot water outside each room, and the missioners appeared, washed and neat, at the communal evening meal, with whoever was staying overnight.

Now, it was Friday evening. He had the weekend to relax. Tomorrow, he would watch some of the Independence celebrations and avoid others. On Monday morning, he would collect his car at the Ministry of Works garage. It lay on blocks there, with the wheels removed and the battery drained. He would report back officially at the Ministry, get his instructions and leave for his duty station. Out there in the bush he would be his own man for a while, away from state surveillance.

He changed his clothes, read a little of Madame Blavatsky, and went for a walk. Mature trees, acacia and jacaranda, drew off sun and rain from the long avenue. In their own grounds, colonial houses decayed. Independence had emptied them of whites, and filled them again with black government personnel. Tuaregs drooped over their swords at the entrances, guarding their new masters. Through the split white stonework, lizards came and went.

There were whites still, of course. The ones at the mission, and the Bible-belt Americans flown in to evangelize the country. But they were drained, spiritually exhausted, with a look of permanent anemia. Baturai, as the Africans called them. Men with no skin.

'The Lord sent me here,' the hostess had told him, as she gave him his key. 'Whatever road you take leads to Rome, isn't that right? Rome for me is here, for the rest of my days.'

Not me, he had said to himself. He remembered his son in the States, a married dropout with a job, still pretending he needed subsistence. And the catamaran he had had shipped, at huge expense, into Sri Lanka only to see it confiscated by the state as an illegal import. And the retirement house he was building for himself and his wife in the hills behind Kandy. If it wasn't for these, he wouldn't be risking his middle age in a country like this.

Night fell quickly, at half past six, bringing with it a sharp downpour and the sound of mountain thunder. When it cleared, the stars were out, and the night was alive with the buzzings and croakings of tree-creatures. The flame-trees in the compound were dripping, and their husks lay on the ground. A steward was banging a gong slung from one of the branches, announcing the evening meal. White folk, ethereal as maternity patients in their loose tropical shirts, drifted through the darkness to the refectory.

The Reverend Tony Swan, late of West Bromwich, introduced himself from the head of the table.

'Would you thank the Lord for us?' he asked Chinnakone.

'Let us be glad we have this food,' said Chinnakone, 'this drink, this fellowship of spirit round the table, in God's name, Amen.'

The Reverend Swan tinkled a little bell. Stifled laughter came from the kitchen. Then the servants emerged, carrying bowls of macaroni and cheese, plates of salad and tomato. The missioners, having nothing to say to each other anymore, ate in silence. Only their children spoke.

'Daddy, would the atom bomb blow up England?'

'Don't know,' the answer came. 'Don't follow such things myself.'

'Would it blow up the whole Moslem pilgrimage to Mecca, Daddy?'

'Can't you stop? You're like a clock.'

'Daddy, the whole world's like a clock. We can't stop it.'

Chinnakone thanked God he'd had the sense to stay some sort of believer. Even if his beliefs originated everywhere and nowhere, they had global acceptability. Theosophy was protective colouring. It meant good food and shelter, and the undemanding company of pious souls like these with their spiritual chitchat.

Only the tea offended him. For Chinnakone, the state of the tea was like the state of the world in general. To talk tea was to talk global politics. Only a Sri Lankan could rightly understand that. It was clear from their tea that these people's awareness of the state of the world was a badly diluted version of the real thing.

On Saturday morning, a taxi brought him downtown. In the old days, there had been certain streets along here where the women made themselves available out of sheer innocence. Nowadays, though, they put a price on their sensuality. They bound their feet in thongs of gold lamé. They strutted up and pinched your arm. They demanded a drink and a cigarette first.

But sex was troubling him less, in the last few years.

He was getting careful, in his old age.

They passed a zoo full of halfdead animals, and the beginnings of a museum. Pitiful. Their first attempt to form an idea of their own past. In there were sacred objects, confiscated from the tribes; fatuous memoirs by bored colonial wives about the effect of the first gramophone on the natives; matter-of-fact accounts, by white company men, of the deportation of tribes off the plateau, with statistics of their subsequent plague, disease, death. The bible of the plateau, its Genesis, its Book of Numbers, its Apocalypse, gathered dust on the shelves in there.

Outside the department store, stationwagons caked with laterite were parked in rows. Whites, in from the bush on their monthly shopping trips. He could imagine them in there, stripping the foodracks bare. When he shopped on Monday, there wouldn't be a Western nicety left. Not a decent bar of chocolate. Not a Danish rollmop herring.

The slums swallowed them up, in noise and crowdedness. The music of dance-bands blared in the streets. As the taxi inched through, a woman with rotted teeth gestured to him, smiling, from her balcony. A man wheeled his home past, on a broken trolley. His wife and child lay inside, with the belongings. Three men struggled to get a cow into the back of a taxi that was bogged to the axles in mud. Behind it, a line of traffic hooted wildly, deafeningly. The energy and chaos of a young country sorting itself out – it made him feel old now, tired, irrelevant.

At the Polo Ground, he collapsed on a folding chair and watched the closing of the Independence ceremonies. The governor, a puppetlike figure in white military dress, was ending his speech. An appeal for social discipline. An exhortation to national unity. An allusion to the expatriates, expressing the gratitude of his country for their service. Chinnakone switched off.

The real truth would come later, in his dealings with the Ministry, in the memos at his outstation, telling him his leave had been cancelled, his home remittance reduced, reminding him who was boss.

'Eyes ... *right.*'

Ranks of schoolchildren goosestepped past the governor's podium. The whites of their eyes rolled wildly in his direction, with an attempt at formal unity. The crowd collapsed with laughter. Soldiers on Argentinian bay horses moved in to disperse them with whips and sticks, driving them back to the edge of the field.

They were the poorest people – thrilled by a meaningless spectacle.

The sun climbed to its zenith, a terrible heat emptying the public places, driving the people indoors to eating, sensuality, sleep. A taxi carried Chinnakone to the International Hotel where he lunched alone, surrounded by the unbearable dialogue of foreigners. Unbearable, because he was one of them.

'I basically lost my faith in man,' a voice beside him was saying, in a hubbub of voices. 'America? I hate the system, the way the barmen call you Mac until the next customer arrives, then forget all about you. Japan? Tokyo is like an anthill. Kick it over and see the human hordes emerging.'

'What about here?' another voice butted in.

'Nigeria? Worst country I've travelled to. In the Ministry the other day someone came up to me and said: We've come to a conclusion. Imagine that! We've come to a conclusion.'

'And Lagos ...'

'Lagos? The beggars are dropped at streetcorners by a gangster in a car. He collects the takings later on. The women cripple their children at birth, to make profitable beggars out of them.'

Rainclouds had gathered in the mineral hills to the north. The afternoon cloudburst. He watched it through the picture window on the diningroom terrace, over the remains of his meal. It moved across town towards them, blurring the roofs of the shanties below. And then it arrived, a huge natural force full of freshness and electricity, deadening the voices around him in its steady roar. Soon the Rains would be over. A last, long thunder-clap would usher in months of drought. He would weather those months at his outstation, and the wet months after them, and the whole cycle of extremes again the following year, in the knowl-edge that it would be his last.

On Sunday, the missioners rose an hour late. An hour after dawn, that is. A thin porridge was served them and they drove into the Jos hinterlands to preach the word of God. The older ones adjourned to a reading-room where inspirational literature sat unread on the shelves. Chinnakone flicked through back issues of *Newsweek* and *Time*, while elderly lady missioners in white ankle-socks reminisced.

'I was lightbearer for the church for fourteen years ...'

'... No, the chief wasn't boycotting the service. He was very ill, he couldn't get to the church ...'

'... The church was half empty ...'

'... Towards the end it filled up ...'

'... Psalm 121 ... that's the one I was thinking of ... I will lift up mine eyes up to the hills ... very appropriate to the plateau area ... so hilly ...'

Heat and the shrillness of crickets settled over the compound. The missioners went on reminiscing, quoting instances of the Lord's providence at every turn. Unable to stand it any longer, he toiled into town on foot.

Everywhere, the services were in progress. Breezeblock churches, open to every wind, were a sea of colour. Baptist preachers, perched on tiny rostra, tore strips off their congregations. They sweated, the veins on their necks stood out, their voices had a raw power no white preacher could command. Fat women unfolded endless breasts from the depths of their coloured wraps, pap-fed their babies and listened with languid eyes to the harrowing of their souls.

'There's something very much in love with you, do you know that?' the preacher suggested sweetly to them. 'You don't love it, but it loves you. Would you like to know what it is?'

They all leaned forward.

'Death!' the preacher spat at them, with a triumphant sneer. 'Death is what loves you so much! There's death in your compound, death in your bicycle, death in your hammock, death *everywhere!*'

He had been bellowing an hour at least. Many had passed out shamelessly in their seats. Others rose, their cropped heads rising and bowing in contrition, braying their iniquities to the world at large. Good and evil, laughter and misery, black and white. It frightened him, this love of extremes. All he wanted was a seat in the shade, an hour or two away from the heat of the sun.

It was four in the afternoon before he had slept off the roast beef and Yorkshire pudding of Sunday lunch at the mission. He passed early evening in a downtown picture-house, watching old films. They were showing the Queen's last visit but something was wrong. The Queen was running backwards, at triple speed. Also some Indian B films, with the image shrunk to a third of normal height. On a few of the metal chairs, locals were sleeping. They woke up when Charlie Chaplin started. Chinnakone hurried out, fearing panic and shootings at the screen.

The night was clear and cold after the evening cloudburst. Flying ants, drawn from the ground by the rain, were dying thick and fast against the naked lights of the hovels. The new moon had appeared. Moslems roamed the streets in gangs, celebrating the end of Ramadan. He dropped in for a nightcap at the Plateau Central and found a corner for himself, away from the whores in lurex milling around the flyhatch where drink was served and dusty records played.

'Turn around!' he felt a foot kicking his chair.

His front teeth started rattling.

'This is a good place to sit', the voice behind him continued, 'when you're an artist like me. To see what goes on. I've been drinking today, to celebrate Independence. I started on Native, went on to Local, then to Nationally Brewed, and now I'm on Imported.'

A blind old man, his hand on the shoulder of a child who led him, passed between the tables. He sang nasally, while the child collected alms.

'See that?' the voice behind him spat. 'That's an image of our country – a blind man led by a child. The Americans land on the moon – wonderful! Five minutes outside this town – no water, no electricity, people dying like flies!'

The foot lashed his chair again, in convulsive rage. He shrank into himself, saying nothing. He had spent his life like this, weaving and dodging between creeds and fanaticisms. How many had he met like this – the half-educated products of Independence, emancipated, but only to the point of bitterness.

'I'm giving myself time,' the voice went on, 'but I'm going to show this bloody world there's one Nigerian who can stand on his feet! Were you at the Independence parades? Haha! If you're a

Permanent Secretary, someone dinges your car and it gets in the paper. If you're a little man, the horses trample you to death and no one cares …'

At the flyhatch someone changed a record. African music pounded through the speakers, a steady beat aimed at the blood and loins. A woman glittered in the darkness.

'That's my problem,' the voice changed suddenly. 'That particular bloody whore. I tore up her photograph and she left me …'

Behind him, he heard the crash of a chair overturning. The shadow behind the voice went staggering after the woman. He left his drink and melted into the night.

There was no peace anywhere.

On Monday, he woke to the long hoot of the train setting out on its three-day journey to Maiduguri on the edge of the desert. A steward was sweeping leaves off the compound. He heard a cup of tea being left outside his door.

At the breakfast table, there was only himself and the Reverend Swan. They had little to talk about, except the government takeover of mission hospitals and the score in the Test Match at Edgebaston.

Towards noon, when the Works Yard had finally got his Peugeot off the blocks, he drove across town to the brand-new Ministry building to report back for duty. It was steel and glass now, no more benches in crowded passageways, but polished corridors, closed doors. A Filipino, his wife and two children waited to be called in by some minor official. Did they not realize that they never would be called in? Irish, Filipinos, Indians – they filled him with a sense of shame and vague identification. If they only knew the struggle ahead of them. He thanked God he'd had the sense to leave his wife and children at home. The loneliness, the going with loose women had been a small price to pay. You were really in these people's hands if you brought your dependants as well.

In the early days of Independence, when the foreigner was still god, Chinnakone had acquired a habit he still maintained, of going straight to the top. An Irish nun stood outside the Permanent Secretary's door, waiting to be called in. He stepped past her, knocked on the door and entered at the same time. The Permanent Secretary looked up unseeingly from his desk and motioned him to a seat. A new man, a graduate from an English university, if the sportsjacket was anything to go by. Still familiarizing himself with the various projects. He introduced himself and the Permanent Secretary rang for his file, offering tea while they waited.

The tea, when it came, was strong.

'We had to deport one of your people,' he said. 'About a month ago.'

'Oh?'

'Doctor John,' he said. 'For corruption.'

Doctor John? What did he mean 'one of your people'? Doctor John was an *Indian*. Couldn't he see the difference? Chinnakone felt a rush of hatred for the Indians, with their forged degrees from Kerala State, clamouring for work. The local press was riddled with articles calling for their expulsion. Was he to be tarred with the same brush?

'Actually I'm Ceylonese,' he said. 'Sri Lankan.'

'As a member of the Global Interviewing Board for the country,' the Permanent Secretary said, 'I can tell you – we are cutting down our intake from the less desirable nationalities.'

It crossed his mind to ask which, exactly, these nationalities were. The Philippines? Sri Lanka? Ireland? Newborn countries, torn apart by strife. No different from his own, if it came to that. But Chinnakone kept quiet, as he had long since learned to do.

'The Governor will be touring your area next month,' he was told.

His tooth began its rattle. The tea was scalding – he could have done with a drop of milk. The file arrived, and the Permanent Secretary leafed through it.

'Bridge broken at Mile Seven,' he read. 'New school at Mile Twenty-Two without water. No electricity at the hospital, nuns complaining.'

Well, that wasn't too bad. At least no new disaster had occurred in his absence. Only the same old running sores, still there to plague him. If the did insist on building a school at Mile Twenty-Two, why blame him if there wasn't a drop of water for miles around it? All right, they had millions in oil money to spend. And here they were, trying to impress the world, to raise themselves out of illiteracy in ten years flat. But why be so mindless about it? Why not plan? Why not listen to professionals like himself, Chinnakone, the Resident Engineer? In a month, he would be standing to attention in front of the Military Governor, at the official school opening, receiving a public slap in the face for failing to provide an adequate water supply.

And it wasn't even *his* country.

He carried his orders away with him. It was past one, and the heat-raddled clerks were dozing on their desks behind glass partitions. If they didn't care, why should he have to? He heard shouting and weeping from the Accounts Section, where an emaciated family of whites were claiming for unpaid salary.

It was too humiliating these days.

Make your money, he reminded himself, and get out sane and well.

His car was too hot to sit in. He opened the doors and windows to let the heat escape. While he was waiting, lepers and cripples surrounded him, waving bunches of bananas and tattered copies of magazines.

'*Time* and *Newsweek*!'

Last week's news, from the viewpoint of the Western powers. He had already thumbed through it, in Rome.

The supermarket was empty, its shelves stripped of provisions. What was left? A few packets of frozen bacon. Mosquito spray. Tins of Mongolian preserves. He took what he could find. The rest he could buy from the tribeswomen, where they dragged their wares in baskets to the edge of the highway. It was the season for cheap vegetables, and anyway, by the time the months of drought set in, he would no longer be eating greens. He would be eating rice and meat, unashamedly, in shanty hotels on his local main street.

Afternoon was already deepening when he set out. Three hours and a half would see him to his outstation by nightfall. His fuel gauge registered half, but he knew places along the way where black-marketeers would fill his tank if their palms were greased. Three hours and a half of cloudflown skies, savannah grasses, cornfields tall as a man. Autonomy, in a word, behind a bockety wheel. He would not come nearer than that to being free.

Where the Track Fades

Give me two hours of silence, two hours of prayer and meditation, and I could get my day in perspective out here, the young priest said to himself in the darkness. After all, this *is* Africa. Ahmadu always manages to wake me early anyhow, whether he does it on purpose or not I couldn't say. At half-five in the morning, he's already handling pots and pans in the servants' quarters, cooking for his family, checking what there is in the fridge. Making noise in any case. I must go to town for provisions soon, he said to himself. The cool of the plateau, I could do with that. I could drop in at the seminary too, see a few white faces for a change. There's still an egg or two in the fridge, and the bit of bacon should be okay if the kerosene is still keeping the whole thing cold and the stuff hasn't gone bad.

'Ahmadu,' he called in the darkness, 'a que breakfast?'

'To, fadda …'

He pulled on his undergarments and lit the day's first and most important cigarette, letting his legs dangle out under the

mosquito netting. A quarter of an hour for this, to clear his head
of the previous night's drinking. Perhaps Ahmadu is in a bad
mood over the journey, he said to himself, trying to gauge from
the minimal response of the servant whether he was angry or
acquiescent. They would drive far into the bush today. That
meant sleeping rough, on whatever mud floors were provided,
with the curse of mosquitoes hovering all night over their naked-
ness. Neither of them looked forward to these journeys, but the
priest calculated that if they didn't do one now, the rains would
make the dirttrack impassable for months. He had to remind the
outlying villages of his presence before the rains cut them off and
plunged them back in the Dark Ages again.

On the wall hung a mission map of the locality which Father
Des, his predecessor, had drawn up in his years out here. It con-
sisted mainly of rivers, all of which drained, eventually, into the
huge basin of the Niger. On one of these rivers, marked with a
red drawing-pin, was the outstation where he himself, on his first
tour of duty, was rubbing the sleep out of his eyes. Radiating outwards from the red pin, at distances scaling twenty to seventy
miles from it, a number of white pins showed the position of villages in the bush that had to be visited. Other than these functional points, the map was a comfortless blank, devoid of the least
point of reference.

Outside, dawn broke the stillness with the rustling of cocks
and hens, and the slow awakening of birds on the branches. Normally, he would go down to the river at this hour, to get the first
uprising of sun on the water, the white cattle drinking, the ablu-
tions of naked souls purifying themselves, the first sounds of conversation from the banks in the darkness, the vivid first flashes of
colour …

But today, he had to be practical.

Half a dozen quick moves and he was dressed. Two or three steps and he was on the veranda, in the completeness of his isolation again. Away before him the plains and mountains spread their pure spaces, not yet raised to the power of history, in a shock of growth after the opening downpours. The suddenness of green grass, the glossy new leaves and the smell of the earth, hit him like the first day of Creation, after the endlessness of the Dry Season.

It must have come down heavily sometime last night, he thought. Storms are like monsters here, as Father Des used to say – the black clouds building up behind the house while you look out on a blazing blue day, and taking you by surprise.

'Whatever you build,' the Bishop had warned him, 'put her arse to the east. Everything wet comes from the east in these parts.'

About time the Bishop paid us a visit, he said to himself. He owed them a visit, the people needed a visit, it would do morale a power of good. His priests were alone in their outstations, with their catechists and catechumenates, their strawroofed churches with walls of sodden matting disintegrating in the rain, and the flat, hard chanting of a congregation of illiterates at early morning mass. But thinking of the Bishop reminded him he hadn't done the year's accounts yet. That particular holy farce was still outstanding. I've overspent on beer and whiskey, but we are supposed to be hospitable, aren't we? What else am I supposed to offer visitors who leave yams and chickens at my door out of sheer courtesy? Miserly allowance the Bishop gives anyway. It wouldn't keep a decent man in drink for a week.

On the veranda lay beercans, empty bottles, the litter of the previous night's drinking. The only other white man for miles around, an agriculturalist and communist called Rawitz, as isolated out here as he was himself, had driven over for a mutual air-ing of differences, bringing with him a crate of beer. As they got drunk, they took turns with the priest's .22 rifle, shooting at a beercan in the fork of a tree, to the silent amazement of anyone local watching. And there were always locals watching. He went across in the cold light of day and took the tin down.

In the distance where the hills began, he could see the glitter of roofing where a village twenty miles out and sunk in the darkness of prehistory was catching the first light of day. Father Des researched that tribe once, he remembered. They're an introverted tribe, the Afos. The slave trade decimated them and they withdrew into the hills until the end of the Hitler war. Now they're beginning to trickle down again, to merge with the mainstream of humanity. Perhaps only old women and children will be in the village when I arrive. Who knows? The young women might have gone to the fields for the Wet Season, and the men already have left for the tin mines in the West. Father Des said that's how they managed to have such good roofs for their houses.

'Des has worked too hard here for the last twenty years,' the Bishop had told him when he first arrived. 'I'm afraid he's begun to lose his perspective on things.'

It frightened him to think of Father Des, on whom he had depended for everything in his first months here. Father Des who had established the mission, built the house with his own hands, sunk the wells for water, mapped and chronicled the locality, carried out running repairs on the pickup truck. To think of him sitting in his chair, surrounded by furniture he had built himself, uttering disconnected rubbish whose only theme was a streak of paranoid hate.

'A lot of people come to see me,' he would whine over a bottle of whiskey, 'but not to see *me* ... It's because, at the back of it all, they want something ... and sooner or later they come round to asking for it. I avoid reading these publicized authors like Hans Küng ... There's so little that's written out of personal experience ... It's all just mouthing out what they've read from other people ... *Kai!* Look at those clouds on the Afo hills. It's so clear you can see the shadows moving across the rocks ... We must go hunting together when the grass burns off ... One .22 pellet against a bushrat ... It gives them a fair chance, don't you think?'

One day, the young priest commented on the absence of lockup facilities for the village idiots who wandered naked through the local marketplace.

'Lunatic asylums did you say?' Father Des exploded. 'They'd need to stretch a roof from Cairo to Cape Town if they wanted one of *those*.'

It was noon by the time they were ready. He had a motorbike trussed in the back of the truck, his massbox, and the usual booze for the village chiefs. He went inside to thumb through the books on the shelf. Karl Rahner's *Mission Theology*? The poems of Gerard Manley Hopkins? He decided to take nothing. It would force him to communicate – to try to communicate – with the villagers, even if only from the pressure of his own isolation. It was hard to resist this temptation to bring a book into the bush with him. In overcoming it, he felt he had gained in simplicity of outlook.

You don't know what it's like for us priests, he said to himself, addressing in his mind the antagonist of the night before, the mocking, smiling Rawitz. We might have to sit in a village for three years and do *nothing*, just try to get them to trust us, without even *mentioning* religion. It looks so pointless, but that's how it's got to be done. Father Des, for all his heroism, got it wrong.

Going into a village proclaiming God, and getting put out in the sun with your hands tied behind your back. That's no use.

They were all like that, the priests of the old school. Slugging their servants in the jaw if they didn't obey. Sweating off a dry fever by drinking a bottle of neat whiskey. Drennan of Oturkpo, Osborne in Maiduguri, Mick Simmons in Kaduna.

They drove out of the mission. The truck clattered over a plank bridge across the river and swung into the bush proper. He kept his eye on the dirttrack, scored into channels by flashflooding, and a tight grip on the wheel. Every few miles the track changed colour, with the colour of the wet earth. He liked that. It appealed to something in him he lacked the repose to enquire into. That was the trouble with Africa. It even exiled you from yourself. It dispersed your energies in its vastness, heat and loneliness so that you exhausted yourself just trying to stay at square one. The truck vibrated across corrugations that the Dry Season had left in the dirttrack. Ahmadu sat in the back to make sure the motorbike didn't come loose and topple out.

The track ran in a straight line for miles, to Cana in the foothills. On either side, starved of nutrients, the soil had responded to the early rains by shooting up vegetation to a man's height and letting it die as it came to a head.

'I teach them not to plough near the river banks,' he heard the confident voice of Rawitz saying. 'When the Rains come, I tell them, the good soil will simply be eroded away. Everything has improved since they started handsowing between the stones instead of using bulls to plough up the ground.'

Hunters emerged from the tall grasses, holding a bushfowl they had killed with a stick, or a shining sheaf of fishes. Then there was no one again for miles, nothing but the dirttrack, two irregular wheelruts divided by a shock of green grass. And always the deep blue sky with its fleecy clouds, drawn across the vast savannah to the hills.

'It's the magnetic attraction of the hills,' Father Des had told him, 'that causes so much rain hereabouts.'

The clouds showed no sign of gathering into a storm. He prayed the track would be passable on the way out.

Cana, when they reached it, was sunk in the stupor of afternoon heat. Under a tree in the main square, an Islamic class was in progress. Children chanted from the Koran, overlooked by a thin, ascetic master with a stick. A monkey tied to a tree looked on sleepily. Sick children slept on bamboo mats in the shade, flies buzzing around their nostrils. On his way to the prison, the priest stopped to exchange courtesies with the Islamic master, out of necessary politics. The conversation turned, as it always did at the start of the Rains, to the high incidence of malarial fever.

'If I gave you my blood, Mallam,' the priest tried to joke, 'it would be the blood of a priest in the bloodstream of Islam. What if your son became a priest?'

'That would not worry me,' the Islamic master replied, bowing with exaggerated courtesy, moving back to his class.

Sooner or later there will be conflict between us and them, the priest said to himself. I would almost welcome it. If only I had been sent to some communist country where you know what you are fighting against, instead of this indeterminate limbo, this vacuum of a continent.

He signed himself in at the prison office. A guard in stinking uniform let him through. In the middle of the prison yard was a mango tree in full bloom. In its shade, women were cooking. The calico shirts of the prisoners were laid out to dry in the sun, stamped with numbers indicating dates of internment and release. The prisoners moped about aimlessly, like sick animals in a zoo. A few professing Christianity were put sitting on a crude bench in front of him. Big, powerful men with their caps in their hands and their heads bowed, scratching themselves unselfconsciously in the crotch, they waited for him to begin. He sat on a folding chair and read from the Bible in English, while a prisoner translated into Hausa. When the reading was over, he tried a homily.

'Here we have two stories. The first is about a woman who suffered from loss of blood. She approached Christ, touched the hem of his garment and was cured ...'

His words were met with blank inscrutable calm. Silence. One of the prisoners leaned across and touched the knee of another for illustration.

'We must never be afraid to ask God for what we need,' he continued. 'We must not be ashamed, even though others may laugh at us for our Christian beliefs. We must please God, not other men.'

There was silence. Would it be too much to hope for some response? Some discussion in Hausa?

Evidently it would.

'That's all for today,' the priest said.

No one moved.

'Well done,' he said quietly.

Silence.

'That's all for today,' he repeated.

The first to be taken away was a leprosy case, back to his isolation cell, a mud cavity in the prison wall around which hung the smell of excrement. A fat little policewoman blew a whistle and the rest dispersed, as wordlessly as they had assembled.

The priest signed himself out.

*

They took the left fork after Cana and followed the track along the foothills, which were brilliant with new vegetation. Wonderful! This time next year I'll be due my first home leave, he reminded himself. He remembered the bliss of new priesthood in London, how well he had got on with the parishioners, drinking cups of tea, waltzing with the old folk, feeling his sermons were understood by a congregation formed from the professional classes. Then, a year ago, to be sent to this godforsaken spot, where family and religious ties meant nothing, where all that stood between him and the wilderness was a kerosene fridge, the BBC World Service at nightfall, and trips to a seminary three hundred miles away.

He knew the gorge was coming. At its lip he released the gears, let the car roll down and throttled it hard to get it up the crumbling slope on the far side. Spare us from rain until I get out of here, he prayed. No Father Des now, to rescue the prodigal son when he sticks in the mud.

For the next few miles, the road levelled. The sun was at its hottest and the sweaty back of his shirt stuck to the carseat. Amazing to think of the women travelling barefoot through these valleys, with merchandise on their heads, to get to a market forty miles to the west. Father Des would be walking on his favourite mountains now, in the Lake District. In the space of a few weeks, all the priests had flown home on leave. He would be alone here through the rainy months. Before leaving, they had said prayers for him at their masses in the surrounding districts. Not much use going to the seminary for a visit, either. The priests there had flown out at the beginning of May – to their motherhouses in Rome, to parish work in the orange groves of California. Lucky buggers. They had the best of all worlds, while young priests like himself sweated out their best years on the plains, in the heat and loneliness of the outstations.

Come to think of it, even the Sisters at Our Lady's Hospital would have gone home by now. Who did that leave? Johnny Dunne in Lafia, with his shifty eyes and evasiveness from too much solitude. He won't be glad to see me on a visit. Or old Baggy-Shorts in Kagoro, with his skinny white legs and his stomach pump. Or Fergal Malone, away out in Doma. The last time I made the mistake of letting him know in advance I was coming. He just had time to skedaddle into the bush on his motorbike, leaving a human turd in the lavatory bowl, unflushed for lack of water, as material evidence of his recent presence in the mission house.

They were going the way Father Des went.

The villagers of Afawu saw him coming long before he arrived. A gaggle of women and children, they started running from the fields to be at the chief's compound when he drove in. He eased the pickup across a shallow riverbed and revved through the slushy sand on the far side. Before it stopped, the truck was surrounded by speechless villagers.

The chief emerged, an old man smiling toothlessly, followed by elders and cringing womenfolk. For the next ten minutes, a monosyllable of greeting passed back and forth between himself and the priest. After months of diplomacy and the promise of medical aid, the chief had given permission for a priest to stay overnight in his village. Here the track faded, and in the coming days the priest would ride his motorbike through the bush to visit the outlying settlements.

A line of children carried his gear to a small house, one of three in the chief's compound. It gave onto a triangular yard where a shrine containing straw, bloodied feathers and shards of pottery stood in deference to the powers of darkness. Hens fussed about his feet and the smoke of cooking-fires clogged his nostrils.

A young girl came among the crowd following him and was plucked back savagely by an old woman.

'They are kept out of sight at that age,' Father Des had told him. He was still seeing everything through a haze of anthropology.

His living quarters were mudfloored and dry. Ahmadu set up the camp-bed in the cleanest room. Someone else removed a pile of yellowed newspapers and a pushbike leaning against the wall. A fragment of flowery English, something about Love and the Dawn, was nailed to the door. So there must be one person in the village capable of understanding me, he thought to himself. As likely as not, though, it's that boy who ran away to seek a state education.

They crowded into the narrow passageway and sat down, the priest on his folding chair, the chief and his elders on wooden stools. In the absence of other means of communication, a fresh set of greetings passed between them. Ahmadu boiled tea on a portable stove, and the priest offered sandwiches and boiled sweets to the chief, together with a glass of sweetened tea. The chief mixed the sandwiches, sweets and tea into a mush on his saucer, and lapped it up approvingly.

He seemed to guess the important things that were on the priest's mind. Without further ado, they all crossed the compound in the late afternoon heat to examine the progress of an infirmary the priest was providing materials for. On a patch of cleared ground, mud bricks dried in regular rows.

The priest kicked one of them gently. It fell apart.

'What of the cement?'

Ahmadu translated. The chief smiled benignly, with an air of innocent surprise. Bastard, the priest said to himself. Keeping the cement, using sand instead. *My* hardwon cement.

He smiled and returned the chief's bows. They greeted each other again, continued the tour of inspection.

The shadows grew longer. Sweatflies clung to his arms. He kept brushing them out of his eyes as he walked. Cardinal birds, gorgeous and red, flitted across his field of vision, unbalancing him. He could feel his bowels loosening with the heat. He longed to go into the hills and relieve himself.

'The women have their time of day for going,' Father Des had told him. 'The men go early in the morning.'

That used to really annoy Father Des, he remembered. Getting caught with his pants down by a crowd of curious villagers.

In front of his house, a man was assembling a primitive ladder. He had all the pieces, he was hammering the rungs into the main support. But there was no urgency, no pace. As if the ladder was laid out in some unearthly dimension, the deadline for its completion postponed to infinity. Would the man who eventually used it, he wondered, be climbing into a timeless space?

'He used to be craftsman,' Ahmadu said. 'Used to make statues.'

Of course he meant the fertility gods with huge breasts and genitalia, locked behind glass cases in the museum of the state capital.

The crowd paused briefly at a large straw hut. The chief and his elders beckoned him inside. The figure of a bull dominated the middle space, around which the elders donned huge wooden head-pieces and ceremonial dresses of bloodied straw and feathers. They turned to face the priest.

He raised his camera.

The darkness was split by a single magnesium flash.

'A woman is sick.'

Ahmadu was waiting outside, to take him to her. If it's psychological, dreams and suchlike, leave it to the people themselves, Father Des had said. They have their own psychology. They'll take her out to the edge of the village for three nights in succession, and throw stones into the darkness to exorcize the demon.

But it's probably pregnancy, he thought. That'll mean driving her fifty miles to the nearest hospital, coping with convulsions and cries of labour along the way, putting sand afterwards on the floor to cover traces of the placenta. He knew the routine by now. He had a clean razor in the truck, matches to sterilize the razor with, and thread with which to tie the umbilical cord when he was severing child from mother.

They usually just got up and walked away afterwards.

If only the nuns from the hospital would come out here, he thought, and show their slides on motherhood to the women. If the milk doesn't come they think it's juju, until the Sisters explain that it's malformed nipples.

Then they put the cure down to Divine Grace.

Bloody government are no help either, he reflected. Illiterate bureaucrats rubberstamping the wrong serum, annihilating whole villages by injection. When the villagers see the District Health Official driving up in his white truck, they take to the hills.

In a hut, an old woman lay dying on a pallet. Beside it, a grave had already been dug in the floor. Womenfolk rolled in the dust, crying hysterically. Sons argued angrily as to what kind of burial she should have. She seemed calm herself. Her stomach was hard as wood with the growth of some inner malignancy when he felt it. To shut everyone up, he began to intone a homily about Death, uttering whatever phrases floated into his head.

'We are all here because we love this woman …'

Ahmadu translated. He went on for some minutes in the same vein, haughty and inconclusive. They were not listening to

what he was saying, he knew that. Only to his tone of voice, his
sententious booming. When everyone had gone quiet, he handed
a packet of aspirin to the woman and left.

Only the children followed him this time, as he climbed into
the foothills behind the village. They fell back, under his insistent
waving. He had his moment of relief.

Night arrived with a dark rush of wind across the cornfield as
he came back through the waist-high stalks to the compound.
The ruins of older villages, earlier more timid migrations of the
same tribe down from the hills, showed through vegetation in
razed circles of stone, the blackened sites of fires. That was their
own past. The existing village, with its tin roofs, yellowing newspapers and a pushbike or two, was what drew them into the vor-
tex of world history.

Ahmadu had a meal cooked. They had brought with them
mainly imperishables, such as rice, tinned soup and cans of mack-
erel, a couple of plates and spoons. Later, they could fall back on
local produce, the white cassava sold in the market to make corn-
meal with.

He still found it lumpy and tasteless.

The chief and his elders returned for a last round of greeting
before retiring for the night. Out of the dark hills a hot wind
blew, and they had trouble getting the stormlantern lit. Attracted
by the light, insects crowded into the passageway where they sat.
Green stick insects, flickering about in the guttering shadows,
praying mantises stuck to the wall. He felt the pinprick of mosquito bites on his arms and ankles and braced himself for a night
of torment.

Around now, they usually introduced the question of a woman
for the night. Might he perhaps like one – or two or three – to
satisfy him in bed?

'It's part of their hospitality,' Father Des had said. 'You can't turn it down without violating common courtesy. They think we use the Sisters to satisfy ourselves anyway.'

At the seminary, he remembered, we were always told Never look directly at a woman when you're giving her Communion. Only at the floor. Then we are sent to places like this. We discover what's between our legs, and the availability of women. No wonder there are halfbreeds in the villages. And they'll be well looked after, our illegitimates. They'll be part of the great extended family we're so intent on destroying, while adding to it on the side.

Hypocrisy, as Rawitz had said last night.

They were sitting in silence. You will learn to love silence, Father Des had told him. You will learn the positive and creative thing that silence is, when you have been in Africa long enough. The chief and his elders, nodding and smiling contentedly, seemed by their attitude to agree. After a last exchange of greetings they withdrew for the night and left him alone.

He went outside, and sat by a tree at the edge of the village. The moon had come out from behind the hills, shedding a silver grey on the cornfields and wild grasses. The hot wind blew, and the grasses whispered. He felt the potency of all this, the preternatural intensity with which bits and pieces of bloodied cloth and feathers, the screeching of tethered goats and the bark of a dog drew themselves into coherence after dark.

Perhaps some day he would pass beyond the thinking stage, like Father Des, become so immersed in the whole thing as to have neither time nor energy for reflection. Father Des rose again in his mind – the face of a man punchdrunk with experience, no longer able to react or have feelings or judge what was happening, just going about the huge indeterminate tasks of his mission life like a machine, with one kidney malfunctioning, then the other one going wrong from over-drinking, then the message arriving from the Bishop, informing him that a post had been created for him instructing student priests at mission seminaries in England. He would die there, he would pine away in the sittingroom of a priest's college in London or Liverpool, while the television flickered in winter – lonely, without relations, racked by intermittent malaria.

'I come here,' Rawitz had said the night before, 'and I achieve something. I bring people practical things, the ability to give themselves happiness in this life. But *you*, you simply refer them, in their misery, to an *afterlife*.'

The wind blew, the grasses hissed. The godawful sounds of the village, screechings and bawlings, pierced the darkness at irregular intervals.

Tomorrow there would be Ara, Dogon Dutse, Muroruba ... They all had to be visited.

Before the great Rains came.

Heartlands

Mooing, the white cow was dragged to slaughter off the side of the road. It was thin and scrawny, and its hump had dried to a flap of skin hanging on one side. Pulled by a rope attached to its head, flogged by another attached to its hind leg, it twitched its ears, staggered and collapsed in the dust of the road. Flogged to its feet, it ambled unsteadily down the path, its hide bleeding, pulled and pushed by running men and boys. They smiled at Mister Amos, who had paused on his way along the road to watch the cow's last moments.

It was dusk, the only time a man could walk outdoors without too much discomfort. Amos was going to the dried-up riverbed to dig for water. He was one among dozens on the road at this hour, poor and anonymous, released from the pressure of big ambitions. But there was a difference. His time in the town was up, his time as a cog in the plan to deploy intellectuals to the remote towns in the federation. His life was his own again. In the morning, with his pregnant wife, his two children, his brother and sister and sister's husband – in short, with his current house-hold of dependants, he would journey by the hired lorry back to the village in the Benue forests where his parents, foster-parents, grandparents and great-grandparents lived, at a fork in the road.

With a final bellow and headshake and a clatter of sticks on its bloodmarked hide, the cow was shunted into the slaughtering yard. It had reached the end of its journey, a journey that began in the cattle herds of the North, browsing along the grassy margins of the desert, at the end of the last Rains. Then the long trek southward, an animal among thinning animals following the water south, followed from the north by a cold dustladen wind from the desert. This was as far south as the cattle could be driven – where the new rains, coming north, would meet them. The herdmen came to the doors of the teachers' quarters, begging for bread and water. When they were fed, they were like little children. When they were angry, as the one who cut off the missioner's head off outside his back door had been, they had no good manners at all.

Now, at the approach of the rains, they were slaughtering the weakest animals. Mammywagons, loaded with fresh hides, were parked by the roadside. On reed mats beneath them, drivers slept in preparation for their four-hundred-mile journeys the next day. Small yellow monkeys, chained to the tailboards as mascots, stared about with old, disillusioned faces. Darkness was falling. Spiritlamps glowed in Muslim compounds where families ate the flesh of goats. Unshaven, in a dirty white suit, the bank manager argued with the petrol-pump attendant. Two prostitutes, pounding yams outside the Paradise Hotel, traded insults with an Ibo across the street. A Liberian strongman, passing through on a tour of the outlying towns, was drinking himself under the table.

Amos stepped to one side as a Mercedes revved through the

street and two Fulani horses, new from the wilderness, neighed and plunged. In the back seat Alhaji Tanko sat, a wizened figure in white robe and dark glasses. The blue lights of his pharmacies glowed at every corner, dispensing drugs to the newest poor.

Blessed Ben the photographer leaned out his studio door and smiled. Good days, with so many rising from unselfconsciousness, needing images of themselves for one purpose or another. His lights were burning late. Amos smiled back and greeted him in the English that qualified them both as citizens of the world: 'Live longest!'

Only that afternoon he had taken his family to be photographed here. He and Blessed Ben had hauled the backdrop into the open, propping it against the front of the studio. An idyllic painting of jungle and blue water. The family posed in front of it, smiling. Blessed Ben put a photographic plate in, threw the black cloth over his head, and clicked. Their last day in Gitata, town of odds and ends.

He reached the bridge and let himself down the bank onto the hard sand of the riverbed, by the pilings. Avoiding stagnant pools, he dug a hole a foot deep in the sand where he stood, and watched water strain itself into the hollow, clear and good. When he had a bucketful, he hoisted it carefully on top of his head and started the long trek back.

At five the following morning, the driver idled his lorry outside the junior staff quarters. He and Amos took the last hens out of an iron coop, trussed them and placed them among the baggage, the traps and the breechloading guns at the back of the lorry. They settled there wide-eyed, clucking, alert. The driver honked his horn and Amos climbed into the cabin with his wife. The children sat on the backboards, chewing sticks of sugarcane.

It was still dark when they pulled out of the school compound, past white silent dormitories. The night-watchman slept beside his dog, an ancient sword by his side. When they were twenty miles out, jolting along the narrow lonely road, dawn began to break. It broke in a long steady line out of the east, towards which they were driving, and it brought into clarity the blue plateau ninety miles away where the state capital was, and the nearer hills and forested plains through which they would move all day to the tribal heartland.

Twenty miles further, they struck the highway south. The driver stalled the engine, yawned, got out of the cabin and went behind some buildings to squat. The family climbed out and walked across to the motor park, an area of oil-stained sand under trees, where the trucks and interstate buses changed passengers and the food was cooked. Amos examined the contents of the pots, which the women had steaming from daybreak onwards. They were not his tribe, so he spoke to them in English.

'What kind of meat?'

'Bushrat. Dog.'

He looked at the bushrat, simmering in its skilly. It had been killed a week ago, and the meat looked brown and stringy. The good juices would have gone from it, but the marrow in the vertebrae would be intact and the skilly itself nutritious. It was always better than dog, even if it was not the fresh game he could hunt out of his own forests.

'How much?'

'Fifty K.'

'You have pounded yam?'

'Yam-garri. Rice.'

He gestured in annoyance. Here, in an area that grew beautiful yams, they adulterated the yam with corn and cassava. The good yams went to the state capital, to feed the civil servants and the new rich. The ordinary people ate the hybridized leavings. He ordered enough for his family and the driver and they ate in silence, drinking water in turns from an aluminium bowl. The children went behind buildings to squat while Amos bought two loaves of sweet bread in plastic wrappers as gifts for his family elders. They climbed aboard the lorry, and took the highway south.

The road stretched ahead for hundreds of miles under powerful sun. The first rains had laid the dust of the Dry Season, and the clarity of the air delineated every twig charred by brushfires, every leaf, and the bright blue flashes of birds on the arid landscape. The soil was dead. It crumbled underfoot, riddled with a living legion of ants. The guinea-corn had long since been cut, and the stems lay crisped and rotten in the sunstruck fields, undergoing an odourless putrefaction. Rivers they crossed were gulleys of dry dirty rock, trickles of water through the wastelands of their own meanders. The past, the service to the state, was a memory now. Ahead was life as a free individual. He rested his head on the dirty leatherette of the seat as the miles flew by.

The children in the back – for them it would be different. He remembered his own childhood, one of sixty brothers and sisters by the same father. The government schools he boarded in, though his own people lived in the forests all around him. The wife he had married at twenty, the bearer of his three children. He had said goodbye to the life of his father, that tired patriarch caught in marital complexities, endless procreation. He had gone north to Kano, the walled city on the edge of the desert, and continued his education.

Each weekend, he rode north out of Kano to the outlying towns and villages. After the forests of the south, with their quarrellings between tribes, the desert was a revelation to him. The Muslim strictness, the sense of absolute law from Alhaji to beggar – no wonder Islam was transforming the young politics of his country. Out there, a hot wind blew endlessly. The only hint of water was a damp stain on a wall, or the gelid flash of a bucket being emptied. The surface was a desert, but just underground the water-table spread.

He had loved Kano. His wife and children prospered in the dry heat, the cloudless blue skies of the north. At night it was cool enough to walk along paved avenues, lined with eucalyptus, between which roared a luminous stream of traffic. In three years, he had qualified with high grades in history, and aspired to go overseas, to Europe or America. Instead, the government had sent him to the remote town of Gitata, to a college where teachers were trained.

The driver braked suddenly. Ahead of them on the road an object like the leg of a dismembered cow grew larger, assumed the shape of a naked body, the headless trunk of a dead man. Already, the vultures were feasting at several points. They hopped unhurriedly to the side of the highway as the lorry rounded the obstruction in low gear. Amos leaned out the window and spat. Tribal warfare. A mile further on, they passed a police check and entered a market town. While the driver queued for petrol, Amos bought cans of German beer and stowed them under the seat – gifts for his brothers. The sun was at full strength now and his own sweat blinded him until they were out on the open highway again, fanned by their own slipstream.

Gitata ... he had arrived there at the end of September. The Rainy Season was ending. The rivers were torrents of brown foam. The road they had bumped over was rutted, eaten away, a sea of mud. Amos had a brother studying in the college. Two others, sensing the presence of a breadwinner, arrived out of nowhere to swell the number of mouths to be fed on his monthly allowance.

He believed in God, almost as much as he believed in the power of personal effort. Each morning he prayed fervently that God would provide for himself and his dependants. For the rest of the day, he fulfilled a schedule that put the rest of the staff to shame.

'My discipline is above your wickedness!' he shouted at the students on the hot gamesfields where he kept them from the whorehouses and palm-wine bars of the town. At night, they came to talk with him at his house, by the light of bushlamps. He lay down to sleep at ten, utterly worn out. At five the next morning, he rose to attend to his poultry and set traps for the large herbivorous rats that lived in the long grass by the river. At weekends he went hunting with the sergeant of police, who lent him a shotgun. They shot bushfowl, and grasscutter in November, when the grass was burned away, and sometimes antelope, if the dogs were in good condition. Then the sergeant was transferred to another town and the hunting ended.

Every week he travelled to the primary schools outside town to supervise the student teachers. The school buildings were long and white against green hills. Long before he reached them he could hear the chanting of the children and the high, hectoring voices of the teachers.

He sat at the back of the class while the student teacher proceeded nervously with a series of lessons. Breezes passed through, creaking with shutters. Outside, women prepared food in cooking pots for the children's breakfast. Donkeys and herds of cattle ambled past. Goats bleated, nuzzling against the outside wall, peering in the door. Oblivious, the tots went on forming words on the big lines and spaces of handwriting books.

Who has seen the wind?
Neither you nor I –
The wind is passing by.

Sweat darkened their one-piece shifts, which they lifted now and then to wipe their faces. The support teacher slumped in a chair in the corner doing her nails, the whites of her eyes turned upwards in a daze. This was the nation, coming to historical consciousness.

'You can't just come to school,' the student teacher was saying, 'there must be AIM. You going to be SOMEBODY. There was aims, there was aims …'

He stopped himself from yawning, and proceeded.

'Nigeria got her independence – when?'

'Nineteen-sixty.'

'Nineteen-sixty. WHAT DAY? WHAT MINUTE? This is your country!' He began to speak about the Organization for African Unity, what it was for.

'To live a better life. To live a better life. Not to live in darkness. To, to, Repeat after me. Not to live in? …'

'DARKNESS!'

'Not to live in?'

'DARKNESS!'

'Not to live in?'

'DARKNESS!'

A bell rang, and the children swarmed across the road to get their food. After the classroom had emptied, and the child sweeping straw and unripe husks out the door had gone, and the student teachers in white had gone, Amos sat writing his reports. In ten years, the literate children of peasants would be angry young men and women, in the slums of Lagos, waiting for jobs no one could give them.

'These Yoruba people in the Ministry,' the Principal said to him the day before he left. 'Nkrumah in Ghana – a wonderful man, wonderful, but a Yoruba – headstrong, emotional – you have to do what they say ...'

He sat in the office and listened while the Principal, a middle-aged foreigner with white hair, had pleaded with him to stay, offering him a high salary, senior staff quarters, running water – all the things that formed the spiritual horizon of the expatriate.

He recalled the tempting phrases. Then he thought of the staff-room, the disinherited foreigners lying on leatherette couches, smoking, while their classes sat all morning waiting for them to appear. And the Africans, trapped in status and degree, angry at the cuts of meat given to them for the Muslim festival. All the eyewash of Speech Days, Gubernatorial Visits, Children's Day parades, hiding the loss of values. No, he had been right to leave, to disengage from that large, empty dream. He would work locally, in his own homeland. He would grow smaller and realer, closing the circle, approaching his own maturity.

The driver slowed again. Ahead was a police check. Two oil-drums narrowed the passage in the road. Sleepy policemen, in the shade of adjacent trees, waved them through. The Benue appeared, in a bluish middle distance of forested plains. They rolled up in a line of traffic to the huge structure of a suspension bridge and moved steadily across. Between the stanchions of battleship grey, Amos felt the power of the river. Two hundred miles away, it opened into a sea he had never seen. His own heartlands were the forests that bordered it for a hundred and fifty miles. It was the sources, the channels that irrigated his own backwoods, that drew him now. The sea, and what was beyond it, he would leave to others.

It was mid-afternoon. The clouds that moved across the sky were black and clearly defined, and the light of the sun was hard and yellow. The rains had arrived here, and the road was wet with puddles. Standing green pools gleamed in the forest. There was fresh grass, and the leaves on the trees were new and glossy, the first of the Wet Season. The ground here was black and fertile. Farmers were turning it into yam-heaps with their blunt mattocks. South of the bridge, the traffic spread out again, and Amos began to recognize people he knew – drivers in the cabins of lorries, road-workers or river-blind beggars by the side of the highway.

'That lorry is going to Idah,' he said, 'that one to Ayangba.'

He repeated to himself the old names – Aliade, Oturkpo, Ankpa – as they drove deeper into the tribal heartland. The trees changed, grew huger, more preternaturally real, as the lorry sped south and afternoon deepened to evening.

'Thank you, driver,' he said. 'And we must not forget to congratulate God, for delivering us safely.'

At a small village in the forest, they turned right and entered the local division. Thirty miles from his own compound, Amos gestured at the driver to stop as he greeted the first of his hundreds of relatives. The driver leaned his head on the steering wheel and waited – this was going to be the longest part of the journey. Here stood a collection of huts with a fire smoking in front of them. An old woman, wrinkled almost beyond the appearance of humanity, was sitting on the ground shelling beans. She looked up from her pile of shards and stared at him.

'Amos!'

They embraced, dumbly. Children and women came out of neighbouring huts, touching him, touching the camera by his side.

'Angba'

'Awa.'

'Aaa …'

The language of childhood filled his consciousness, as if there had never been separation, or ever would be again.

Those Who Stand and Wait

Years later, I see him again by chance as I draw money from our joint account in Baggot Street. Du Moulin. I make myself invisible, though he is safely outside the window, pushing an old bike along Haddington Road. His head is bent in to his chest and he is talking to himself, laughing silently at his own jokes. Lost to the world. A ghost in his own lifetime. Is that what comes of playing God and using women? Still, if he is a sick man, someone should take him in.

'Hogan,' I say to the teller, 'Brian and Breffni.' Young and pretty, she still remembers me after two years out of the country.

'There's been no movement in the account for months,' she says, running a quick scan on our balance.

'We've been in London for the last two years,' I tell her, pocketing the money. 'But we keep the account open. We'll be back next year.'

'You're over for a visit,' she smiles.

'Subpoena. They fly me over as a witness.'

I am losing eye-contact. She is less impressed than she should be.

'Anyway,' she says dryly, 'the account will stay open as long as it's a penny or two in the black.'

Private-sector women. They smile behind glass and you never get close to them. Look but don't touch. All smiles while they check, behind your back, on your creditworthiness. And that smell of prosperity they live in, discreet as aerosol, hanging around their air-conditioned premises. What age was I when Father opened an account for me here? Eight, I suppose, at the end of the Fifties. Tellers, columns, polished wooden floors. A smell of cigarette smoke, disallowed now. The weight of new-minted coins, rank in the palm. Poor Father. Already an ageing man, he had set us up by then, in a semi at the seaward end of Claremont Road, with the stretch of Dublin bay in the distance. Everything since those days, in the dim and distant past, has gone from reality to abstraction.

'Have a nice trip back,' she says.

Hardly through the door, I bump into Sharkey. The second person I least want to meet around here. He is on his way back to the office from the pub around the corner, where he has finished his lunch and circled advertisements for spare parts in the motoring column of the *Evening Press*. Miss Flahavan, Bearded Betty and Miss Sugrue pass on the other side of the road. All going back after lunch. And Siobhán waves, a real lady now after five years in the city. Felix, no doubt, is still in the pub. All the old faces, from the bad old days of Aliens.

'Are they feeding you well in London?' Sharkey grins.

He is looking me over, my old superior, with the cold eye of one just a rung ahead on the ladder. Still, if they gave me the Labour Attaché post in London, he must have thought well enough of me to file a good report. My loyalty, no doubt, over poor Du Moulin. No, where the Department is concerned, my prospects are good. A Principal Officer job when I come back. Trips to mainland Europe. A strip of green carpet on the lino floor of my office. Private space at last, after years in the sweatshops. But you can never be too careful.

'Look at the paunch on me,' I reply.

Quickly, he updates me on the latest. Two years Redmond got in the end, after a plea for leniency. Straight to Mountjoy prison, and bring your pajamas. I know all that, I remind him. Aliens had already been set up. It was Du Moulin who moved into Redmond's empty seat. In any case Redmond is ruined now, Sharkey says. Ruined. Only that the Minister in that previous shower intervened, it would have been the boat for England. Instead, they have taken him back at ground level, wheeling envelopes on a trolley, like old Proinsias. As for Du Moulin, at least he took the hint when it was given him, and never came back.

'There are days', I say, 'when I feel I shopped Du Moulin.'

'You did the moral thing,' he reassures me, with that paternal squeeze on the arm of his. 'Next time you're over, call in to the office. And give my regards to the wife.'

When he has gone, I have Baggot Street to myself. I feel as I did in those days as a junior civil servant when I had clocked up enough hours to take a half day off. Twelve, thirteen years ago that must have been, in the late Seventies, when the city was different from what it is now. Then, it was a place to get out of, as Du Moulin had done for a while, unless you were pressured into the Service early, as I had been. Since then, the harness has settled around my shoulders – the hours, the career, the way of life. There are times when I have looked with envy at colleagues on the fast track – university boys, economic advisors to the Minister.

But I have seen, too, how the years have taken the shine off them. By the time Du Moulin joined us, I was well dug in. He had a taste of freedom, and the harness was too tight. He could never adjust to it.

And now look at him.

I cross the road to the phone-box, and put through a call to Breffni in London. Only this morning I left her and our two young ones, for the darkness of Archway Station. God, how green it is here, after the greyness over there. Ashen, I would call it. The ashes of the spirit, as Father Paddy, our local curate over there, expresses it in his sermons. But here it is green, even now in the autumn. I take it all in as the number rings through. The bright new frontages of pubs where I celebrated promotion once, and engagement. The eating-house on the corner, with its heavy fare, where Breffni and I ate after work. We were the only jack-eens there. Everyone else was an outpatient with a cardiac prob-lem, up from the country on a visit to the redbrick hospital since closed down. The young nurses, who idled away their lunch-hour in starched white tunics here, are gone. I miss them now, as I miss my own best years. After all I courted them, under the West Stand of Lansdowne Road, at the end of so many rugby club dances, until I was thirty-four.

'Breffni,' I blurt, as soon as she picks the phone up.

'Who else.'

'Any news?'

'The young one is crying after her shot. I took her to the clinic this morning.'

'And Brian Junior?'

'He's expecting you to bring him something.'

'I will, I will.'

'Do you need to be met tomorrow?'

'Don't worry, I'll take a bus.'

'Listen – can you hear them in the background? Do you want a word with them? – I'm up to my ears at the moment. How was the court case?'

'Oh nothing. A five-minute job.'

'Good – that's Daddy on the phone, can you hear him? – I'm taking them up to Waterlow Park now, for a walk.'

'I'll see you tomorrow.'

As I leave the glass booth, I feel like someone who has just stepped out of his own life. The kind of thing I used to read about all the time in Du Moulin's journal. For a moment, I know how it feels to be Du Moulin – to be neither here nor there, to be an outsider, an onlooker. For some reason, I would give anything just now to be immersed in functionality. In the Department, in London, anywhere. Immersed in things, as Breffni is. Breffni, always so level, never subject to the highs and lows as I am. That, I suppose, is what makes our marriage work, unglamorous though it is. Marriage and work, our strength in life. Yet here I am, seized by depression in the space of a minute. Oh, not a terribly deep depression, a vague sort of gloom about things, a tightening of the sinuses, I have known far worse. At such times, and they happen more as I get towards forty, I see what Du Moulin and his journal have been about all along, and how much a part of me that strange character is.

When he was late for work in the old days, I used to watch for him from the window of Aliens. He didn't walk, he dawdled, like a man going nowhere in particular. It was others who walked, or marched up and down Baggot Street to whatever drum was beating inside them. Today it is I who dawdle along Baggot Street, on this bright, dry autumn afternoon. And something of his vertigo takes hold of me.

I stop for coffee, to bring myself round. A fastfood joint, with high stools and plastic ledges clamped to the walls. But there is one table, by the front window. On it I place a white coffee and a large creamcake – a gesture of freedom from Breffni's strictures on weight. Eating it, I already feel better. My first free moment in ages, between one thing and another. Ridiculous I should be here at all though, on a matter of such insignificance. A technicality. For the fact is that once, about ten years ago, I had taken notes at a tribunal before which a worker in an independent radio station appeared, claiming unjust dismissal. A standard meeting, one of dozens I sat in on at the time. Five of us, including the chairman Sean Prendergast and the two representatives, in a vast hearings room at the top of the house. And now, an issue of principle had arisen out of Prendergast's judgement on that day, and a court case. What could I be expected to remember of this meeting among so many? Were it not that Prendergast himself had died in the meantime, my presence would not have been required at all. But, as usual, nothing was expected of me. I was spoken for. Protected.

'You are, are you not, Brian Hogan?'

'Yes.'

'On the third of June, 1979, did you minute an Unfair Dismissals case brought by – against – ?'

'I did.'

'Are these minutes, to the best of your knowledge, a true and accurate record of the proceedings?'

'They are.'

And that was it. My day's work was over. And I sit here over a coffee, wondering would Du Moulin have had a case against us if, instead of easing him into indefinite leave, we had fired him outright. But there are conflicts too intangible for courts of law or tribunals to resolve. Another set of values is involved. One way or another, the wind blows colder now on Baggot Street, and time has passed. Where are the young economists, the brightest minds of the Eighties, who filled the pubs along here? Everyone who can has taken shelter against the cold. And for those who cannot, it is already too late.

2

Tonight I am staying in Sandymount, with Mother. She has me in Father's old highbacked chair by the fireplace. The TV is on, with evening news and sport. She has wheeled in a full meal for me, on a trolley. This although she is in her late seventies. And it isn't as if she has the house to herself even yet, with that brother of mine still hanging around.

'How's Gearoid?' I ask her. I hope not to cross paths with him at all.

She sighs.

'Is she still taking money off you?'

'I can't deny him a pint with his mates after a match in Lansdowne Road, Brian.'

'I would.'

'Anyway he's doing the garden for me. When he's not too hungover.'

I lived in this house until the day I was married. The marine end of Claremont Road, with the sea-wall around the corner, and Howth across the bay. Two sounds dominated my childhood – the moan of the foghorn on winter evenings, and the Wexford train, rattling past our cabbage patch twice a day. A standard suburban upbringing. Happy enough, you might say. We were once on TV, when the tide came over the sea-wall into our garden. Father, already old then, had retired from the civil service. All he wanted was to be left in peace in his highbacked chair while the three of us – Nessan, my elder brother, is now a chartered accountant – did our homework. One grey afternoon, he took me to a rugby match at Lansdowne Road. London Irish (who I now support) versus Rest of Ireland. Rest won, nine points to three. A try and two penalties to a penalty. Much of my life has been lived in the shadow of the West Stand; the school I went to, where Du Moulin and I first met; later on, the lounge bars of Ballsbridge, and the dance floors of Wanderers and Lansdowne rugby clubs. Just as I was getting a bit old for such places, I met Breffni. In hospital, as it happened. To be exact, she nursed me through the aftermath of a minor operation for the removal of hair from my back passage. No one can say our marriage hasn't a realistic base.

'Do you ever see Tommy these days?' Mother asks, as she takes away the trolley.

She has a soft spot for Du Moulin, ever since the night of the blizzard in winter seventy-nine, when he turned up on our doorstep. He was living around the corner at the time, in a bed-sit at seven pounds a week, and his heating had gone on the blink. He was trying to write, poor idiot, living on savings he had brought back from foreign parts. For some reason, he never took the dole. I was between girlfriends, so we saw each other over a pint some evenings – both lonely in our own ways. He has a beautiful attitude to life, Mother declared, as soon as he had left. From then on, he was fed like the rest of us when he came around. Now, it is Gearoid who sees him, on and off – so much the worse for Du Moulin.

'Haven't seen him in years,' I tell her, switching channels. I don't want to talk about it.

A restlessness seizes me. Am I going to sit here like Father, in this same highbacked chair, being fed and ministered to, growing old before my time? Mother is fine for a while, but there is not much we can talk about. Her main means of communication is food.

'I'm going out,' I tell her, 'if I can dig anyone up to go out with.'

Upstairs, I unearth an old address book with scads of women's names crossed out as soon as entered, and a list of male friends to be phoned, in descending order, on dead Saturday nights. Stokie, Old Man Murray, Lucky Burke. Married now, mortgaged into housing estates, they would need more advance than I can give them.

I will have to make do with Fergus.

Half an hour later, off we roar in his convertible. He is delighted I phoned him, delighted. We will have a few pints in Ballsbridge and take it from there. Much as I pity him, I have never hesitated to use Fergus as a last resort. The old reliable. Let's face it, Breffni and I did him a few favours in our Belmont Road days, in the first years of our marriage. How many times have we had him in for lunch and a few beers when the internationals were on television? He has always been grateful for anything that would get him through the hell of an empty Saturday.

'Did you bring me back anything special from London?' he asks.

'Would you still have space for it under your bed?' I reply in kind.

He lets out his rumble of insinuating laughter. We are back on the old wavelength. Infantile regression, after the heavy duty of matrimony. Poor Fergus, with his tonsured head and pebbleglasses, trampled in every scrummage except the one at the bar.

These days, even Ireland has left him behind, and he walks Dun Laoghaire pier of an evening, with only the great blue yonder to look forward to. And the sad thing is, he is such a decent man. A woman could do a lot worse and frequently has around here, with the loose-head props and second-row forwards some of them lead by the nose to the altar. But his manner belongs in the age of chivalry. To have had any chance, he should have been born five centuries ago.

He whisks me along Sandymount Road to the Merrion Gates, then back in towards Ballsbridge. Behind the wheel, he is surprisingly fast and aggressive, taking on cars twice as big in bursts of brinkmanship that have me glad to be well strapped in. A breakneck tour of my old stamping grounds. For fifteen years, I wove a tissue of white lies around a number of women here, in the name of romance. One, I gave an engagement ring to at sixteen. Another I absconded with to Italy, a dash for freedom ending when Mother informed me I had been called for the civil service. And the most recent disaster, with whom I had been doing a steady line for years till her girlfriend – they always have their spies – spotted me in a darkened car in the forecourt of a Dun Laoghaire nightclub, having it off with someone else. Years of innocence, the rough and tumble that teaches you about life and readies you for the moment when the right one comes along.

'Baby-snatcher,' Fergus rumbles with laughter. 'Isn't that what they called you around here?'

The lounge-bar has a quiet midweek feel. Women out with their women friends, men with their mates. The usual lizards, making it clear to their wives that home isn't what it's about where they are concerned. No way. So there *is* life after marriage, we joke to each other as we wait for the pints to draw. I have known them since schooldays, but they went on to college, while

I pen-pushed in the Corporation. These days, we have little in common. They are in the fast lane. I see it in their coats and cars, the women with fake English accents who glamourize their reception areas and hang around with them after hours, glum and silent, waiting to be spoken to. Our only common ground was the big matches, the chartered flights to Edinburgh, Cardiff and London, the drunken binges, the fake camaraderie. I envied them at the time, but thought them cheap and vulgar too. I had less money, but I felt superior.

'Hope you brought your wallet,' I say to Fergus as I put the pints down.

'Who do you think I am?' he laughs. 'Du Moulin?'

For a while we talk about Du Moulin, that bottomless fund of gossip. How he cooked nothing for himself, preferring to eat readymade dinners in places like this, at ludicrous expense. How an X-ray unit diagnosed a shadow on his lung in the bitter winter of seventy-nine. His hatred of lifts and closed spaces. How he read and read and read. His orphanhood, which none of us asked him about. And strangest of all from our point of view, how deeply women were attracted to him.

'Did I tell you I saw him today?'

'He's a candidate,' says Fergus, 'for John of God's.'

He goes up to get another couple of pints. I look over the talent, and get no response. When he comes back, the conversation shifts to other topics. How the steel broom of the Eighties is still sweeping through the building societies, where small fry like himself cling to their jobs. How Stokes had rung around in a panic when it seemed he might lose his. Stokes with a wife and two children, a second mortgage. Do I remember Stokie? Do I what. Hadn't we watched blue films in his living room with Old Man Murray a few years back? God, they were so boring. Completely moronic. Yet the wife seemed to turn a blind eye, as if they kept him off her back. No, Fergus insists, they have a lot going for them. They get better the more of them you see. Stokie has increasingly varied supply now, one of the best in Dublin.

'What about Old Man Murray?' I ask, my eyes flickering about the place in the hope of spotting an old flame. Anything to change the subject.

'Ah, that's a sad story,' he says. 'Murray's moved in with a much older woman. A Protestant, would you believe.'

'At least he's broken free of the mother.'

'About time too.'

All this is vaguely depressing. Not what I have come out for at all. Small talk, with the stream of life flowing away beneath it. As a vision of what faces me when we move back, it doesn't add up to much. And Breffni insists we are moving back. I may be a few pounds heavier and nearing forty, but I still have life in me. Yet here I am preparing to pack it in well before closing time. I drink off the dregs of the pint and suggest to Fergus that we make a move.

'Are you game', he says, 'for a quick tour of Dublin by night?'

Off we speed in the direction of Leeson Street. The darkened streets are empty of traffic, the Georgian terraces ghostly red. The clubs are still alive, faintly flickering basement signs defining the pleasure-ground in the direction of Stephen's Green. Couples and groups drift in and out of some, but it is clearly an off night. I have hit the clubs occasionally in the past – after an office session, for instance, when the younger staff were still on for a dance. But the drinks are costly, the clientele ritzy and old. Not the regular crowd at the rugby dances. A jaded extramarital set, their wedding-rings in their back pockets, out for a bit on the side.

Fergus glides us into Fitzwilliam Square.

'I like to keep an eye on what's going on here,' he says, trying to sound authoritative. 'There's always something new to look at.'

In the shadowy parts of the square, in twos and threes, women are huddled. Their cigarettes dilate quietly in the darkness. A light flow of cars moves round and round, and Fergus eases us into it, his eyes widening when a car in front pulls in beside a woman.

'I get hypnotized,' he says unnecessarily. 'I'm still here an hour later.'

Some of the women are beautiful, though their faces, when we cruise at close quarters, look tired and old. Not that I would do in a million years what the losers around here are doing and pick one up. There is the disease aspect for one thing, Fergus and I agree. Besides, as we have been taught, one should feel sorry for fallen women, thrown onto the streets by life.

'Just one more spin,' he says. 'There's a tall thin one I want to take a closer look at.'

We are just clearing off down a sidestreet when we are pulled in. Blinding light in the mirror, a single motorcycle policeman. Exactly as in my worst nightmares. A torch beams in our faces, we are ordered out, the boot is opened. Fergus hands over his papers to be looked at. Our voices as we respond to inquiries are contralto with terror. If a word of this gets out, I am utterly ruined, whatever about Fergus. The policeman pokes about, prolonging the agony, while we wait for the moment of truth.

'Gentlemen, those are nice coats you're wearing.'

'Thank you, officer.'

'Around here,' he says, 'they're called Wanker's Coats.' He looks at Fergus. 'I've seen you here before. If I see you again, you're in trouble.'

I swear again, as we drive away, that there will never be any irregularity of this kind between Breffni and myself. True, there had been that one time after an away match in Cardiff when I had shared a bed with one of the rugby women. But that had been an accident. Where we are now is different. I feel eerie, out of my depth. This is Du Moulin territory.

'He was only trying to intimidate us,' Fergus says, when he gets his breath back.

'You stupid pervert,' I snap at him. 'Don't ever do that to me again, do you hear?'

The poor sod, I can see he is hurt. But I am shaken myself. We drive back in silence, through the night streets I know like the back of my hand. The kiosks, the bus-stops where I had seen people off or waited for morning transport to work. Familiar ground, but seen now as Du Moulin might have seen it – *from the other side.* How he didn't go mad back then I wonder. Anyway, it is clear enough why his life is disintegrating at this stage. Christ, what a dismal night.

'Listen,' I tell Fergus as the night air off the sea clears my head, 'stay with us in London anytime, but keep your mouth shut about this. Think about the Twickenham game in February.'

'Brian, I'd love that,' he says, and off he drives. I know we will see him in February.

Hardly have I closed one door when Gearoid opens another. For a man in his thirties, living off his mother and the dole, he looks pretty content with himself. As well-fed as ever, his glasses tinted, his stubble pretentious as well as squalid since he started doing bits and pieces of artwork for brochures and getting ideas above his station.

'No rest for the wicked,' I say out loud, whether to him or myself I am no longer sure.

'Guess who I was with tonight,' he grins. 'He sends his regards.'

'Don't mention it.'

'He thought you might like to have this,' Gearoid laughs, handing me a notebook, 'as you've read most of if already.'

I will not be allowed to forget Du Moulin.

3

By eleven the next day I am airborne. Nothing could be further from my mind than the court case, or the future of Gearoid, or Mother's endless past. What stays in my mind, as Ireland ebbs away on the horizon, is that frightening glimpse of yesterday. The man himself, his hair already grey, pushing a wretched bike. The twisted smile, the self-communing. The difference that five short years have made.

Du Moulin – once a friend, now a shadow.

It was five years ago he joined us in Aliens. I was just setting it up. Well, not exactly setting it up, for something of the kind had always existed, but putting into place a new updated section adequate to world realities which, in spite of our best efforts, we could no longer ignore. Changes elsewhere that were sending us immigrants as never before.

'Take Hong Kong,' the Minister said to me affably, as I sat in his office with the Assistant Secretary. 'The Chinese who leave there now don't stop in Britain. They cross the channel to us, where the going is easier. Each time I eat in a Chinese restaurant, I wonder how legal these people are.'

It was one of those brief hallucinatory visits to the top of the tree that so rarely punctuated my life back then. I balanced a cup and saucer on my knee, feeling disembodied, partly out of fright, partly from a sense of release from the sweatshops I was going back to shortly, on the floors below. This was the top floor. The Minister's aides and tennis partners had moved in with their sports gear, till the next election booted them out. Only one of our own people, a whey-faced personal secretary selected from the rest of us, stayed up here. He sat in an anteroom, waiting to bring in tea on the fine service or letters for signature. The office itself was a sea of blue carpet with a commanding view of the Dublin mountains. It had a wide desk, suspiciously clear of working documents, on which unread copies of *Le Monde* and *Die Zeit* reposed. From the stark horror of the lower offices, everything up there had been rarified out, to a single-page text, to a quiet word in the Minister's ear.

'Brian,' he recalled my name with effort, 'congratulations are in order, I believe. When is the Big Day?'

'In three weeks' time.'

'Ah well,' he smiled at the Assistant Secretary, 'it's not the end of the world. You can always get light relief in Strasbourg, like the rest of us.'

They laughed their worldly laugh. I joined in, halfheartedly. 'Of course,' the Assistant Secretary added, as if the thought had just occurred to him, 'you'll be taking on Du Moulin.'

He had heard of Du Moulin. Even the Minister had heard of Du Moulin. Du Moulin had been sitting in the personnel office for six weeks, in the limbo between sections, waiting for someone to take him on. Tired of watching him read the daily papers, they had given him a couple of legal files to tidy up, a submission to draft. After all, they were paying his course fees up at the Inns. It was said that he had produced an amazingly concise submission, which had come straight to the Minister for signature. But he was restless, bored. He couldn't understand the procrastination, the delays in appointing him somewhere. What he didn't know was that no one wanted him. He had a 'past'. Nothing specific, just an attitude problem. He was always a bit naïve, poor Du Moulin.

'Yours is the desk by the window,' I told him that day in April as I showed him in. 'I'm here in the corner.'

'I know the score, Brian,' he said. But of course he didn't. He didn't at all.

To establish this section, I been given half of a large room overlooking the canal. The other half, a vipers' nest of elderly spinsters known as Disablement, had been occupied by Miss Flahavan and her underling Bearded Betty for the past quarter of a century. As I worked, I could hear the obsessive rattle of bottles as they dosed themselves – nerve pills, diet pills, blood pressure pills. Miss Flahavan had refused to leave the building on several occasions, and had rested, for brief periods afterwards, in a mental institution. Her manners, when not denouncing Bearded Betty in private to our mutual superior Sharkey, were those of a flirtatious convent girl. Together, they were putting a priest through seminary for the African Missions. And since it was Lent, above their desks, like temptation, hung unopened bags of their favourite sweets. I looked across at them and saw the last vestiges of the dark ages in Ireland. I thought with compassion of what Father had endured over a lifetime in these offices, to see us through to adulthood.

But this was the spring. I was setting up a new section, on new, enlightened lines. I had known my own dark night of the soul, the horror years at the bottom of the pile, coming in each morning to a line of parked Morris Minors, a boss in the corner whose eyes I felt boring into my shoulder blades each time I looked out the window or daydreamed. By now, though, it was me in the corner, the overseer not the overseen. My field of vision from where I sat was wide and, I like to think, fairly liberal in terms of lateness, sickness and actual hours on seat (I allowed a certain fictionalizing of this each month). Unlike most others in the Department, I had no regular tea-partners, morning or afternoon, and sometimes accompanied Felix or Siobhán, my two clericals, to the cafeteria. They were still finding their feet in the city and Felix in particular, with his speech impediment, benefited from any extra time spent on him. Whoever was left took the incoming calls while we were out of the office – the lines, after a month, were already buzzing with inquiries from worried foreigners. Besides having a new section, and Du Moulin to boot, there were the wedding arrangements and the house in Belmont Road to think of. Looking back on it now, five years later, I see how it marked the end of my old life in one moment as brief and hectic as the blossom on the trees along Pembroke Road, and as quickly blown away.

'See that old telephone beside your desk?' Felix said to Du Moulin. 'It belongs to the bank next door. If it rings, shout Fuck Off into it, slam it down, and let them pick up the flak.'

I left Du Moulin with a set of newly minted registration forms for Aliens. I wanted him to check them for spelling and layout, and by so doing, to acquaint himself with the complex tripwires of cross-reference hidden beneath their apparent simplicity, tripwires Sharkey and I had dreamed up in our drafting sessions. Sharkey, even more hung up on promotion than the rest of us, took the view that these people were leeches, parasites on our young economy. That, he said, should be our starting point. Whether or not they were legally in the country in the first place should be checked out with our contact over in Justice. They should be given the third degree in the office downstairs when they came to explain what work they were engaged in, or what business they proposed to establish. Most especially, attention should be paid to their marital status – had they married into this society at all, he wondered, or were they just darkies riding on the backs, if I would excuse the phrase, of young Irish women who were keeping them on the quiet? All this, and many other matters, legal and administrative, we thrashed out over tea-dregs and cigarette smoke in his office across the corridor, while desks and computers were moved in, and the orange plastic telephones whose incessant blip was to rule our lives, and a command structure was set up.

For the first week, I left Du Moulin alone. I took it on trust he was learning the job, sifting through what files we had, getting his mind inured to the procedures. When I looked up, he was as inscrutably hunched over his desk as we all were, for what that was worth. Spot the corpse, as the saying goes around here. But he seemed anxious to make a good impression, and I appreciated his sensitivity to the border between work and friendship – he was to be a guest at our wedding. We were in a difficult situation, we both knew. In any case, I was in no position to judge the application of my colleagues. In those busy April days, my mind was usually elsewhere too.

There was trouble at home. Gearoid, who was to be usher at the wedding, was acting up. He had never held a regular job in his life, and his attitude towards me was ambivalent. On a winter Saturday afternoon when an international was showing on television, he was part of the household. But if we bumped into each other in a Ballsbridge lounge where he had been drinking with the rugby crowd, he was sour and bullish, sarcastic towards Breffni if she was with me. Now he was threatening to boycott the wedding altogether. Nessan, who was to be my best man, was called in as head of the family to have a word with him. He is insecure, Nessan told me. He sees the years passing, and this is his way of expressing it. But my tolerance was low – there was Mother to think about, and how she would live after I left – and there were times Gearoid and I barely stood off from physical confrontation when our paths crossed, usually late at night.

Then there were the practicalities of the wedding itself – the clear soup, the roast beef to follow, the trays of sherry on arrival for the guests. We had to visit the hotel – on the north side of Dublin bay, convenient to the airport – to check the seating, the arrangements for the band. Would we want a free bar? If so, for how long? Rooms upstairs to change in? It went on and on, and although we were happy in the abstract sense, Breffni and I were probably never more separate than in those final weeks.

It had become my habit, at that time, to sleep for three or four nights a week in the new house we had bought in Belmont Road. It was still uncarpeted and bare – we were redecorating it to the skirting boards – but there was enough of our stuff there to need looking after at night. Strangely, as I lay on a crude mattress on the floorboards of what was to be our home, I found I enjoyed the bareness, the solitude, the absence of things and people cluttering my mind and my life, as they had done before and were about to do again. Those few short weeks of spring, with the light increasing in the mornings, were, you could almost say, my bachelorhood, the single life I had never known and now will never know. I look back on it sometimes with real regret, as at a glimpse of a lost life I might have found happiness in, rather than the dull contentment I grow old in now. It was sheer coincidence that I first looked into Du Moulin's journals at about this time, and found he had been sleeping on floors most of his adult life.

I admit it – all my life I have been curious about other people. Sometimes when talking with them, I see them drawing back physically, and I realize I have been leaning too close to them, especially women. Crossing the invisible line, as they say. And the same is true of anything left lying about. Since I was a child, I have peered shamelessly into people's diaries and private correspondence. In the Department, I quickly noticed, there was no shortage of these – no lack of frustrated people, their minds and personalities driven inwards by the constraints of the job, committing their thoughts on paper to the bottom drawer of their desks. Mostly it was the usual half-subversive whining of inverted souls, but Du Moulin was a different story.

In his second week, we let him onto the phones. They were blipping around us as if our very existence, announced by the advertisement in the papers, had awoken a panic in the shadowy sectors of Ireland. There is always a moment of curiosity when a new colleague handles his first enquiry, and we listened as Du Moulin dealt with this one. Clearly, he had grasped everything. His telephone manner, which was to catch on like wildfire among the clerks, made us all sit up.

'He has a great command of the English language,' Felix said reverently.

While he was still on the phone, Sharkey walked in. It was just before morning tea-break, the usual hour of his visit. He made sure of receiving greetings personally from Felix and Siobhan, casting an eye over what was on their desks as he exchanged pleasantries with them. Then he made his way over to my corner.

'Listen,' he said. 'I've had an idea.'

My heart sank. The last thing I needed on top of everything else was a new idea of Sharkey's to complicate matters just as they were sorting themselves out.

'A fee,' he said.

'What sort of fee?' I asked bleakly.

'An administrative fee,' he answered firmly. 'We should be charging them fifty quid a trick for administrative purposes.'

'We should not,' said Du Moulin with equal firmness. He had just put down the phone.

Everyone went on working, apparently. I heard the rattle of nerve pills from Miss Flahavan's end of the room. I, too, pretended to be busy.

'That's a bit strong, Tommy,' said Sharkey, adjusting an imaginary defect in his tie. 'I'd suggest you get to know the section a bit better before coming out with remarks like that.'

'Administration', said Du Moulin, 'is what we get our salaries for.'

'I might remind you, Tommy, that the previous occupant of that seat of yours is now in Mountjoy prison. Keep that in mind, would you, like a good man.'

Sharkey's bald head vanished through the door. I did not join in the outpouring of breath that followed. Inwardly, I cursed Du Moulin. I knew what the future held, and the part I would play in it. But I was damned if I would let it get in the way of my own approaching happiness. Let Sharkey worry away at it. The Redmond scandal, that amateur fraud, was his one claim to fame. He had tasted blood already. His appetite was whetted for a little more.

'That fella!' Miss Flahavan spat quietly, as Du Moulin left for his tea.

'Are we going to have our tea?' Bearded Betty intoned catatonically.

'Don't you remember?' the other one snapped. 'They confiscated the kettle. It was dripping through the floor below us. That bucket by your feet, woman, is to catch the drip from the floor above.'

'Do you know,' said Bearded Betty, 'it's been there so long I'd forgotten it.'

The pair of them trundled out to tea. Siobhán and Felix had already gone. I looked, as I so often had, at a sea of unprocessed files. The telephones blipped in the empty room – two, three at a time. It was hard to tell which were or were not ringing. I crossed the room to take a call at Du Moulin's desk and saw, among his files, some personal writing. Another journal. The umpteenth. As I was dealing with the call I sat in his swivel chair and began to read.

4

July 28, 1984
New address, new journal. Is it the energy released by change of residence? Since mid-July, when I moved in, the neighbourhood settles around me like an old jacket. Neither happy nor sad, just waiting for autumn like so often before, in the August interim while everyone is away. Fine dry weather, a cool steady breeze bringing the first leaves down. As it was in the last place, the August I moved in there. Or Sandymount, so long ago. Or any of the other places since, all over Dublin.

A Monkstown basement, with a grassy bank in front by way of outlook. Set of iron steps, at the top of which Dublin bay and the long curve of seafront to Dun Laoghaire, and the green trains shuttling through on the commuter line to Howth, its headland swimming in and out of mists and weathers, at the north end of vision. Inside, pure simplicity but for books. A room floored with bare boards, a mattress on a frame against one wall. Washbasin and mirror in one corner, worktable of rough wood in another, a battered armchair by the hearth. A kitchen with greenish light through cracked panes from the plants and grasses outside, a shower and toilet out back. I have what will satisfy me, after the ersatz gentility of the last place, the camelhair coats there who refused to return my deposit, claiming stains on the toilet bowl not there when I moved in. The owners, who live upstairs, are away on holidays in the Seychelles. Simon, a therapist from France, who inherited the house, and his wife and daughter. They have just moved in themselves, to what used to be a warren of sublet rooms through the Sixties and Seventies. There are still one or two of the old guard left. Tadhg, who teaches painting up in Thomas Street, lives in the room above mine. Abandoned wife and children for one of his sitters, Germaine, who occupies a small room at the top of the stairs. Part of the floating population of Dublin, like myself. We shared kitchens and bathrooms before, and will again. A lost, frightened woman from a foreign country. Tadhg is a father figure. Tells her little jokes to put her at ease before making love. When I hear her upstairs beginning to giggle like a child, I turn on the radio and pick up a book.

August 12

Instead of a holiday, I take days off. A dip in the sea, then drying out with the other pale bodies in the suntrap on the lee side of the sea-wall as the trains spark and whisper along to the city centre.

After swimming, as I crossed the road back to my basement room, bumped into R. Unconscious suffering, beneath solid marital exterior. Wheeling a new baby, so her crisis of last year quite clearly over. What news, she asked me, with an air of bright impersonality. No news, I replied. Ah well, no news is good news, she said, stalking off into her own realm, pretending not to know me.

I remember her differently. A panicky phone call out of the blue, a year ago, at the old address. I had not met her in ages, and there she was crying down the line. My husband neglects me. Does his job then sits behind his paper all evening. Not a word out of him. My fault perhaps. I married him for status. I was wrong, I admit it. I've slept with others since. I need affection. I think you need affection.

We met, later that night, in a place down the road from where she lived with her indifferent husband and their two children. Liaison territory. For the first and last time in my life I was part of a liaison. She seemed unconcerned when we met, turning aside to greet and chat with this or that acquaintance, as if I was not there at all. Later, as I drove her back, she indicated very smoothly a sidestreet near her house, and told me to pull in. Lifting her upper garments, she allowed me to kiss her breasts. Small nipples, that did not react under the pressure of my lips. You're fond of them aren't you, she said in a dry, detached sort of way, her mind on other matters.

The second time was no different, except it was at my place and we went all the way. She arrived dressed to kill, under one arm a bottle of wine, in her handbag a protective device. Talk to me about Theatre, she said. Talk to me about the Books you have read, the Art you appreciate. I don't go to plays, I told her, and I rarely visit galleries. Her attention turned to the little flat I was living in. The groutings in the kitchenette. The specifications of the toilet. You could have them before the courts, she commented sharply. You could get good money out of them. When we had exhausted this topic there were others and the wine. Then, in a businesslike way, she suggested we go to bed. That over, it was time to get back. This is the beginning, she said as she was leaving. No, I told her, it is the end. You have manipulated me, she cried out then, with that mock outrage I have come to despise. No, I said, it was you who wanted this. The rest would be falsehood. She walked off into the night, the sounds and lights of traffic, bitterness etched in her face. I did not hear from her again.

A distant sound. An evening train through Seapoint station. She on one side of the tracks, me on the other.

August 16
Feel clean here. No wish to invite anyone for the moment. Maybe ever. No people, no compromises. Just to sit here a while and watch the light travel around the wall. Silence, light and warmth. A space in which to breathe. Conditions for redemption of lost years.

Orphanhood. I come from nowhere, I am going nowhere.

August 22
Upstairs before going to work this morning, to check the post. On the hall table a telephone that takes only incoming calls. A tenant called Anya flitted, leaving an unpaid bill.

Two letters. One from the Inns of Court, acceptance for autumn studies. Normality. Not real normality of course, which is a kind of inner balance, established out of years and abysses that have to be worked through gradually, as I have gradually worked through mine. No, not real normality, but a necessary social mask that I crave, just now, more than anything. To be apprenticed, indentured into ordinariness, my mornings in smoke-filled rooms doing business, my evenings up at the Inns, my mask in place.

And the other one, a card from A. in Liege, on her annual visit home. That afternoon in late June, when something passed between us. Her nimbus of physical attractiveness, drawing in others besides myself. The young musicians she hangs around Dublin with, the clubbers, the undergraduates. A glamorous blow-in from the landmass of greater Europe, in her exploratory phase. The Clontarf house she shares with several others. The hours spent swimming, on the long white strand beyond Bull Island, the dunes, the tidal grasses, the huge natural amphitheatre from Howth to the Sugarloaf, with the big skies passing away. The jokes, the cook-out smoke. Levity. Spirit of play.

An enigmatic woman, emerging from a cloud. And the single word Uncertainty, in bold black print.

September 5
Bourgeois sleep of Monkstown on a Sunday. Newspaper reading, empty silence. Ritual walkers on the sea-front after lunch, among them R. Grey sea, and the lights of homing ferries from Liverpool and Holyhead. The mist-wreathed shape of Howth across the bay.

Went walking on Killiney beach again. Beachcasters' rods propped on the foreshore, lines streaming outwards. Sunday afternoon anglers in black waters. Not happy, not sad, more like something washed up by the years, by the darkness and depth of what went before.

Tea alone at the outdoor cafe. The last time this season.

September 15
Owners back. Last Thursday held open house for us in the apartment they occupy on the second floor of the building. Panorama over roofs of houses across Dublin bay. Hypermodern furniture

in glass and steel, Japanese screens, giant bookshelves crowded with art books and therapy manuals. Coffee table with magazines on good housekeeping, interior design. Easy talk, laughter and conviviality as Simon and his wife dispense drinks and snacks. Undertone of unease, beneath assumption of shared liberal values. Ours come with a price – social anathema, expulsion from family, loss of income. Theirs, on the other hand, the icing on the cake of power and money.

Imperceptibly the tone changes, the smiles freeze. Simon has it in mind, he tells us in his brisk up-front way, to refurbish the house from top to bottom, necessitating the closure of certain rooms and a reduced, if not entirely eliminated tenantry in the long run. Sure, it was a great house in the Sixties and Seventies, we all remember the camaraderie, the communal living. But there were problem people too, remember? People whose heads weren't entirely together. For instance in your room, Tommy, he turns to me, the man before you set fire to himself in his bed. He, Simon, had snuffed it out quickly and efficiently. And there was Anya, with her telephone bills to India. So there was a bit of straightening out to be done. For a start, Germaine would be moving to a mews annexe at the end of the garden. Her old room would be converted into an office. There, Simon would see clients, now he was moving into private practice. We would soon see his new plate on the door. This was all just to let us know a few transformations were going on, if we heard banging and hammering about the place – but not to worry, we were alright for the winter.

We smiled. We understood. Would we be reasonable about it all? Of course we would be reasonable about it all.

September 25
In the back garden, chatting with Germaine. Appletrees by the

high walls, windfalls on the ground. She supervises the daughter of the house, who plays in the flowerbeds. Child-minding her only work now, apart from photographic modelling. I have to be careful, she says, what kind of modeling it is.

Makes me tea in her new room. Even more austere than the old one, if that is possible. Her entire goods fit in a sailor's trunk, which she moved out a week ago. All your life you feel you are being edged out, she says wearily. Her father, a sculptor, split up with her mother. She left for Paris, lodged in a room above a sex-shop on rue Budapest. Slept with everyone, all her hair fell out. Became a camp follower of Irish folk bands and ended up in Ireland. It was Tadhg who put her together again, precariously, like one of his openwork sculptures. I will never forget what he did for me, she says, though now we are growing apart.

October 13
The Wexford train. Passes, without stopping, through the suburban stations. Steady roar, then silence. Does anyone else I know hear it the same moment I do?

5

I put Du Moulin's journal down, knowing I would take it up exactly where I had left off. A stupid habit perhaps, but one inculcated in me since childhood, when I was obliged to read, for self-improvement, a chapter of Dickens every day, till the book was finished. Reading the journal was like looking into a dark pool and seeing someone like myself reflected, but with all the blacker depths coming through. That way madness lies, I had long ago concluded, after a few fumbling attempts to look into myself on paper. I left it where I had come across it only ten minutes before – where I knew I would find it again. I salved my conscience about reading Du Moulin's private words with the knowledge that they had been written, most of them, in office time.

In ones and twos, the others drifted back from their tea break. I borrowed Du Moulin's newspaper and headed upstairs. There were only a few people about. In front of me at the counter, Bearded Betty was ordering a second cup of tea.

'You need the rodeen on your backs, the pair of you,' said Róisín behind the counter. 'To wake you up.'

'Is it very dead,' Bearded Betty turned to me with her catatonic stare, 'or is it me?'

'Both,' I answered. I had given up trying to spare her feelings.

Alone at a table Sharkey sat. Propriety dictated I sit beside him. He was so peculiarly nondescript that he actually stood out. I had noticed him in the canteen on my first day here. His hairless head, his bloodless face, the collar of his shirt perpetually curled inward like the corners of an uneaten crust. He shifted from group to group rather than having one of his own, as people in here tend to do. It took me a while to realize how afraid of him most of his colleagues were.

'Brian,' he said as I sat down, 'are you all set to walk the plank?'

'As ready as I'll ever be.'

'I don't deny that marriage is a good thing,' he said, becoming paternal. 'But by Jesus you've got to work at it. Every day of your life you've got to work at it.'

I let him ramble on about his own marriage, the money he had saved by going to Rome and standing in the queue, money he was afterwards able to invest in a car. On Saturday afternoons he tinkered with it in the garage of his house in Blanchardstown. I knew of his mania for motor mechanics. I had seen the magazines on his desk, pushed aside quickly when I entered. He was always doing little deals over the phone – my togglescrew for your carburettor, that sort of thing. His other interest in life was military history. He had retired recently from the F.C.A. with the rank of Corporal.

'To think that this day forty years ago,' he sighed. 'Hitler was defending Berlin against the Commies.'

It sounded like his masterplan for Aliens. But I didn't say so. I wanted a break from Aliens.

'I'm having a Stag tonight,' I told him. 'Join us for a drink if you like.'

'I'll give that one a miss, Brian,' he said quickly. 'I always find myself buying a round for twenty people.'

He got up to leave. I watched the back of his sand-coloured suit vanish through the door. I was the last in the empty cafeteria. I clung to my cup, to my two minutes of peace, as Róisín's dishcloth swept the Formica surfaces of tables all around me.

'The rodeen,' she said bitterly. 'That's what all of you need to wake you up. The rodeen on your backs.'

That afternoon, the phone on my desk rang. It was Sharkey again. Would I step into his office for a minute? My heart sank. Stepping in there was like stepping into water of unknown depth. To my relief it was only a presentation, which I had half expected. We were always making speeches and presentations in here, when we moved from one desk to another, blew our noses, broke wind. In a place where time has no other definition, I suppose it is the only way of noticing an event. Sharkey made a short formal speech and handed me a card and cheque, from contributions

I had furtively watched being dropped into a paper bag in the previous weeks. To my disappointment, it came to only seventy pounds. At least it would pay for the evening's drinks.

When I went back to my desk, everyone had vanished upstairs for afternoon tea. The far end was empty but for the bucket on the floor. It was quiet enough to hear water plinking into it from the kettle on the floor above. At my end, only Du Moulin sat working at his desk, or at least writing something, I didn't enquire what. I left him to look after the telephones and went for my tea.

The canteen was unusually crowded. For eight or nine to squeeze around a table for four, even with nothing to say to each other, is, in my experience, quite normal here, such is the terror of aloneness. But there are also times, and today was clearly one of them, when the tide had gone out so far that unusual fauna were exposed. Seniors who normally took tea in their rooms, battleaxes from the dispatch room and the stationary office. I saw Miss Sugrue, whose nephew dwelt among the savages of the Orinoco. A lesser tributary of the Orinoco, she corrected me. And Proinsias, our baby-faced porter, whose afternoons were spent destroying Confidential Waste, had parked his shredder in a corner and was quietly drinking tea.

'How is Blanche?' I asked after his imaginary wife as I sat down beside him. He measured me with his gaze, as if sifting the depths of my personality.

'Do you know,' he said. 'That woman has never given me a day's trouble in my life.'

For one horrible moment, it occurred to me why half the Department might be down here in the canteen. I flashed back a few years, as Proinsias rambled on about Blanche, to the time of Sharkey's marriage. The unnatural crowds, tipped off in advance.

The shadowy entrance of an ash-blonde woman in a gabardine, too fabulously good-looking to have gone unnoticed beforehand, had she been one of us. God knows, you would need a broad definition of Woman to cover some of the horrors in here. Her standing over Sharkey as she took her coat off, with only g-string, black stockings and suspenders on underneath. The whole place cheering as he was led by the ear to the head of the canteen and placed across a chair. Bearded Betty, Miss Sugrue and Miss Flahavan with her nerve condition clambering onto the tables to get a better view, as he waited, numb as a sacrificial victim, for the blow to fall.

'Has he been a good little boy before marriage?'

'No!' Miss Sugrue yelled.

'Then should we teach him a lesson?'

'Yes!'

The nonsense with the riding crop was the easy part. The hard part was answering the questions in between. By now, Sharkey was shaking uncontrollably. It was no longer funny. It was ritual humiliation.

'... And I will never ever EVER look at strange women the way I used to ...' he repeated, in a small lost voice.

Roars of approval. Proinsias, I remember, crawling between the table-legs to get at the chocolate bars behind the counter, and feeding unconcernedly while attention was elsewhere.

'Well then,' she said, 'as you are clearly a good clean-living Catholic family man in the making, I've a reward for you. The last one before marriage.'

All the men craned forward. Knock-kneed seniors clung to the wall for support. Here and there, a flashbulb went off. From her knee to her thigh, she sprayed herself with a squiggle of whipped cream.

'On your knees,' she said. 'And lick it off.'

She was gone as quickly as she had come. Wild words flew around everywhere. Why shouldn't there be state-funded brothels here anyway, Miss Flahavan was crying out to anyone who would listen. Can't they sleep together if they want to, Bearded Betty said, alluding to an affair much whispered about in the corridors. What harm is there in it, Miss Sugure agreed. They're both cripples anyway.

As the place cleared gradually, I realized that the same thing would not be happening to me. I drank my tea, lukewarm as it was, and thought of all that people are put through, in the name of marriage and having to live. Wasn't it better, then, never to get beyond the age of innocence, and stay wedded forever to an imaginary wife?

'For the fact is,' Proinsias was at me again, 'Blanche and I have never been happier.'

I strolled down Pembroke Road on a fine spring evening. The trees were a mass of white and pink blossom. Homebound traffic stalled at the changing lights. I knew it all so well. I had sleep-walked through it for half a lifetime. In a strange way, I loved it – the news kiosk, the railings and great houses of Lansdowne Road, with the stands of the rugby ground looming behind them. The taxi-rank I had used so often, last thing at night. Bus-stops, sweetshops, the fluorescent light of a filling station, public bars with their padded upstairs lounges. My stamping ground. In a few square miles, from the salt air of Sandymount to the terraces of Baggot Street, my life, such as it was, had happened to me.

My crowd were waiting, in the usual place. There were fewer than I had expected. Fergus, of course, already past redemption. Stokie, Old Man Murray, Locky Burke. The quick and the dead.

Seventy quid's worth of drink would see us through. It was easiest for Fergus, he had no domestic commitments. The rest had children, their wives kept them on a short leash. Locky Burke had married a Carlow woman and was lying low in a Lucan estate, except for working hours. He looked old and wizened. But he had always looked old and wizened. Was that what accountancy did for you? Stokie, with his blue movies, was as gentle as ever. He had lost a lot of hair since I had last seen him. I never could understand the stream of slurry that ran through such an average suburban life, so like my own. I rush home these days, Brian, he said. I love to see my daughter. Old Man Murray, too, had crawled out of the woodwork. He was still living with his mother around the corner, in a riverside cottage none of us had ever seen.

'Drink up, Brian,' he raised his glass. 'You're only middle-aged once.'

We had been at it a good hour and a half when Du Moulin dropped by, just long enough to pay his respects. No one knows the food here better than you, Fergus shouted at him as we studied the bar menu. Would you recommend the Passion Fruit Salad or the Queen of Puddings?

'Fergus,' Old Man Murray read from the evening paper, 'here's one for you. Chaperone for an elderly lady ...'

I was embarrassed on Du Moulin's behalf, and yet angry at the same time. Why should I have to split myself in half for his sake, and stand outside my own natural self as it laughed and chatted and went along with things? His icy calm unnerved me. I preferred seeing him on his own.

'Tommy,' Old Man Murray fastened on him, 'has the well gone dry these days?'

'He's a busy man,' I answered quickly, on his behalf. 'He hasn't time for any of that.'

'Beckett,' said Old Man Murray, 'is the one for me. The bit about tying your shoelaces. Which book is that?'

'I can't imagine you having trouble with your shoelaces,' I told him. Every day, through my window in the Department, I watched Old Man Murray strolling to work along the canal, at exactly ten o'clock, as punctual and dapper as Immanuel Kant.

'Tying the knot,' Fergus said. 'That's his problem.'

'Speak for yourself.'

'We can take you to water, Fergus,' I said, remembering the many times Breffni and I had dropped him off at dances, 'but we cannot make you drink.'

It was unfair, I know, like blasting a sitting duck out of water. But some people are, unfortunately, the butt of every assembly. While the others ate, I had a few quick words with Du Moulin. He had drifted in and out of the group for years, out of loyalty or loneliness I didn't know which. But he was always different. I had never met his women, whom he kept hidden away somewhere.

'Brian,' Locky Burke buttonholed me drunkenly, 'is it time for your bath yet?'

We had thrown Locky Burke into a bath of bright yellow curry the night before his wedding, ruining a good office suit. It still rankled.

'I've had a long enough day already,' I said.

I could see Du Moulin didn't want any part in what was coming. He shook my hand and said goodbye.

'Don't go,' Fergus threw after him as he left. 'You're great crack.'

At one the following morning, naked to my underwear, blackened with boot polish, bound hand and foot to a goalpost on the back pitch of Lansdowne rugby ground, my head began to clear. Above me, the posts swayed slightly in the breeze. A train sped past the back of the stands on its way to Connolly station. My childhood train, the one I knew by heart. Here, locked and barred, were the clubs I had gatecrashed time and again, on the nights of the big matches. I felt a cold wind on my exposed parts. The cold wind of middle age, of realism. I was glad I wasn't Du Moulin. I was glad I was me, myself, Mister Normal. I wondered if anyone would rescue me.

6

About this time, the effects of our first media blitz began to be felt. People started coming forward. Small, frightened people, crawling out of the woodwork. Brash, confident ones, whose money was used to talking. All the races, all the colours. I would not have believed how many could come to the surface, not to mention all those still cowering, conscience-stricken, out of sight, hoping the steel brush of Aliens would pass them by. We'll flush them all out, Sharkey said grimly. We'll be running for years. I knew from experience how long a section, once established, could stagger along, its staff going grey, cobwebs linking their chins to the desks they sat at. I only had to look at the far end of the room, where Miss Flahavan presided, to see what would happen if world events outstripped us.

For the moment, though, I was obliged to believe in Aliens. Sharkey, who belonged to an earlier epoch of Irish independence, held to it fanatically. His ideal would have been to command an F.C.A. platoon in defence of a blazing General Post Office against alien invaders of suspect race. A combination of departmental fire-drill and Search and Destroy. My own patriotism extended no further than roaring Ireland on at Lansdowne Road.

Like everyone else, I had absorbed our tragic history at school. It had gone through me, most of it, like a dose of salts. If a few outsiders came in, so what? I enjoyed a Chinese meal like the next man, or a takeaway late on Saturday night. I was no fanatic.

Du Moulin, meanwhile, took things to the opposite extreme. Every case became an issue of principle, to be followed up with Justice and reamed out with innumerable consultations, in the front office, with the persons themselves. It was he who dealt with them down there, the East Europeans and the dark-veiled Moslem women, the Chinese restaurateurs and the lovestruck students overstaying their welcome. When he bounded back upstairs, he was already on their side. Between himself and Sharkey I sat uneasily, balancing the demands of the job with the loyalties of friendship, feeling in my bones this would not, could not last.

Where Siobhán and Felix were concerned, it was their ignorance of world affairs in general, and Aliens Registration in particular, that worried me. By the first week, Siobhán had developed a fake English accent for telephone queries, in which I overheard her one day advising clients simply to get married, and solve all their problems and ours in one go. Besides, as she put it, it's a good thing to do. As for Felix, well, he was a good lad, but to be blunt, he was barely house-trained, stinking the place out with his unchanged socks and farting with tremendous power into the airless space we shared with the ladies at the far end. More importantly, from a public point of view, Felix was afflicted with a stammer. Normally loquacious, he seized up completely on the telephone, producing agonized sobs and gnashings of teeth in his efforts to explain our policy. Long minutes passed while we willed him to get the words out. I feared for the image of the section, not to mention the country in general, in the mind of whoever was calling. Usually, they hung up in despair. We decided, Sharkey and I, to take Siobhán and Felix off the phones, except for basic matters, until the section was properly under way.

So matters stood at the end of April. The telephone bleeping, answered or unanswered. An ever-mounting surf of applications, each with a clipped-on photograph of some dark-skinned man or woman jammed in a metal booth. Du Moulin and I sorted the more complex applications and I noticed between us a discreet competition to handle the more attractive women. Felix and Siobhán, instead of their usual cafeteria lunch, took to frequenting Chinese restaurants in the city centre. I had to warn them against accepting patronage, before the sense of power went to their heads. A pair of jewelled slippers arrived for Siobhan, and a multi-coloured fez for Felix. I ordered both to be returned. Not that their superiors were setting them any example. While we dealt with the riffraff in the front office, the Minister was dining out with half of Chinese Dublin, and following up on his free lunch. Every second day the door opened, and Sharkey ferried in the latest batch of requests that had landed on the Minister's desk.

'Deal with these urgently,' he said with a worried air. 'The rest can wait.'

On the afternoon before my departure, I sat across the corridor in Sharkey's office. For the three weeks I would be away, it was agreed Du Moulin would head the section – reluctantly on Sharkey's part, I could see that, but there was no alternative. Besides, he had done nothing wrong. His attitude was wrong, that was all.

'He has to take a few days' leave,' I told Sharkey, 'in the middle of May, for his law exams.'

'His law exams,' Sharkey repeated.

'Yes,' I said. 'It's been cleared from above.'

To be honest, I wondered about Du Moulin and the law. I knew the type that went in for that sort of thing, and in all the years I had known Du Moulin, he had actively avoided such people. When will you be taking silk, I ribbed him now and again over a drink. But he only smiled his noncommittal smile and changed the subject. Sharkey, however, did not see the funny side of it all. We are paying for this, he said, but we are not in a position to see if the ordinary taxpayer is getting value for his money. If they took attendance at the Inns, he said, I would have put through a discreet call to check it out.

'Keep an eye on our friend,' he warned me.

I nodded and said nothing. I wanted no fuss at this stage. Let all that come to a head in its own good time. We moved on to other matters not less problematic. There was the question of the administrative fee Sharkey wanted charged to each person for the services of the section. He had pursued it up the line and approval had come down. We are in business, he said. If they're in any doubt at all about their position in this country they'll think twice about applying when we slap this one on them. I listened and said nothing. I had seen the semi-literate minute that had gone up to the Assistant Secretary. So, unfortunately, had Du Moulin. He pronounced it in earshot of its author, while refusing to implement it if it was approved. Now that it had been, the pair of them were on a collision course.

'It's so hard,' Sharkey sighed, 'getting the perfect wording for these things.'

I looked at the typed minute on its single sheet clipped inside a file marked 'Policy'. I remembered the agonies of drafting and re-drafting, out of Sharkey's turgid ramblings. He was not one of nature's stylists.

'Reading that man's words', Du Moulin said, 'is like eating polished ricegrains. The nourishment has been scraped off. Only the lifelessness is left.'

Language, I knew, was a tricky issue with Sharkey. He had been the object of a ballad on his bald head, composed by Redmond, Du Moulin's predecessor in the window seat, and widely circulated. The balladeer now reposed in Mountjoy prison, after a six-month covert investigation by Sharkey uncovered the siphoning of public monies into a private account. The jaws of the trap had shut slowly, but everyone remembered the day Redmond had been summoned upstairs. He had taken his coat off the back of his chair and calmly wished everyone goodbye. No, Sharkey's sense of humour was restricted. He was unhappy with the free play of language in official matters.

His office overlooked the car park at the back of the building. An uninspiring view at the best of times. The bleeping bonnets of cars, Proinsias out for a fag or furtively unzipping his flies at the far wall, the wooden bar at the entrance raising and lowering itself rhythmically as cars entered or left. The state sector's phallic salute to the private sector. They had all the prettier women. I had admired their shapes swimming in the distant office lights during the tedious hours of meetings in here when Sharkey and I had ratcheted together the schemes for Aliens. He seemed to guess what was on my mind, for he leaned across paternally and tapped me on the arm.

'Brian,' he said, 'when we are ready it happens. It doesn't matter what the lady looks like. God knows, mine is nothing to write home about. But when we are ready, it happens, that's all. Look on it as the first day of the rest of your life.'

It dawned on me how carefully I had prepared for myself, over the years, an exclusion zone from which everything unpredictable was about to be shuttered forever. I knew, more or less, what I would be doing every day of my life from now on. Every weekend, every mid-morning, every two-week break in summer. I was being fed advice, calmly and reasonably, by this monster of realism across the desk. My mouth felt dry, as if I had eaten sawdust.

'There goes our friend,' Sharkey said suddenly, looking out the window.

Du Moulin was crossing to his car. Leaving early, I supposed, to be over at the Inns for his lectures. I admired his noble bearing, the straightness of his back. I thought, through a film of misery, of the depth of his secret life. His women, of whom I knew almost nothing, except that the ones I had seen him with from afar were beauties. Above all, perhaps, the whiff of freedom in his life that was about to be snuffed out of mine forever. I didn't want to broach the subject with Sharkey just yet, but Du Moulin had already spoken of taking leave at the end of the summer.

'Brian,' he said, 'would you do one thing for me when you are leaving tonight? Would you check whether our friend has taken out his key?'

Back behind my own desk, I felt easier. Here at least there were a few potted plants. None would have survived the metal and linoleum aridity of Sharkey's office. Everyone had left, into the light spring evening, except for myself and Bearded Betty at the other end of the room. We were both up to the same game, trading off our after hours for our early mornings or free afternoons, shifting the sandgrains of official time as they dribbled through the hourglass.

'So you're getting married, Brian,' she said, bolt upright and staring into space. 'Well, good luck to you.'

I thanked her. At least she wasn't delivering the kiss of death in the guise of good wishes. Put a couple of drinks in Betty and the ladies and you never knew what outrageous wildness would emerge. Sex and violence, drunken fathers, helpless mothers, the depths of Irish life they had run away from to make a life for themselves. I had known the ladies for many a year, and watched them drop into the black hole of retirement, wandering about town with newspapers under their oxters, propped over quiet teas. Occasionally their names cropped up again, found dead in lodgings from the Dodder to the Tolka. A lost generation. The withered branches on the family tree of Ireland.

'I'll send you a card,' I said, but I don't think she heard me. She was deaf, into the bargain.

I crossed to the window and looked out. There was Sharkey below me, emerging from the front entrance, his coat open. A dead leaf skittering along the pavement. Stripped of the fear and subservience factor, he was nothing at all. I remembered my father coming home, the pause as he hung his coat in the hall, when I wondered what state he was in. How great and powerful he had seemed to me as a child. Now, as I enter our front door on Highgate Hill, I see my own children looking at me in the same way. And I am ashamed, for the world I come in from is smaller, not larger that theirs.

A breeze blew down the canal, freshening the new green leaves on the bankside trees that all leaned gently in the one direction, in the invisible current of air. Women basked in the sun by the heavy wooden lock-gate. A man threw a stick and his dog splashed after it. At lunchtime, Du Moulin and I had done the circuit along the grassy bank on the far side. In the low water, just below the outflow from the Leeson Street lock, he showed me something I had never noticed in all our walks. A pike, long and striped and still, swaying among old ironwork at the bottom of the canal. A predatory spirit, ghosting the freshness of the place.

'Who does that remind you of?' he had asked.

As I was daydreaming, the door burst open. Like human tempests, the cleaning-women entered, dunting and crashing about with their Hoovers, dragging black plastic bags behind them, into which they emptied the Confidential Waste that Proinsias's shredder had made tapeworms of. Bearded Betty, lost in a daydream of her own, lifted her feet automatically as they swept beneath her, and put them down again. If they had chucked her in with the rubbish, I doubt if she would have raised a murmur of protest. Housewives, they asked me sharply had I a job for their husbands. Frightening voices, from the real world outside. They ran a cloth over my desk and Siobhán's, both of which were tidied of everything bar a glass with a few biros. The other two desks, piled high with ill-assorted files, they ignored. You could almost tell, looking at the desks, whose life was destined for order and whose for chaos. As the cleaners worked their way down the room, in noisy and wordless brutality, I sat into Du Moulin's desk and carried on with the journal where I had left off.

7

November 10

It has happened with A., as I thought it might. Back from Liege since last September, working as a childminder now in Cabra, three days a week. Leaves Clontarf at the crack of dawn, and cycles in through the quiet streets of Phibsboro. At weekends, I sleep over.

Yet she has never been here, in this room, and never will be. A loose connection, neither asking questions. What she does for the rest of the week, who she mixes with, I know only vaguely. But there are others. The music people of the Dublin underground, and the students at the Institute. And those unknown souls who phone her out of the night, for advice in their crises. The floating population I see around the place when I stay over, or meet at the bars when I am out with her in Dublin. For them she is young, foreign, an object of desire and fascination, the carrier of a different, perhaps larger, mythology than their own, into which they escape for a while from the local cage of this city.

The other residents of her house – Rourke, the owner, a self-proclaimed atheist, who makes candlestick holders for half the Catholic churches of Ireland. Has a specially nice manner with the clergy. His girlfriend Clare, who has lived with him for over a year in the hope that they will marry and settle. If not from conviction, at least from inertia. At night, when A. and I come in from the city centre, there they all are on the long leatherette sofa watching television, the two of them plus Sean, Rourke's unemployed brother, who supplies the soft drugs. A line of heads on the sofa, dope haze between them, and whatever late-night movie will see them into the small hours.

'What is the food situation?' Rourke shouts over his shoulder at A. when he hears us coming in.

They like to play language games with A., a foreigner after all, who does not handle our idiom as well as she might. Beautiful but a figure of fun, to be condescended to. She accepts it, as one must when money is scarce and one depends on the goodwill of others. Would you like a puff of this situation? they ask her. Are you taking that situation upstairs to sleep on your situation? Hahaha.

'It gets tiring at times,' she smiles uneasily.

As white a body as I have ever seen. When her clothes come

off, the old-maidish clothes she uses to keep the world at bay, I am taken aback. Full breasts, stamped with the heavy coinage of nipples. A dark thatch of sex, between immaculate thighs. Am I trying now to possess what then possessed me? In vain. Her red lower lip, like a bitten cherry, closing over mine in the morning, in a half-lit room filled with winter birdsong. Her smoker's cough, her long white arm reaching across me to her things on the night-table, for a cigarette. The essence of those mornings – bliss of sensual plenitude, into which I sink again, remembering.

And the silence of the kitchen at that hour. The others upstairs, in their various room, snoring. We are the first down, to make breakfast. Coffee, eggs and bacon. The eggs bring out her Flemish side. It annoys her if they are not done to the right consistency. A home-maker. The children she minds in Cabra love her more than their own mother. She leans against me softly in the after-atmosphere of lovemaking, and squeezes my waist. Very gently, after a considered pause, I disengage, and she half understands. I want no real involvement.

'What is the food situation?' Rourke shouts from the top of the stairs, his face a mask of shaving cream.

Soon, they are all down in the kitchen. Sour, crotchety, having overslept, with the whole of Sunday already shot to hell. Rourke packs his brother off for the Sunday papers. That waster, he snaps, it's the least he can do. He opens the fridge and his fat lips part in a smile. Ah, he says, the food situation is good. He beams with genuine regard at A., who besides her rent, keeps them all in good cooking. Clare across the kitchen stares at us stonily. She works in a garage in Raheny. She is playing a waiting game. If not love, then attrition. It may take a year of living in sin with Rourke while her parents scream at her godlessness, but the day will come when this house will be swept clean of outsiders, and she will face Rourke, a chastened, overfed, middle-aged Rourke, alone across the dining-table. And what will God have to do with that?

'I had to send the wine back last night,' he says, still fishing around in the fridge, 'at a place by Howth harbour. It has to be exactly sixty degrees, I kept telling them, or it's unacceptable.'

When Rourke begins to whine, it is time to go. We get in the car and drive – anywhere – through the grey drizzle of a November Sunday. To the cliffs of Howth head, the sea below trailing foam into the teeth of a north-easterly. To the flat shoreline of Malahide and Skerries, the desolate stone bathing shelters where A. lights a cigarette out of the wind. To the empty stretches of road behind Portrane, lined with bare winter trees. Or further north to Drogheda, through the Sunday sleep of Balbriggan, its rain-lashed ice-cream stands and newspaper hoardings. The Sunday sleep of Ireland, from which only movement can awaken us. Sometimes I drive, sometimes A. takes the wheel. At times, we go the back road behind the airport and park in the flat fields at the end of the runway, watching the planes roar towards us and lift off over our heads going God knows where.

'When I go back to Liege at Christmas,' she says, 'I will fly for the first time.'

She has problems with Liege. Family problems, problems of history. What do you do when your father, a wealthy brewer, is a rabid Flemish nationalist into his old age, unashamed of his Nazi links in the Second World War, even after they sold him down the river? You get out, she says. You find a country that doesn't have blood on its hands.

'You've made a strange choice,' I tell her.

I drop her off at her house, where the rest are slumped already in front of the television. We will meet again next weekend, somewhere in the centre. I drive back through the winter twilight, along the grey curve of the North Strand, with the docklights and refinery lights shining across the deepwater harbour. Then the Liffey tollbridge, and the flat bird-haunted sands before Merrion Gate, past Hogan's house in Claremont Road and out to Monkstown. In the empty basement kitchen I boil a pot of tea and take it inside to my bare-floored room, light a fire and read, in the stillness and solitude, till it is time to sleep. Unthreatened by entanglement, the self floods back to me. Ineffable peace.

It has been like this, now, for weeks.

November 22

After work, into the night of Dublin city. Over the bridge at Ringsend, past empty docks and flourmills, their rotting grainships anchored by the outflow chutes in their walls. Over the Liffey and past the decayed redbrick of Capel and Dorset streets. Pink fluorescence of night eateries. I grab a bite before parking behind the Inns, that ruin from the Age of Reason. Boards, tarpaulins, scaffolding rattling in the wind. Desolated grounds looking west, into a night of traffic and filling stations, satellite towns. Dublin out there, the Dublin whose deeds and misdeeds we dissect legally for three hours each evening.

At the head of the lecture room a coal fire. A barrister yammers out key cases, we take notes. The law is not Justice, he warns us. It is not ethics, it is not morality. The law is the sum total of the judgements of not particularly bright, sometimes imbecilic judges of the past. One golden thread runs through the fabric of law, he adds ironically. Go away, buy the cases, study the dicta, he cries. My colleagues laugh – they are on the solid ground of cynicism now, they know their footing. Company managers acquiring new weapons of attack and defence, civil servants solidifying their qualifications for middle management, young women out of business and insurance, paid for by their offices. The reverse of A. Seductively dressed as if to attract, but shrinking into themselves, like anemones, at the slightest touch.

Driving back across the city. Workers coming up and off shift. Streetwalkers at the docks, taking up position. The yellow of carbide lamps floating coldly on the Liffey.

November 24

Fee simple. Escrow. Deeds. The concept of absolute ownership. Who is the absolute owner of this place, in the bowels of whose earth I am buried, sitting here in a basement room, as the hammering continues? Surely not Simon, who is upstairs doing the hammering, transforming, day by day, Germaine's old room into his office. On my rare visits to the top of the house, I see the new pink plasterwork and paintwork extending downwards, advancing upon us, not even the relative owners, day by day. Tenants, holding on by a thread to our own threatened reality. Simon, coming from some privileged nowhere of his own, has acquired a Dublin identity as well as the house. Bang, bang, bang, he goes, muttering away in Dublinese, in his friendly but brisk manner. One day, friendly but brisk to the end, he will rip us out of his life like dead skirtingboard and fling us on the scrapheap.

Public nuisance. Private nuisance. Limitations of privacy. What constitutes actionable noise and intrusion? I lie in bed and hear Tadhg's radio, long past midnight, through the ceiling. He falls asleep in his chair, Germaine tells me. Sleeps so deeply you would need to shake him hard to wake him. One day, the music stops. There has been a row between Tadhg and Simon. In the small hours, Simon entered and switched off the radio. Unpardonable intrusion, according to Tadhg. Simon claims he knocked and knocked before entry, but got no answer. Right and wrong on both sides. But there is no doubt who will be the ultimate victor.

December 2

I take a night off lectures, not for the first time. Treat Germaine to the cinema. Beyond bare subsistence, she hasn't a penny to her name. If you don't have money, she says sadly, you don't have friends either. She is still friends with Tadhg, but they live in the ashes of a relationship – he in his big front room piled with nudes he painted of her when he first left his family, she eking out existence in the mews at the end of the garden.

'Besides,' she says matter-of-factly, 'he brings home another woman now.'

French film. Sexual intrigues between members of the bourgeoisie, artfully hinted at against background of dining-room furniture and fine kitchenware. And to think these people and their actions are considered important, she says wearily, as we emerge into the wet Dublin night. They are worthless, as Simon and his wife are worthless. Empty people, with nothing but sex and money in their lives. People without values. To think I left France because of these people, and found myself living amongst them once again.

Stark austerity of her room at the end of the garden. Narrow bed with basic coverings. Personal linen, clean and threadbare, stacked on a shelf. In a glass on the sill, a sprig of garden flowers. On the wall a chaste, almost sculpted nude photograph of her sitting on a glass table, head fallen, arms tucked around her knees, drawn up into herself, exposed to the world, vulnerable, yet closed and virginal as a flower.

December 10

Changes at work. Yet we go on as usual, brokering agreements between workers and management. A small team, reliant on each other, not part of the Departmental mind. So it has been for me now, this past two years. But the Department needs extra bodies for its undermanned sections. I have done well here, everyone tells me so. Yet I am the last to know, and the first to go. Late last Thursday night, as the Chairman and I sprawled exhausted on seats in the corridor, while the two parties conferred in their separate rooms, he opened up.

'Tommy,' he said, 'you've heard the rumours?'

'Yes.'

'You've done a good job for us,' he went on. 'You're efficient, the unions and management like you, you're bright. You're so bright I wonder at times what you're doing among us at all.'

'Is that a question?' I asked.

'In a way it is, Tommy,' he said, 'a question for yourself. Are you one of us or aren't you? We are all good men and women here, but if you threw us out tomorrow, we'd only be fit for cutting turf. But you have a better mind, perhaps too good a mind …'

'People always say that', I answered rather bitterly, 'when they are looking for an excuse to get rid of you.'

At that moment, the management called us back in to hear their final offer. It is always like that in here – the dropped word, from which you construe your fate. We never took the matter up afterwards. Now, I suppose, we never will.

December 15

She passes, back and forth. What long walks she must take, R., out along the sea-wall on the west pier. What is she walking off?

8

The night before my wedding, I narrowly avoided a car crash. I was driving through Ringsend in a car I had borrowed from Nessan – bringing home my suit. Two streams of traffic, in and out of town, passed each other in the half-light. A car coming the other way veered on to my side. I feinted towards it as a warning, and we passed. I saw in the rear-view mirror it had gone out of control twenty yards behind me, bouncing drunkenly along the pavement before tipping over. I didn't stop. I was in my stream of traffic and it carried me on and away from the scene, even as I saw that car burst into flame. There is no way anyone could have known I was the cause of the disaster, perhaps someone's death. The last thing I saw was the wreckage burning as I carried on out to Sandymount and was gone. I felt strangely neutral, as if part of a process from which something or someone else had been eliminated.

Next morning, as Nessan drove me across to the church in Clontarf, I passed the place again. A mangled heap of burnt-out bodywork, bulldozed to the side of the road. Whoever had been driving couldn't have lived. Neither of us passed any comment on it. We had other things on our mind – the speeches we would make, and the bother about Gearoid. Regarding to the central thing, I was composed in my mind. No uncertainties there. It was almost a side issue to ensuring the day went well for everyone else. I wanted everyone to have a good time.

'No dirty telegrams,' I warned Nessan. 'As little smut as possible.'

It went like a dream. Perhaps it was a dream, for all I know. The drive past the rubbish heaps of Ringsend with their storms of gulls. The light grey spring weather over the bay, with a ferry homing to the North Wall. The trees greening in the flat expanse of Fairview Park. As I waited at the head of the aisle, the lads came up to wish me well. As Breffni and I exchanged rings, I watched Gearoid out of the corner of my eye. He circled slowly in the offing, with a reel of film – we could add music afterwards. He had decided, thank God, to co-operate. Other than that slight worry, I felt no emotion, not even nerves. In fact, it was all rather functional. My mind was on the meal, the arrangements, whether Mother was bearing up. Afterwards, there was the fuss and backslapping outside the church, the local residents looking on through the gate. As Breffni and I were getting into the Rolls for the short drive to the hotel, Fergus rushed up and pushed a small bottle into my hand.

'A Baby Power, Brian,' he said fervently. 'To get you going.'

As we stood for the official photos on the front lawn of the hotel, I could see poor Fergus knocking back pale sherries as fast as he could grab them off the tray, laughing his inane belly-laugh that tailed off into a kind of hysteria. What do weddings do to people? Nessan promised to keep an eye on him while I steered Gearoid off to the bar and bought him a pint. A reward for good behaviour. He was inordinately grateful, so that was alright. The rest of the lads were with their tough, hardbitten wives and handlers. Du Moulin stood off in a corner, quietly nursing a pint. Old Man Murray, growing more sardonic with every drop of the hard stuff, was the only question mark.

I didn't enjoy the meal. How could I, knowing I would have to speak at the end of it? I sat in my ill-fitting monkey-suit, faintly aware of how ridiculous all this was. I could hear the noise-level rising like a tide until Nessan tapped his glass with a spoon and began to speak. I heard myself spoken of as a child, the middle child who would always turn out well, after a spell, and the less said about that the better, of trial and error. Now, a welcome new member of the Matrimonial Club. And wasn't it amazing that someone as quiet and – in a manner of speaking – ordinary as Breffni could catch such a lounge lizard, he wondered out loud, to a scattering of ironic laughter. To Big Brian the Disco Lion, he read from a sheaf of telegrams, Watch Out I'm Still After You. From the Car Park Attendants at the Intercontinental. From the Ladies-in-Waiting, Fitzwilliam Square – See You in Two Months Time. Hahaha. Just when they were starting to be in bad taste like that, Nessan wisely put the pile aside and signed off with the wish, on behalf of himself and everyone there, that for Breffni and I there would soon be the patter of little tax deductibles about the place.

As I rose to reply, I took a drink of water. My hand was shaking. I embarked on a stilted speech of thanks to all those the etiquette book told me I should thank. Just as I sensed I was starting to bore everyone, Old Man Murray, of all people, shouted from his table Remember the ferry we took from Cork to Roscoff. Suddenly I became my natural self again, improvising memories to the hoots and jeers of the lads. Of course I remembered the ferry, all those years ago – my first paid holiday from work. Strange how an image could stay so long in the mind – myself and Stokie throwing beer bottles out to sea from an upper deck, seeing them collide and smash in mid-air before vanishing into sea. I remembered that, and other trips, like the one where Stokie finally got someone to go to bed with him, and how smart and cocksure he was afterwards – I didn't go into that. I went on instead about my early dash for freedom to Italy, leaving out the inappropriate bits, and how glad I was now that fate had called me back.

'Ah get off the stage,' Old Man Murray shouted, to general laughter and applause. 'Let the real performers on.'

The three-piece band we had hired were quietly setting up at the back of the room. Blurts of an organ, a crash of cymbals, the singer ahemming into the microphone. One-two-three, one-two-three, and then we were off. I shuffled Breffni over the cleared floor in a passable imitation of a waltz Nessan had taught me in our front hall, and soon half the room was up and dancing. Never have I heard such hysterical screaming as I did from Breffni's friends during the quicker numbers when they all joined hands. That peculiar wildness that comes over people at weddings and deaths, as it did when Father was being waked in an upstairs room in Sandymount. Not that I felt it myself, strangely enough. I wasn't unhappy, but there was a central kind of numbness, as if I had died sometime previously and was being waked myself. I came out of it briefly though, an hour later. The dancing had thinned. I could hear the voice of Old Man Murray, unpleasantly loud and insistent now. He was haranguing Du Moulin.

'Get on up there,' he shouted, as Du Moulin chatted to a glamorous cousin of mine. 'Give us a performance.'

'A recimitation,' Fergus tittered, into his cups.

'The green eye of the little yellow god on the slopes below Kathmandu,' Old Man Murray went on relentlessly.

'No, not that,' Fergus interrupted benignly. 'You need to wear a cap for that.'

'Get on up there!' Murray roared. 'Show us what you're made of! Do you hear?'

Du Moulin signalled to my cousin that he would be back in a moment and went to the stand. Breffni and I looked at each other. I went cold with fright, realizing how complete a stranger

Du Moulin actually was to me. What would the fucker do? Take his trousers down and bare his arse to the aunts and uncles? Bring disgrace on us all? Instead he had a quick word with the organist and returned to his place.

'Let us all stand,' said the organist condescendingly, 'for the National Anthem.'

We sprang to attention and sang, while Du Moulin went on chatting. Even Old Man Murray was jerked into line by the general will. I breathed a sigh of relief and went back to being dead. With what sounded like a loud, deliberate fart from the organ, the band called a halt until later in the evening, when we would be gone.

In twenty minutes we had changed into our going-away clothes. We reappeared, to be serenaded, given the bumps. We were fed through the human tunnel. Our new life had begun.

We had a flight to Rome at nine the following morning, and Nessan drove us to the airport hotel. As we pulled out, I saw Old Man Murray heading back to town on his own, dapper as ever I had seen him through the office window. But the face a broken mask, Immanuel Kant in tears. As we sped up a back road to Clontarf, who should I see getting out of his car and entering a house but Du Moulin. Would anyone be left at the hotel for the rest of the night? I was too tired to care. We hit the airport road and joined the traffic flow. I found myself thinking again of that wreckage from the night before. I wondered who had died.

What can I say about the next two weeks? Tiredness. We were tired flying out the following morning, and tired as we went about the business of being happy on our honeymoon. Are we, I wonder, the kind of people who are unequal to the happiness life sends? I do not know. But tiredness stayed with us then as it has ever since. Life has become a task, that is all, to be carried out well or badly.

We were hardly airborne before Breffni began getting anxious about hotels. Why hadn't we arranged for accommodation? We were winging it, I told her, it was part of the adventure. But she insisted. Perhaps Rome would be crowded, overbooked. I was irritated and refused to answer. I looked down at the sweep of Dublin bay and wondered what Du Moulin was waking up to. A damn sight more than I was, I suspected. I ate in silence, while the green patchwork of England and France slipped away beneath us. I was in one of my moods. I do not deny that certain difficulties the previous night had contributed to it, but it had been there before, and has been ever since. As it was, the loveliness of Europe, the white rumpled chain of the Alps and the blue of the Mediterranean, were lost on us.

'Never mind,' I said finally, to break the silence, 'it will all work out.'

But as usual, her practical self was proved right. From the moment we stepped into the blast of heat at Fiumicino, we were taken for a ride. Literally, in a yellow taxi from the airport to the city centre. Instead of enjoying the yellow and green fields of corn and rapeseed in the outskirts, and the parched brown streets of restaurants and gelaterias shuttered at two in the afternoon, we waved a piece of paper with the name of a hotel on it in front of the driver, who nodded and followed his own route. He left us at a concrete block on a street corner, beside an entrance piled high with rucksacks, and dispossessed us of seventy-five thousand lira. Upstairs, we collapsed on one side of a jerry-built partition and tried to sleep, while a German couple climaxed repeatedly on the other.

Breffni decided she hated Rome. Everything about it got on

her nerves. The heat, the thunderstorms, the astronomical money units, not knowing what was on the menu and always choosing the same thing. And most of all, after she had spent the whole first day writing cards to people she had seen only twenty-four hours previously, the scuffles at the post office window. We lasted a day and a half, before heading south.

On a hot afternoon, we took a train to Naples. The sea was on one side, on the other the burnt-out scarps of the Apennine foothills. I went into the corridor for some air. Men in shirtsleeves hung out the carriage doors into the cool slipstream. I liked the wildness and freedom south of Rome. It brought back to me briefly the only time I had ever struck out for my own life, that once, for a fugitive month.

But Naples proved no better than Rome. We found ourselves in a doubtful hotel on the top floor of an old apartment building. An understanding proprietor oversaw the comings and goings of short-term guests into the small hours. A blare of all-night traffic rose from the streets. Down there, beneath blue-lit grottoes to the Virgin Mary, crippled women sold themselves.

When we booked, at last, into a hotel on the Amalfi coast, things began to settle. In the afternoons we stayed in bed and that got better. I cannot say I was physically attracted to my wife. It was all on a functional level. But I did find myself learning new virtues. Patience, consideration, a new kind of tenderness. Not very exciting perhaps, but they have stood me in good stead ever since. In the evenings we stayed in our room and watched gameshows on television. A girl taking off her brassiere, a wheel spinning, an ageing roué tickling the ivories. We were frightened by the sumptuous floorshow downstairs, the waiters sneering as we fumbled through the menu, the cold indifference at reception. Had it not been for the bedroom, we would have checked out.

The day before we left, I slipped on the marble floor of the lobby and broke my wrist. I thought of Compensation, but we were too afraid to make a case. We travelled north in a bad mood. The usual setback, just when you get on top of things. The story of our lives. That night, before flying home, we looked at the silvery litter of coins in a Roman fountain. Carefully, Breffni fished a worthless five-lira coin from her bag and threw it in. We watched it settle slowly, almost weightlessly, among the real coins at the bottom.

'Brian,' she said, forestalling my objection, 'we never were the sort of people to trust our luck.'

9

It is Saturday morning in London. If the December fog has lifted enough over the city to let the Dublin plane in, the Irish newspapers might be available at the kiosk outside Archway station, at the bottom of the hill. I can pick it up after taking Brian junior for his Saturday swim at the public pool. And then there is the library, and then there is the Christmas fair at the church in the afternoon. Breffni is taking the younger one with her to brave the mobs on Oxford Street. How little we see of one another now, even on weekends. Perhaps for the better.

'Will you cross the road for me,' she says as she gets the little girl up, 'and buy a pint of milk, half a pound of Kerrygold and the nearest thing they have to a loaf.'

'What about eggs?'

'I don't trust their eggs,' she says. 'Pakistanis aren't clued in on eggs. I'll get them at the supermarket where it's cleaner.'

True, the Pakistani shop across the road isn't very clean. I'm sorry to say it, because it seems to be run by an old Irishman who hovers around silently, shifting things from shelf to shelf between pulls at a fag and watching sport on a tiny portable TV behind the counter. He has the air of a man savagely disappointed in life – who could blame him around here – and we do not talk. But I often speak with the Pakistani lady behind the counter – or is she Filipino? He changes them so fast. We are all good honest work-ing people in this area, she is always assuring me, with the des-peration of one trying to set up a clientele. The bad apples are all at the bottom of the hill in Archway. The sour old Paddy glances at her and she goes back to her calculations. He is usually in the front of the shop, rearranging piles of girlie magazines on the top shelf. Poor Fergus will have a feast for his eyes when he comes over in February for the Twickenham game.

We are halfway up Highgate hill – just on the lower half – in a rented redbrick house. If we were on the upper side, just across Cromwell Road, we would be different types altogether. We would be leafing through English papers this morning, drinking cappuccinos in Frenchified cafes in the village at the top of the hill. Instead, we go downhill to the grey of London away in the distance over the roof of Whittington hospital, where wine mer-chants, newsagents and greengrocers fall into the pit of Archway. Drunken blacks and Paddies huddling out of the wind in the sta-tion entrance, smashing their own bottles on the pavement. No, where we are at the moment, above all that but below the Eng-lish money, just about sums us up in the scheme of things.

'Father Paddy called,' Breffni says when I come back in. 'He wants to see you for a drink this evening.'

I am getting a bit tired of Father Paddy. He has latched on to me as a Labour Attaché, a useful man to know, on behalf of his parishioners. Still, he baptized our youngest and the church is a point of reference. When we first came to London it was weird and disorienting. The tides of filth blowing along the streets, men and women lurching half-naked about the public places with crushed cans of Tennants in their fists. Shop-windows splashed with the telephone numbers of local prostitutes. And the rottenness behind the façades of terraced streets around here – subdivided, sublet, the middle classes moving out, the immigrant poor moving in. Far gone, as if the bottom had dropped out of everything and all that was left was the stink of garbage. So we count ourselves lucky to have the church at least, where we are among our own.

'If he's running in and out of the pool,' Breffni warns me as she goes out with the young one, 'don't forget to change his wet togs.'

She has this absurd idea that walking around in wet togs will hamper his development as a male. She picked it up from the childcare manuals I am leaving back at the library. But I am too tired to argue with her. On matters of health she always gets her way.

Down at the pool, there is the usual Saturday morning scrimmage in the changing rooms. Not a decent body in sight. The women are slackbreasted stretchmarked housewives like Breffni, the men balding and double-chinned like myself, all bad breath and dark circles under the eyes and bellies slopping over the edge of our trunks. I hurry past the mirror these days, to avoid seeing the damage that fifteen years of office life has inflicted on me. If I saw myself I would be depressed for the rest of the day.

The pool is a huge shallow kidney dish of warm water. All the races of the world wallow democratically in it, while a wave-machine washes water over us and disco music thunders in the background. It might have done Sharkey a power of good to be dunked in it a few years back. I lie in it myself as in the stream of life, blissfully conceding victory to the forces that have formed me. Wages, domesticity, the procreative impulse I hardly understand in myself though it has produced two children already. Above the glass roof skies pass, grey, unremitting, featureless, sometimes blowing rain on the silent panes up there, sometimes opening so a shaft of light quickens the green waters where I lie. At such moments, I realize with perfect clarity that I have given up, become passive for all my running around, yielded to the organized madness of life. And I no longer care. I have not cared for many years. It is for others to do better.

The library is just as crowded. Is there anything I do that others do not do at exactly the same time? While I queue to return the childcare manuals, I read the fliers pinned to the noticeboard. Drop-in centres, touchy-feely encounter groups. You would think people would be happier here, given how much is done for them. But they sprawl, inert, stupefied, workless, on leatherette chairs, flicking through dailies and supplements, basking in the free heat. I avoid eye-contact with them, as a rule. Half of them are ours, from across the water. At least we taught them to read and write before sending them packing. I must have met some of them at the Irish Centre. Or did Father Paddy introduce me to them?

'These?' says the fairy librarian, taking the childcare books.

'And this,' I slide a weekend video towards him.

He runs it all through the computer. A true public servant. Then he flashes us a bright smile and sings out Good Day. He always smiles brightly. He is always happy. I am beginning to loathe him.

'When are we going to eat?' Brian asks.

'As soon as Daddy gets a paper.'

A freezing draught howls through the entrance to Archway tube station. The couple who run the newsstand have no Irish papers. They haven't come in, or have all gone out already. They can't remember, or they don't care. They pretend not to know me, though they see me every day. But this is London. So off we go down Holloway Road, past the Irish ballrooms with their groomed photos of crooners over from Roscommon or Sligo. Public houses gape open – dusty frowsy joints as wild as saloons in the Rockies. Brokenfaced men and women hog the counters, their hair falling like unkempt curtains across their faces. The metronome of Country and Western ballads ticks over the tannoy, to the whine of pedal steel guitars. I never set foot in places like these, even when I am with Father Paddy. These are not my people. The nearest I want to get to them is on an official form in my office.

'No,' I say, anticipating Brian's question. 'They don't allow children in there.'

At the corner of Holloway and Seven Sisters Road, in a white plastic cafeteria, I sit Brian down with a burger and myself with a coffee scalding from the machine. Old women hog pots of tea at dirty tables, mothers laden with shopping fight to get chips and ketchup into four-year-olds. Arsenal supporters in white and red scarves fortify themselves for the cold stadium around the corner. This is as near as I will come to relaxation all weekend.

We take a bus to Finsbury Park station, but the Irish papers have vanished there too. Under the railway bridge, three men and a woman are having it out. Hunkered around lager tins, they stagger to their feet to face each other down, or pretend to wander off into the distance, only to drift back again into the trapped circle. Are they ours? They are more remote to me than the Asian fruitsellers, the Nigerian butchers of halal meat along Stroud

Green Road. It is as if I, and Ireland through me, had struck them off our books forever, leaving Father Paddy to pick up the pieces.

'Will Mammy be at the fair?'

'No, but her cakes will be there. I'll show you her cakes.'

Father Paddy, when we arrive, is up on the improvised stage of the strobe-lit church basement he uses now as dancehall and social centre. He has his collar open, his shirtsleeves up and he is shouting into a microphone, jollying and hectoring the diffident groups of Irish bachelors and the mobs of local black women into buying raffle tickets. Behind him are prizes – tins of biscuits and bottles of whiskey, hairdryers and electric irons, and the bumper prize, a small microwave oven, donated by a local discount store. He shouts out a number and an apologetic bachelor shuffles forward to receive a bottle. A little girl in a party dress stands behind him, at the wheel of fortune.

'Give it one last spin, Agnes,' he shouts, 'and then we'll have a song from a man we all know well, Dan Prunty, a great and much-loved character on the local scene.'

We all know Dan well. He hangs like a shadow at ten at night outside the off-licences, cadging cigarettes or a slug of beer from laughing teenagers. No self-respecting seller of drink will serve him now. He roams the streets by day, shouting incoherently at the top of his voice, breaking into a song, as he does now, that is all brokenness and vibrato, with somewhere in its depths the traces of early training. After a few minutes he is led off to embarrassed applause, and a group of cheerful Nigerian ladies shuffles on-stage to dance to an African beat. Father Paddy jumps down and makes a beeline in my direction.

'Brian! Good of you to come.'

'I wouldn't have missed it, Paddy.'

Well I would have missed it, if truth were told, but London Irish are playing away this weekend. I would have to admit that the people I drink with at the clubhouse there are more my kind of people. Doctors and solicitors over from Ireland like myself, for experience and promotion. There is a kind of animal warmth here, the animal warmth of Irishness in a cold world, that I draw back from. Father Paddy grips me by the arm and leads me to the bar, chattering away about the Donegal-Derry match and the closeness of the result. I know the result – I make it my business to know – but my interest is feigned.

'A lemonade for the boy,' he says delightedly, getting behind the bar and serving us himself, 'and for you, I suppose, a pint of the black.'

'Thanks, Paddy.'

'We'll save our real drinking for this evening,' he says, turning businesslike. 'I have a lot to discuss with you.'

'I know, I know.'

'I was round at the Bank of Ireland yesterday. They were saying the brikkies and chippies used to make a line halfway round the block on Thursdays to cash their paycheques. Now, apparently, you could count them on the fingers of one hand. So that gives you an idea of how bad things are for our lads over here at the moment.'

'I know, I know.'

Of course I know. But what the hell does he expect me to do about it? I do a job, that's all. I cover myself and my family. I don't operate on gut loyalties, like Paddy, and my spiritual conviction is weak. One year they employ me to keep aliens out of Ireland, the next year to get Irish aliens in somewhere else. I throw out one rule book and take on board another. It's what I'll do for the rest of my life, it's all I'm fit for. But am I supposed to believe in it?

Paddy would say yes. So would Du Moulin, and look where he is now – adrift in Dublin, not far above Dan Prunty, who gets his hot dinner and lodgings in a welfare hotel around the corner. What more can I say? I am a tepid soul, one of those the Gospel condemns for being lukewarm. All I have learned in life is how to save my own skin.

As night falls, we board a greyline bus back to Highgate, packed with Saturday shoppers. Headscarfed women, their legs like tree trunks marbled with varicosities, lugging plastic bags full of merchandise from the immigrant stores at the cheap end of Stroud Green. Irishwomen, Greeks, Asians. They pour off the bus in a flood at the redbrick council blocks before Archway. Breffni will be home by now, on the tube from the West End.

'Whose cat is that?' Brian asks as we trundle up Highgate Hill.

'That's Dick Whittington's cat. He looked back at London, and he loved it.'

I am back in time for the sports results. I sit in the high-backed chair and let myself be deluged in a flood of statistics while Breffni cooks in the kitchen. I might be my father. I might be dead. I might never have left Ireland, for all I know of London after these years. The whole thing might be a waking dream, dreamt by an ancestor in Ballinasloe centuries back. Who do we know besides our own kind, in luck or out?

'When is Fergus coming over?' Breffni asks from the kitchen.

'February. For the Twickenham game.'

'We always get the lame ducks,' she says. 'What about Du Moulin?'

'What about him.'

'You never talk about him these days.'

'I feel guilty.'

'You shouldn't,' she says. 'You did the right thing there.'

You reach a point in life where every moment is mortgaged. You owe it to something or someone else. Either you scream out loud and get taken away in an ambulance – and I was close to that with Aliens – or you dull the pain by shutting it out. Counting your blessings, as Breffni calls it. That we are the envy of half of Irish London, for example. That we have a house to go back to, prospects in our own country. Or there is one other thing you can do, in my case, when the depression sweeps over you. You can call to mind Du Moulin, asleep on his bare floor. You can leaf through his journal, as I have done this past month or two. But Du Moulin, his life for better or worse, is not something you talk about. Like conscience, you commune with it, if you commune with it at all, in secret.

10

January 11, 1985
I live in a world of the id. Car, habits, restaurant food and moving images. Someone to sleep with at weekends. Plunged in the instinctual, a chain of appetites. But aware all the time of this as a phantasmagoria to be lived through.

January 17
That silly contraceptive joke of Rourke's in his bathroom. A little glass case on the wall with a condom inside, and the caption, 'In case of emergency break glass'. And she? How does she manage? Trips to the bathroom after lovemaking. The sound of running water. Why do I never ask?

'I tried to have a baby with someone,' she said once, 'but it never happened.'

We drive further now, into the snowy fields of Meath. Slane abbey, where the wind howls in the ruins. The cross of Monasterboice. If I was like my father, she laughs, I would photograph it from all four points of the compass. Thus we get through the dark grey January days.

But she has gone further. Midweek trips to the west with others. Midnight pillion rides to Old Head, with the moonlit wastes of the Atlantic beyond. And that Belgian company man, a lonely divorcee, who wants her to retire with him to his house outside Galway. Dogs her everywhere, including the Dublin pubs. He smiles at me conspiratorially, as if we both have a stake in the same property. Look at yourself in a mirror, she snaps at him, losing her temper. Check your birth certificate, for God's sake. The pubs are crowded with her acquaintances. Refugees from the Dublin estates, in black deathshead punk. They eye her, these Dublin punks, with awe. A European underground figure. At times, resentment breaks through. You are a rich kid experimenting among us, they sneer.

'They are fascinated by my past,' she tells me. 'They want War memorabilia to wear.'

She must leave this country soon, if her work papers do not come through. A matter that concerns me. Meanwhile, she bicycles out to Cabra every week. An element that keeps a marriage together?

'If a man is satisfied,' she says cryptically, 'his wife and children will benefit too.'

February 6

The business of the rats. It began back in the autumn, when I started Law. A faint cry, almost subliminal, as I lay on my mattress and listened in the dark. Only audible after dark, when everything else was quiet. Difficult to pin down where in the room it was coming from. Here and there on different nights, with whole days or even a week of silence. Then it came again, this time with a grinding, gnawing sound, somewhere beneath the floorboards. Ever more piercing and piteous sounds. Then silence. And a few days later, the smell began.

At first a light, barely noticeable change in the atmosphere. A thickening, slightly sweetish, when I entered the room at the end of a working day. Gradually, unmistakably, a heavy putrescence, everywhere and nowhere, swimming in the warm waves of air by the radiator, acting on my mind like depression, the source of which is hard to identify. A sewage leak perhaps? It got worse and worse through January, until I could no longer feel it was noticeable only to me.

Last week I called Simon in and he solved the matter in a flash. Sniffed around like a rat himself, then pounced on the floorboards under the desk, ripping the nails out with the back of a hammer and tearing back twin planks with frightening intensity. There, he said smiling with his fine white teeth, is the solution to your problem. I saw, beneath where the boards had been, the decayed remains of two dead rats, one having half eaten its way into the other. Poisoned, Simon said with satisfaction. I remember we put down poison here years ago. He went off to get a plastic bag and some aerosol. It was strange looking into the grey undulating sand of the foundations, that hollowness through which the rats had run, beneath the whole terrace. He came back, swept the remains into the bag and blasted half a can of aerosol into the subterranean darkness, before banging closed the floorboards again and dumping the rats in the bin outside. I thanked him. I was grateful, even if he frightened me. I felt I was living again in a clean space.

Have been fooling myself with law. Will take the exams, to satisfy my employers. But no more.

February 20

Changes at work. I am to be transferred. Called in yesterday, by the head of personnel. Swivelled on his chair with the deepening night of Dublin behind him – traffic, warehouse lights, a ship moving up the Liffey in the grey dusk, the web of static and moving lights that is this city. You have done well, he said to me. There will be a good report going with you when you leave. Why me, I wanted to ask. What is it that will accompany this report, to blight me?

Two years in these offices. Two years of early mornings and late nights, in the smoky back rooms of depots and factories, in the plush managerial conference rooms and hotels, in the linoleum of state corridors, where the haves and have-nots battle it out. Dead time, filled with tea-dregs, sporting gossip and newspapers, while the two sides stand off. Murderous silences over bargaining tables, broken by ribaldry, the whole place rocking with laughter. Boot and Shoe men. Electricians. Bakers and Confectioners. Effete media types. Security guards. Pigs and Bacon men up from the country once a year. Men and women from the supermarket chains, in jazzy suits. The ones who drift in late and drunk, the ones who phone their women to say they'll be late, the ones who quote Shakespeare and John Donne over the percentages. Half the humanity of Dublin, the days and hours of its light and darkness, the wages of its sweated labour, the stones of its docks and streets I will leave behind me. I have written them up in countless meetings. I have expressed them better than they could express themselves.

March 1

Late at night, after the pubs close, Tadhg brings home his new woman. I hear doors opening and closing upstairs, the brief kerfuffle of shoes and clothes on the floor that is my ceiling, then the rhythm of the bedsprings and the crescendo, mutual moans and shrieks trailing off into silence. The strangeness of sex, when you are not involved in it yourself. And yet Tadhg is not happy. Instead of nudes, the paintings in his room now are grey studies of sea-mists coming and going on Howth head, across the bay. A man biding his time, between leaving his family and waiting for Simon's hammer finally to fall.

Bang, bang, bang. Simon works in his spare hours, refashioning the house after his own image. He is down to the first floor now, with brief forays of terrifying efficiency into the bowels of the building to check a pressure-gauge or adjust a boiler. His office is carpeted and pine-furnished now, his plate on the door. On the steps outside, I see the troubled-looking couples, the parents and children who come to learn the secret of happiness. For a fee, of course.

March 5

No word from A. these past weeks. We need a rest from each other.

March 15

I sit at a desk in the main Department building, and wait for a section. I have been here two weeks now, just waiting. You're a legal man aren't you, they say, as they shove some unfinished files in front of me. Well, get together a submission on this while you wait. They watch me on the sly, the maiden aunts and spinsters who have wormed their way into the cool haven of the Personnel section. I feel like a stylite perched on top of a pole. Every so

often, heads of sections peer around the door and look me over.
Should I flex my biceps, like a servant at a hiring fair? In no time
at all, I finish the submission and hand it back. Brilliant, they say.
It has gone straight to the Minister, tomorrow it will be signed.

No, it is not what I do that is the problem. It is what I am.

'What section are you in?' Brian Hogan asks me over tea in
the cafeteria.

'I am nowhere,' I tell him.

'For a man who is nowhere,' he laughs, 'you look remarkably
substantial.'

A noticeable emptying in the lecture hall at the Inns. Some
have given up, others like myself will cram up the cases and dicta
from the library. How could I explain to anyone there that the
results mean nothing to me now, that this whole episode, so fool-
ishly entered into, is no more than a chapter of my moral education?

March 23
Bright breezy weather. Half of Dublin out for an evening walk on
the East Pier at Dun Laoghaire. By general consent, Spring has
arrived. If you stood here long enough, your whole life would pass
before you. Brian Hogan, and his bride-to-be. Poor Fergus, muttering to himself. Simon, his wife and child, tanned as if winter
had never happened.

In the open waters of the bay, the low hum of a motorboat. I
see it is a police boat, trailing, twenty feet astern, an anonymous
bulk that makes its own secondary wake. Others have noticed it
too, it is clearly a body. As the boat enters the harbour, an ambulance and police car race along the pier and draw up at the moor-
ing steps. A few, possessed by curiosity, crane over to see, the rest
walk on as if nothing has happened, as if the fabric of south

Dublin life had already sewn itself whole again after a rupture. The body, bloated and pockmarked, but recognisably female, is graiped ashore. Six weeks in the water, one of the police says. I think of R., who I haven't seen in ages. Could I have helped her back then, in her blackest hour?

March 30

Still no word from A. I telephone to break the silence. Rourke answers. Launches into the story of his recent trip to Africa, to sell candlesticks to the churches there. Ended up in jail, briefly, in Lagos. For not having a work permit.

'And the worst of it was, they took away my tapes and my headset ...'

I get him back on the subject of A. She comes and goes, he says, but just now she is away. In England, he thinks. Her stuff is still in her room, but Clare doesn't want her around anymore. She may be leaving soon.

April 3

They have finally given me a section with, of all people, Brian Hogan in charge. It calls itself Aliens Registration, or just Aliens – and I am more an alien in it than most of those who apply for permits. Besides ourselves, it is staffed by two clerks who wander from telephone calls to permits half-tapped out on a typewriter, in a haze of dispersed consciousness. In the deserted midday hour, they titter over their Lenten diet and do bicycle exercises lying on their desks. The floor is yellow linoleum, the walls a bile distemper. The windows, permanently grimed from the traffic outside, are sealed with adhesive tape. Inside is the slowed time-world of a government office, at the far end of which, under a Marx Brothers reproduction, two middle-aged spinsters sit.

'Isn't it time,' says one, noticing it is Spring outside, 'we took down the Christmas decorations?'

'We'll think about it,' the other says firmly. 'They might do for next year.'

Once around the canal, at lunchtime every day, with B.H. I talk of my dissatisfactions, my need to take leave in the autumn. He grabs me by the arm and adopts his most confidential manner.

'Mark time,' he says earnestly. 'Take the attitude that Yes I'm delighted to be where I am. They like that, the self-important bastards. If I weren't getting married and buying a house, I'd be taking leave too.'

Funny he never noticed the pike, until I pointed it out to him. A long streak of misery, that will pass for the one member of staff not mentioned above.

'Who does that remind you of?' I ask him.

'Tommy,' he smiles at me sadly, 'you're a lost cause.'

II

Angry and disgusted, I laid aside Du Moulin's journal and went on sitting at his desk, thinking. I was even tempted this time to leave it open as an indication I had been reading it, though I doubt if he would have cared. Was I wrong to see in all this the barren self-preoccupation of a man at a dead end, socially and emotionally? Even three weeks ago I might have seen Du Moulin differently, envied him in a way. But since returning from Italy, it was as if a whole season in my life had passed away. I don't know whether it was the sleeplessness and difficulties of moving into a new house with someone still more than half a stranger to me, or the problems I had faced that first day back in the office, but my attitude to Du Moulin, the freedoms and excesses and the odd circumventions of reality in his life, had hardened.

That morning, warming the seat in my corner of the section, I knew I really was confronting the first day of the rest of my life. Much though I feared and disliked Sharkey, I was painfully aware of the truth of his remarks about things in general, most especially those concerning the need to work every day at marriage. Three weeks into mine, I was sweating like a stoker in a hold. There were evenings when we sat across the kitchen table from each other, Breffni and I, in the silence of our new quarters, with nothing whatever to say to one another. It was as if we both had a stone in our hearts. There was nothing to do but wait, in humility and despair, for the mood to pass away. We were part of a process, that was all, and we had to co-operate with it. Breffni's part in it was to stop nursing almost immediately, the better to conceive, for we had decided subconsciously to fill the void between us, as soon as possible, with children.

Then there was Gearoid. He had been given the run of our place while we were away, on the understanding that he would mind it. Instead we spent our first day back cleaning up after him, his half-finished cans of food in the fridge, his empties littering the front parlour. He was back in Sandymount now, living with Mother. The dole wasn't enough, he was bullying her out of the few quid Nessan and I gave her each week. He was pissing it away in the locals and doing nothing to make a life for himself. By now, our truce was over. I lumped him together with Du Moulin, as one of life's failures.

So much for the home situation, then, as I faced into the problems of Aliens. I would have to negotiate a middle way between the twin obstinacies of Du Moulin and Sharkey. I would have to pick up the stray threads of policy and knit them into some coherence. Policy? There was no policy, Du Moulin snorted. There was simply a primitive terror on the part of closed minds for what they did not understand beyond themselves, rationalized into a set of regulations. Deep down, I agreed, but the time for such high principles was past. I knew which side of the fence I would be on if decisions had to be made. Meanwhile, Felix's lockjaw had to be loosened and Siobhán weaned off her addiction to happy marriage if we were, as a section, to establish meaningful contact with the outside world. The chickens hatched in April were coming home to roost now, in early June. The honeymoon was over.

'This place,' I warned everyone, 'is neither a Moroccan kasbah nor the Imperial Court of China.'

It was eleven before Sharkey appeared. During this lull, while I apprised myself of the full horror of the situation, Felix ground out an obscene joke about my fist, and the Italian chocolates I had brought back went around. They were being fought over, with barely concealed savagery, by Miss Flahavan and Bearded Betty, when the door opened. That motor salesman's face. The bloodless pallor behind which a world of deviousness lurked, and behind the deviousness the real stupidity, unknown even to itself. There are moments when reality bears down on you with a crushing weight, turning your world into ash and sawdust. I noted the crookedness of Sharkey's front teeth. I was looking, closely, at the face of the Gorgon.

'Brian,' he said, smiling as he shook me by the bandaged hand, 'I needn't ask how it went.'

Everyone tittered nervously and went silent. The staff had switched suddenly to that rigid appearance of thinking deeply about administrative problems while bent over a file that I knew from experience is hard as plexiglass to break through. It was quiet enough, as Sharkey moved from person to person, to hear the rattle of Miss Flahavan's nerve pills as she dosed herself. He honed, inexorably, on Du Moulin.

'Tommy!' he cried in fake bonhomie, for the rest of us to hear. 'Are you well?'

'I was,' sighed Du Moulin, 'until a minute ago.'

'And the law exams, Tommy. How are they going?'

'They're finished,' Du Moulin looked up patiently, as if explaining to a child. 'They finished a week ago.'

'God, Tommy, you're a mine of information!' he cried, staring wildly at us all. 'What about the results?'

'Don't worry,' Du Moulin said. 'The Department will get its pound of flesh.'

Sharkey asked us, with his resigned smile, to participate in his sadness. We smiled bleakly, each after his own fashion. There are shades of neutrality only a job like this brings out in you. Sharkey's face took on an expression of feigned solicitude.

'Tommy,' he said with a troubled air, 'you forgot to remove your key the other night so I took it out for you. You might like to deduct the two extra hours when you do your monthly reckoning.'

'Our m-monthly work of f-fiction, as Brian calls it,' Felix ground out, in an unfortunate attempt at a joke.

Sharkey drifted back to my desk, and the tension went out of the air. The listening silence at the far end of the room was broken again by the rustling of the Italian chocolates. The ancient telephone on the windowsill, linked to the bank next door, purred like a bronchial cat. Felix lifted the receiver and shouted Fuck Off. We were back to normal.

'See me this afternoon,' Sharkey said in parting.

I made my way upstairs to the canteen. Ahead of me in the queue, a shuffling dumbshow of elders prevaricated over their usuals. You all need the rodeen on your backs, Róisín snarled behind the counter. That would wake the lot of youse up. Yes, Brian, the same as always. Welcome back. No longer a virgin, I hope. Two chocolate biscuits and a coffee with a dab of milk and no sugar.

I hesitated before sitting down. I always hesitate in here. About whether to sit with this group or that. About which word to use in a sentence. About whether to go to the jakes or not. I have spent most of my working life cultivating indecision, praying the problem will melt away of itself, as it usually does when the real world stays beyond sealed windows. In through those windows the sun of early summer was shafting the plastic tables. There were gaps now, people were already on summer leave. At the far end, by himself, sat Du Moulin. Halfway up, two old men were debating the decline of Irish life since the collapse of the Cult of Our Lady, while a young man beside them, with the beginnings of a bohemian moustache, held forth on animal imagery in Ted Hughes to a group of glazed juniors. There, he said with satisfaction, we have raised the tone of another coffee break. We should have serious discussions like this every morning, to keep our minds in trim. A little further along, two economists I saw in the bars of Baggot Street after hours, retailed to each other the Minister's peccadilloes in Strasbourg. I nodded to them in passing, and headed for Du Moulin.

'What possessed you to put in for leave so soon?' I asked him. 'You've hardly begun here.'

'Brian,' he said, putting down his paper for a moment. 'I've a lot on my plate.'

'I can see that,' I said. 'But why did you join us in the first place?'

'I didn't join,' he said. 'I infiltrated.'

I gave up, and we both went back to our papers. I would miss him, all the same. It wasn't that he ever said much. It was more the quality of his silences, which were extremely restful. The absence of empty chatter. He was possessed of a peculiar inner peace, as if he existed at the eye of various storms he generated around himself. Sometimes, as we strolled through the long grass by the canal at lunch, an almost mystical quiet settled over the pair of us. If I was fair, I would have to say that for all the troubles he caused, Du Moulin also gave me a great deal.

'Tommy,' I said eventually, 'don't be ridiculous.'

'I've enough saved,' he said, 'for a year of simple living.'

'Simple living? You mean the life you had in seventy-nine, when you ate at our place?'

'It's pointless to talk about it,' he said.

'My mother fed you,' I went on, 'as she feeds that wastrel Gearoid now.'

'You sound like an old married man,' he said.

'At least I made a decision,' I answered, feeling the anger rising inside me. 'At least I committed myself.'

'No one would ever persuade me to get married,' he said calmly. 'No one ever will.'

When he had left, I regretted my outburst. He was right in a way. Hardly married, I was already using it as a stick to beat others with. I felt angry at myself, and sorry at the inevitability of both our lives, mine in the groove of home and family, his with a black night of orphanhood somewhere behind it. Róisín came by, ruthlessly sweeping away my cup, and I left. On the way downstairs, I paused at the Men's and communed with my bladder. Did I or didn't I need to go in? Could it wait, more profitably, until later? I pushed through the door and saw the line of cubicles with their stamped rolls of paper. Saorstát Éireann. I could hear, from two that were shut, the settled rustling of newspapers. Felix? I would know when I went back. Proinsias? But his shredder wasn't outside. As I unzipped my fly at the urinal, I was joined by Sharkey and his superior Cathal Flynn.

'Have you read the book about Haughey?' Flynn said importantly, as they unzipped their flies beside me.

'No, Cathal,' Sharkey said anxiously, 'but I was wondering about the submission I made to you …'

'It's called *The Boss*,' the other went on. 'I'm saving it up for my summer break.'

'It sounds good, Cathal. But about that submission I made to you …'

I felt my bladder drying up. I would have to come back later. There was no peace anywhere.

That afternoon, in his hot little office stacked with motoring magazines and popular histories of World War Two, Sharkey filled me in on the past weeks. Things had ground to a halt. It was up to me to get them moving again. Du Moulin was refusing to levy an administrative fee. It was on the brink of changing from an issue of principle to a disciplinary problem. Our friend, as he described Du Moulin, was spending far too much time downstairs talking with foreigners. Because of the delays in processing, all kinds of exotic specimens, as he put it, Indian rope-dancers, Chinese hatchetmen, women from the burning sands of the Sahara who claimed to be circus performers, which he very much doubted, were floating around in the front lobby, causing embarrassment.

'Darkies are flooding the lower corridors,' he added. 'One even peeped around my door the other day.'

When I had calmed him down, I promised to deal with the most urgent cases myself, exacting the fee while Du Moulin did the processing and some limited consultation downstairs. An interim measure, I said, thinking of the bucket catching the drip, and hoping for the same stay of execution. With luck, even Sharkey might forget. But no, he hammered on, Du Moulin must be pinned down on this one. He, Sharkey, would see to it. As for the darkies, nine out of ten should be sent packing, or they would flood the whole country.

'Guilty until proven innocent, Brian,' he said. 'Let that be your yardstick.'

He was distracted by the blurting of the telephone on his desk. He put his ear to the receiver and brightened, like a schoolboy in a sweetshop. He was talking to a mechanic on the Tallaght road. His car was in for servicing. They discussed bleeding batteries, accelerator cables and the tuning of the engine. As he was relaxing into big ends and overhead camshafts, I gently made myself scarce, leaving on his desk the potentially explosive issue of Du Moulin's leave application, which we had not yet discussed.

Sunlight flooded the building, and work had slewed to a halt. The doors of the abandoned offices stood open, the desks of whole sections were empty but for one toiler minding the shop. The rest were outside, sunning themselves on the canal bank. For them it was early summer. For me, summer was already over. I was left with the torrid minutiae of a section in chaos, and the silence of the house around the corner in Belmont Avenue, where Breffni waited. I slumped into Du Moulin's chair and looked out on Baggot Street – the shirtsleeves, the brisk women's legs, the life that has somewhere to go. Depression flooded me, the depression that has come and gone ever since, that I have never found a reason for.

At the far end, Miss Flahavan made to go. Bearded Betty had won the war of nerves. She could stop pretending to work. But the door burst open again and the cleaners entered, catching us both in the same trance. Automatically we both lifted our feet as they swirled like dervishes around us, cursing the bucket in the middle of the room. At such moments, there existed between Bearded Betty and myself a complete unity of mind, tuned, beyond the duntings, shovings and cursings of the cleaners, to the drops dripping into the bucket with the measured regularity of an exquisite oriental torture. Time itself. Empty cubits of official time we sat in the middle of, neither of us, for our own reasons, wanting to vacate it until we absolutely had to. What had Bearded Betty to go back to? Silence, absence of communication. What had I to go back to? Silence, absence of communication. Angry and disgusted with myself, with Du Moulin, with life itself, I picked up his journal again and discovered just what he had meant when he told me, only that morning, he had a lot on his plate.

12

April 19

At last, a long letter from A. I should have known what the matter was. She made the discovery weeks back, and took the decision alone. To England and back, living, now, at another address. I didn't want to consult any of you, she writes. Any of us? How many of us were there? The family man in Cabra? The boys in leopardskin at the underground clubs? The motorcyclist on Old Head? Or the industrialist who has shadowed her all winter? We are all responsible. She has decided for all of us, and let us all off the hook.

My own cruel egotism as I check back on dates and times. As likely or unlikely as anyone else. Next, the dawning realisation of her circumstances, the sudden destitution that is her reason for writing to me. Money. I can get it to her straight away, and in the longer term some provision. The car. Then, her work papers. To push these through regardless. Not to wait. They sit, unprocessed, in the pile on B.H.'s desk.

After work, across town to Mountjoy Square, where she has taken a cheap room on the top floor of a run-down Georgian building. The front door sags open when I push it. Wide hallway, bikes propped against the wall. How well I know all this. Stairs of untreated wood, spiralling upwards past doors behind which music or arguments sound, or the blurtings of rented televisions. Progressive impoverishment as I climb through the floors to a bare-board landing and a door to an attic at the back. Unchained. I push and it opens to a stonefloored kitchenette running with unwashed pans – not her style. In the distance, through the kitchen window, night and the Dublin docklands, its scheme of lights blood red or magnesium yellow and white, the steady drone of heavy machinery, loadings and unloadings, that carries from Alexandra basin. I listen, in the darkness and silence up here. I smell Dublin, the rank fumes of its harbour life blown inland, its industrial chemistry. In spite of everything, I am waylaid by the city itself.

'In here,' she says, in a small voice.

She is curled on the bed, under a light duvet. Fully dressed, as if she has crawled in after some half-completed activity. She is still moving in. Black plastic bags of clothing stand unopened in the middle of the room. Items of ironed underwear are already on the shelves. But she has crawled back into bed. Exhausted and weak, in the aftermath of everything, letting the room grow dark around her. I touch her on the shoulder. She smiles a gently accusatory smile, as if I have been caught cheating in a parlour game, and shakes me off. How long has she lain here, how long it is since she has eaten or drunk, I do not know, and I hesitate to ask.

'Poor Tommy,' she says, 'you were never much good at saying how you feel, were you?'

'I've made a mess of this relationship.'

'Relationship!' she echoes ironically. 'Where has all this sudden commitment come from? Help me up.'

She heaves herself upright and swings her legs onto the floor beside the bed. Sitting there in the dark, in the lurid wash of light from the East Wall, she reaches for her tobacco pouch and rolls herself a smoke. The ash glows and dilates as she inhales, thinking, not speaking, not including me in her world as I have so often not included her in mine. Not unfriendliness, more indifference, an acknowledgement that there can be no real connection between us. Ships in the night. Leave it dark, she says, as I go to boil up some tea on the battered kettle. When I come back in, she has a candle lit on the table. I was ever impatient with her love of shadows, but now I see it, with relief, as a return of normality.

'Don't worry about me,' she says. 'I am much stronger than any of you. All I want from you now is money and a chance to work.'

As she smokes in the darkness, in the iron din of the dockland night, I tidy up around her, putting away clothes on shelves, washing up the scummed cups and saucepans in the kitchen. I don't know who else comes in and out here – there are different butts in the ashtray – but she is able to manage. I will do what I can for her. Perhaps others are doing the same.

'I won't ask you to stay,' she says eventually. 'I'd rather sleep alone.'

May 6

The steady, regular rhythm of days – stupefying, numbing, anaes-thetising. Their painlessness, their lack of intensity a form of death. If I put it down to experience I would call it the price to be paid for Belonging. How much longer will this go on for me? End of summer, perhaps. Meanwhile I sit at the heart of the sit-uation, fully conscious of being trapped. All I can say in justifica-tion is that here, for a while, I was taken off the streets, after the terrible years that went before.

Sitting at B.H.'s desk I do two things therefore. Approve A's application for a work permit, and tender my application for leave.

May 9

'There, in these grimy offices which we walk through as fast as we can, men in shabby coats sit and write; first, they write a rough draft and then copy it out on stamped paper – and indi-viduals, families, whole villages are injured, terrified and ruined. The father is banished to a distance, the mother sent to prison.'
– Herzen, *Memoirs*

May 15

A few free days during which, as a matter of intellectual pride, I read up on key cases in the woodfloored library at the Inns. Examinations in Criminal and Land law, the law of Torts. Dis-secting, for the last time, the human life of Dublin into motive, accessory, intent and consequence. Around me, filling foolscap pages, the representatives of a mercantile class consolidating itself. I fascinate them, not because I belong to any class they aspire to, but because of my classlessness. If I have done anything these past years, in private and work relationships or alone in a room, it is to de-categorise myself. I am, as far as is possible in this city, a member of no known class.

The rustle, after three hours, as the papers are collected. Have fulfilled my obligations to the State. The last time ever I will try to Belong.

May 20

Phone call from two men in the motor trade, interested in my car. Am I free this morning to take them out on a test drive? Can they come over to the office directly? Leaving Felix in charge upstairs, I meet them in the lobby, hand them the keys and let them take me for a drive in my own car. The one time Sharkey might have been useful to me, if we were still communicating. A strange feeling, like being a passenger in your own life. Outside, the greening trees of Wilton Place and Leeson Street, the lamplined length of Morehampton Road, with its old associations; two and a half years passing out of my life. I hand over the keys to those who properly belong in the old life. We speed down Waterloo Road and find a parking space in Baggot Street. They mean business and we do the deal there and then. Keys and documents to them, and to me two thousand pounds in cold cash, wads of grubby blue tenners counted out on the front seat. As they drive away, the lightness comes over me, the lightness of no possessions. Looking up, I can lipread Felix at a front window as he shouts Fuck Off into the ancient telephone and slams it down. As if I were on the other end, bereft already of power.

Will get the money to A. later in the month.

May 23

Hello, Simon said, as I was walking out the front door after collecting my post yesterday. I jumped six inches into the air. I hadn't heard him padding down his freshly carpeted stairs. You gave me a fright, I apologised. Did I really, he said without batting an eyelid, how interesting. He makes us all feel like that. Inadequate. Nervous misfits. Not that he does it on purpose. No, it is something innate, an emanation he is unaware of. Even as he squeezes us out he tries to be friends with us. What is it then? That beneath his urbanity he believes in nothing but power, while we, for all our disorganisation and failure, have never believed in it.

He likes me best of all, because I have regular money and pay on time. The rest have their marching orders for the end of the month. I hear Tadhg padding around upstairs, gathering up his gladrags. And the other day, for the first time in weeks, I knocked at the door of the mews and got no answer. She's gone, Simon's wife sang out across the garden from an upstairs window. She left two weeks ago. I can give you her address if you want. I thanked her and said no. I would wait until we bumped into one another on a Dublin street one day. By then, I would probably be homeless myself.

May 29

Warm night. Moon three-quarters to the full over the calm waters of the bay. Crescent of lights on the north side and further in, the dark mass of the power station as the green suburban train shuttles me through Ringsend and the docks, across the river to Connolly. Wrought-iron gloom and platforms, the rumble of porters' carts. A point of entry to the city. What possessed her to come here, of all places? Our 'life of the spirit' after the grey deadness elsewhere. I must ask her someday, if I still continue to know her, which now seems unlikely.

Spiritless drift of uncollected rubbish, at the station end of Talbot Street. Children kicking tins on the hot asphalt parking spaces of Gardiner Street, where once the tenements stood. Demolitions, reconstructions. I am the last of a line, existing in myself and not for the sake of a future. If I lived by will and not passivity, I would square my shoulders and assert equal citizenship as a member of this city with every other. But I let it float through me as though I had no stake in it. I register it coldly, under another imperative. The publicans in Parnell Street rumble their iron barrels down wooden ramps to the cellars, the nightclub owner sweeps the pavement outside his entrance. Each sweats for his place in the city, even as I give up mine.

The silence of Mountjoy Square. High buildings there when my Huguenot fathers entered, in flight from elsewhere. Now it is her turn to make these streets her own. And she is taking possession, if the babble of conversation behind her door is anything to go by. There are many here already. I am no one special.

'Go in to the other room,' she calls from the kitchen, where she is talking to someone.

The room where I sat alone with her two weeks ago is full of smoke and hubbub. Three are reading Tarot cards at a low table. Others fiddle with a black and white TV she has somehow acquired. What has happened to her? A musician who works the clubs for pittances is arguing nastily with his manager, a young man with a stutter. I remember now. She told me he lives in the front attic. He is always crying at night and having crises. A painter of medallions sits crosslegged, chatting with two Belgian women in black leather, friends of hers who have abandoned their jobs and followed her to Ireland.

'Welcome to Bohemia!' they yell without irony, as I beat a retreat to the kitchen.

She is leaning against the stone sink, smoking. In the haze that envelops them both, he has his arm around her shoulder. No, I am not mistaken. The sad industrialist who shadowed us all winter. As he smiles at me self-evidently, I can scarcely believe my eyes. But then the penny drops, as it should have done months ago. Bohemia, the other side of the rich man's coin ...

'They are waiting in there for you,' she says with an edge of impatience. 'I told them all about you.'

'I only came in for a minute.'

'What brought you here? Me?' She glances at the other. He smiles and looks at his shoes.

'I said I would leave you this,' I put the brown envelope on the sink, 'in case you needed it.'

'Oh, Tommy,' she says, pulling me outside for a moment, 'that's the second nice thing you've done for me today. The first arrived in the post this morning. Not that I need to work just now. I'm alright, as you see. But can I keep this in the meantime?'

'I won't need it until the autumn.'

'Think well of him, Tommy,' she says as she steps back inside. 'He's a friend of my father's.'

For a moment, on the landing below hers, I listen to the noise and footsteps on the floor above. I am certain I will never see her again. With renewed clarity, the thrumming of the Dublin dock-lands carries from beyond the East Wall. On the river, in the far distance, yellow and white semaphores of coming and going call to each other blindly in the summer dusk. And nearer, no less otherworldly, the storm of gull-cries in the hush of Mountjoy Square. Why is it always the same? Why do I always feel this sense of release, of inner freedom, walking away from the false-ness of human relations?

May 31

And the hot summer of Dublin begins. The deep blue air, the heathaze over the bay. Empty sunlit offices all over town, abandoned for the Bank Holiday weekend. Today Tadhg leaves, so the depths of the house are mine until September. A lifting of tensions now, as twelve months' falsehood comes to an end. No need for anyone now, just to move anonymous through the summer crowds, less and less a person, more and more a disembodied spirit.

13

I remember that summer as one long trauma of adaptation to work and marriage. The sun shone on emptied desks at both ends of the room. Siobhán had gone home to the country for her summer break. Miss Flahavan, Bearded Betty and Miss Sugrue from upstairs, whose nephew was still taming the Orinoco, had left for the Bible country. The canteen was quiet and Róisín had put away her rod until the autumn. Young economists lingered over coffee there – ministerial aides, products of the universities, coming and going from the top floor with their sportsbags and steel rackets, gossiping loudly about what the Minister had said and done, what the Minister had got up to after hours. I sat alone and listened, swallowing my coffee, with the horrors awaiting me downstairs. I had never been on a free trip abroad. I was putting in my engine-room years. I was determined to rise, after my own slow fashion, out of the mire of Aliens.

For a quagmire is what Aliens had become. Not that we weren't working day and night to move the mountain of applications from extended Chinese families of twenty, Afghan kebab merchants, Moroccan fire-eaters and sword-swallowers who had turned our lobby into the greatest public spectacle since the Crystal Palace exhibition. No, the piles were going down, we were being ruthless left, right and centre. If a telephone rang, we let it ring. Felix took the old phone on the windowsill off the hook. We shut our doors and our ears to the growing cacophony in the front lobby and considered each application purely as a piece of paper. We stopped looking out the window lest it unnerve us. In the evenings, we exited down the fire escape at the back. In this way, once contact with the actual world had been broken and abstraction took over, things went like clockwork.

'Are we near the gates of Moscow yet?' Sharkey stared in anxiously twice a day. 'Are the Mongol hordes being driven back?'

'We're round about Smolensk,' I said, to get him off my back. The Nuremberg trials would have suited him better.

Felix, who could barely grind out a fricative to save his own life let alone a labial to save ours, found it in himself one day, having picked up a stray call from a journalist, to fill her in on conditions in the section, not neglecting, in his helpfulness, to throw open the issue of the administrative fee, and concluding with a statement as to the likely effect of our policies on global migration. Hardly believing her luck, she sped around to view things, as it were, from the outside. Improvised kebab stands lined the canal bank. Circus artists were giving impromptu performances. The following day, a feature appeared in the paper.

'You're in the news, Brian,' Proinsias said, trundling in the papers on his trolley. 'Save the bit you need, and I'll shred the rest this afternoon.'

'By then,' I told him, 'I'll be in the shredder myself.'

Felix barricaded himself behind the black door of a cubicle in the Gents, and when the call came from the Minister's office for

Du Moulin and me to go upstairs, I wished I could join him in the one next door. But as I remember now, it was nothing serious. It never is in here, once crisis gets diffused around the place. We stood around the Minister's office, admiring his vast empty desk with its unread foreign papers. We weren't nervous, we were in the eye of the storm. After all, this dapper little gent who greeted us affably would be gone with the next full moon. It was our own kind downstairs we had to watch out for, the Sharkeys and Flynns who emerged from their offices like pike from under a stone.

'How's it going?' he asked companionably, as if he hadn't read a word in the paper.

'Teetering,' said Du Moulin before I could stop him, 'from one ineptitude to the next.'

Ha, ha, ha. He thought that was a good one. He appreciated the frankness of it, he said. Besides, it ministered to his sense of us all downstairs as barely human. And what might your name be again, he questioned Du Moulin. Know the name, he said, know the name. He was always saying that, on his handshaking forays through the department.

'Listen,' he said, getting serious, 'we've all seen the mobs downstairs. Black, yellow, white. Personally,' he applied the common touch, 'I don't care if you wipe your holes with those application forms. It's the image I'm concerned for. My own, the country's in general. Would you keep an eye on it for me, like good lads?'

Sharkey, having reported sick in the morning, dragged himself in that afternoon. I found him downstairs with Breege, our liaison officer, composing a rebuttal of the lies put about in this unflattering article. Breege, her hands palsied to the point where letter-writing was impossible, had seemed to our superiors a natural choice as intermediary with the external world. We had worked with her on other occasions, with limited success. The pair of them, when I entered, had been wrestling a long time with the finer points of the English language. Breege, her hands trembling uncontrollably, was gathering up bits of paper on which versions had been scrawled, crossed out, wedged with conditional clauses and peppered with officialese.

'These swine from the newspapers,' he snapped, after she had gone, 'they know we're bound and gagged.'

'It's what we're paid for,' I said, trying to sound philosophical.

'Will you watch that fool Felix in future,' he went on. 'And get him to change his socks more often. How about his professional development?'

'He's on speech therapy,' I said, 'if that's what you mean.'

'And the other fella?'

'He passed his law exams.'

'So we don't owe him anything,' said Sharkey.

'What about his leave?'

'We'll be rid of him by the end of summer,' he said, to my immense relief. And then he added, 'There was something I meant to ask you.'

I felt myself tensing up again.

'An application,' he said, 'for which no fee was extracted. Accountancy asked me to ask you about it.'

It was then, I remember it clearly to this day, that I left Du Moulin in the lurch. I let the middle ground I had cultivated so carefully between Sharkey and himself slip from under me. Ever so subtly, of course, but the damage was done. Oh it was nothing serious, I told Sharkey. A sin of omission, as it were, in respect of a permit that had gone through in May, when I was away in Italy. Our friend, I was careful to emphasize, had not profited in any way. But the State had incurred a small loss.

'There was', I added fatally, 'a personal dimension to that particular case.'

'Brian,' he shot me a glance, 'leave the rest to me.'

When I got back to the section, Felix was working away, trying to make himself invisible. I left him under Du Moulin and told them both I was going for an early tea. I would be back at six-thirty and they could sign off then. I slipped out the back down the fire exit and hopped on a Donnybrook bus at Leeson Street bridge. I jumped off at Belmont Avenue and walked the fifth yards of redbrick terrace to my own entrance. Breffni was there, as she had been all day. She had given up work, to concentrate on the other thing. She had always been tough physically, but thin, whippetlike. We could not be too sure. Her days were long, full of silence that hung over her as it hung over me. She was at work at the table in the back room when I came in, making curtains on a sewing-machine. She hadn't expected me, and that was what made it a good moment for both of us, for habit was deadening us even then. She looked up and I could see she was ready for me. It was one of those rare moments between us when words were not necessary and it began a short period when we existed for one another in something other than a practical sense. Not that we didn't speak. We did. We made small talk and brewed tea, but the feeling was there, that feeling I wish I could recapture now, since the birth of our second child. We locked the front and back doors, took the phone off the hook, and we went upstairs.

It was six thirty when I got back to the office. The limbo dancers and trapeze artists had dispersed until morning so I came in the front entrance. August heat had emptied the building, but the Minister's car was still outside. His spare suit dangled above the back seat, his tennis racket in its steel frame propped beside it. God knew who he was entertaining upstairs at this hour.

Felix had knocked off already, but Du Moulin was still there writing. His journal, I supposed. He didn't give a damn if I saw it or not, and I was past caring too. We both knew it was a kind of communication anyway. He didn't look up until he had finished writing, and I settled myself behind a pile of unprocessed applications for an hour or two of undisturbed overtime. I was feeling expansive, pleased with myself for a change. He closed his pen with a snap.

'How long have we known each other?' he asked.

'You tell me.' I knew something was up.

'Brian,' he went on, 'you shopped me.'

'What do you mean?' I said, knowing perfectly well what he meant. I could see in my mind's eye Sharkey arriving five minutes after I left, with a polite enquiry.

'Brian,' he went on, 'I would never have done that to a friend.'

'Tommy,' I said, 'start living in the real world. Stop letting your heart rule your head.'

'What do you mean?'

'You know what I mean. And you know *who* I mean.'

'I see,' he said. 'Marriage isn't enough for you. You have to live my life as well.'

'I may not have beautiful women,' I answered, feeling the strength of my position for once, 'but I've never stooped to picking them off the street.'

He shot me a queer, sad smile. I saw at a glance the dark hells of his early Dublin years, when he lived around the corner from us and came in out of the nights that were blowing snow off Dublin bay, from the cold room he inhabited then, a room I had never seen, as I had never seen the rooms he lived in since.

'We never knew each other,' he said simply as he walked out the door.

I knew I had gone too far. But it was too late now. We had taken up with each other ages ago, as unthinkingly as children in a playground. Now, it was the parting of the ways. Again, I saw his face from decades ago, in the back row of an old school photograph. A grain of dust in the reproduction had blackened into a smut obliterating his nostril and part of his cheek. And that, to me, was Du Moulin – a face with a hollow eaten into it, where God took the place of common humanity. For years, he had come and gone. Now, through the vanishing point of his journal, he was about to become a shadow.

'That fella!' Miss Flahavan spat, having followed every word from the far end of the room.

The ladies were back from the Bible country. They had decided, after much hesitation, to leave up the Christmas decorations through to the coming December. A power concession had occurred, in that Bearded Betty now sat facing her overseer. The issue of the bucket, however, was still under review. On the floor above us Miss Sugrue, her nephew trapped in the Orinoco, was fighting a last-ditch battle against the canteen. I heard the clunk of her squareheeled shoes on the ceiling, and waited for our evening visit.

'Has anyone got three tea bags?' she asked, looking in a minute later.

'As this is the State,' Miss Flahavan looked weightily at the bucket, 'we'll give you two.'

14

A week before Du Moulin left us forever, we called him in. We have all been called in in our time. To be called in means confronting two of your colleagues, being at a disadvantage. To call someone in means being in the company of at least one other when the person called in arrives – in other words, being at an advantage. To everything that is said, therefore, there is a witness or an accessory, depending on your point of view. In the case of Du Moulin, it was Sharkey and myself who did the calling in. One afternoon at the end of August, he lifted the phone where we sat in his office and politely enquired of Du Moulin if he was free for a moment and could he pop across the corridor and join us. Then we sat back, our papers in order, our faces set for this distasteful aspect of the job, and waited.

'The final skirmish,' Sharkey said, 'before the fall of Moscow.'

We had our lines prepared. Du Moulin's file, which would go back to the personnel section, sat in front of us. It would follow him through the years, if he ever came back here. It would shadow any reference given to him if he didn't. Not that he was a criminal like Redmond, just that he was – different. He represented trouble. And people picked up on that. People wanted peace. I wanted peace. Instead of which I had reaped a whirlwind in the opening months of running the section, and lost a friend as well.

'Go easy on him,' I said to Sharkey. 'Remember, he's leaving us.'

'If he has any sense, he won't be back.'

I had seen Sharkey in worse moods. For all that he and his family had been rained out in Achill, his summer break had relaxed him. And Aliens, its mad paperstorm through spring and summer behind it, was at least on top of its backlog. It was now possible, as he put it, to walk through the lobby without darkies leaping at you from every corner. His phobia had reverted to an officially acceptable level. His phone was longer hopping off its hook. His most difficult underling was about to pass out of his life forever. After a torrid summer, sweet autumnal breezes were blowing through the corridor. A new era was beginning.

'Have you seen the new lad?' he asked me.

I saw in my mind's eye a young man dressed in what looked like a Holy Communion outfit, sitting in Personnel where Du Moulin had sat, awaiting his section.

'Nil deperandum, Brian,' Sharkey smiled, and patted me on the shoulder.

Just then, Du Moulin came in. Sharkey leapt up and directed him to an empty chair opposite us. It couldn't have taken him more than a few seconds to figure out the point of the meeting, but he kept his peace. What else was he to do, the poor bugger? I didn't like my role in this whole business any more than he did. But at this stage, I knew which side of the fence I was on.

'Tommy,' Sharkey began, 'it's the practice in here when someone is leaving to cast our minds collectively over the high points and at times the low ones, of bygone days …'

Du Moulin closed his eyes and laughed soundlessly. In spite of myself, I joined in, mainly out of relief that he was at peace with himself. Not that he would ever again be at peace with me, but it made things easier.

'What about the law?' Sharkey said awkwardly, shuffling his notes. 'Could we begin with that?'

'I think we know about that already,' I said. 'We know how well Tommy has done.'

'No, we don't,' Sharkey went on, with a wounded air. 'Every time I ask Tommy, I can't get a civil word out of him. I can go around this section and share a joke with everyone, but not Tommy.'

Du Moulin said nothing and looked on. It was incredible how often that happened with him. Without talking, he could make himself the centre of conversation.

'In any case, Tommy,' Sharkey recollected himself, 'the point is this. You were recommended to us as a legal man who could help us with the finer points of our regulations, but not only have you contributed nothing in this regard, you have abandoned your studies as well.'

'True,' he said.

'Could we note it down, then,' Sharkey said immediately, 'as part of our final report on you? Wouldn't that only be fair?'

'Of course.'

'On that very score,' Sharkey bored in, 'could we talk a moment about the regulation for the administration fee? Now, Tommy, you and I have differing views on that. We'll ignore that – though without it, God knows how many darkies would be cluttering up this island. No, leaving that out entirely, Tommy, what bothered me a little was a case you yourself pushed through in May, while Brian was away, without asking for the fee. Would you care to comment on that?'

'No,' said Du Moulin flatly. 'I wouldn't.'

'Why not, Tommy?'

'Let's be frank, Tommy,' I interrupted hastily, 'we both know there's a personal element in this case. No need to go into the details – we've already exchanged words on that. But it's advisable to acknowledge at least that it exists.'

'If it's a question of money,' he said, 'I could pay it myself.'

'Tommy!' Sharkey exploded in mock outrage. 'We wouldn't *dream* of asking you to pay it! No, Tommy, you seem to be missing the point. The point is, did it happen? Would you acknowledge that?'

'Of course.'

'Wouldn't it be fair and proper, then, to make a note of it in the final report that goes upstairs?'

'I suppose so,' Du Moulin said wearily.

'Now, Tommy,' Sharkey switched to paternal mode, 'we've all had our off days. But Brian and I have always been here if you needed us, if there was any deep anxiety affecting your work or life. Is there?'

For an instant the dark space that had blotted out part of Du Moulin's face on the school photograph so long ago came and went like a blush.

'This is an embarrassment,' he said.

'Ah now, Jesus,' Sharkey smiled indulgently, 'give us a little credit, can't you? You're an intelligent man, as we all know. But I'd have to warn you, Tommy, if you came back here I don't know who would have you. That said, though, we all wish you well. As they say in here, you have done the State some service.'

'Iago,' he smiled.

I didn't know what he was talking about and neither did Sharkey, who shook his head gently and changed the subject. On we went with this conversation which we were not handling well, which circled aimlessly around the destructive report we were about to file on Du Moulin, with his consent, as regulations required. Sharkey, having got what he wanted, was in a relaxed, even philosophical mood, insofar as his mind stretched to such matters. He had heard how well read Du Moulin was. There had, he said, been great literary characters in these offices once upon a time, who had left for better things. Had either of us heard of them? They had gone away and made millions writing books. Du Moulin said he had no intention of writing books, let alone making millions. As I sat there watching him, I had mixed feelings. It was like seeing my younger self, or a part of myself I had never wished to explore too deeply, sitting in the dock under judgement. But the summer had passed. I had made my verdict.

'Tommy,' I said, 'it only remains for us to tell you, quite frankly, that the report which you've heard and approved, is not good. We couldn't, under any circumstances, recommend you for other work here.'

'If the positions were reversed,' he said calmly, 'I'd have felt the same about you.'

After he had gone, we avoided directly mentioning him for a while, and concentrated instead on putting the right complexion on the report. On the whole it was charitable, but concluded with the kind of subtle indictment everyone in here would recognize. It was not that he was fired, more that he would be unwelcome back. It was a play on words, we both realized, in which someone's future was at stake.

'I feel I may have shopped him,' I said suddenly, for the first of many times.

'Brian,' Sharkey laid his hand on my arm, 'you've been in a difficult position these last months. It hasn't gone unnoticed by me or others further up the line.'

'What are my chances?' I whispered.

'It'll stand to you,' was all he said. 'Believe me.'

At that moment I was prepared to believe anything he told me. That Moscow had fallen, and Hitler had won the war. That the Mongol hordes had in fact been driven beyond the Urals. That Aliens would one day be for me a thing of the past.

'What about Redmond?' I asked, now that the important stuff was over.

'I keep these,' he smiled at me, 'as collector's items.'

He took from a drawer in his desk two small sheets of paper. The first was an old newspaper cutting. It referred to the conviction of a minor official in the department, and mentioned the vigilance of a certain Sharkey in uncovering the fraud. His proudest moment. The second was a crude scribble on a sheet of jotter paper from Redmond himself, saying he had seen Sharkey from the window of a prison van as it crossed Dublin, and expressing the hope that they would meet again – preferably in the exercise yard of Mountjoy.

'There goes our friend again,' said Sharkey.

Du Moulin was walking away, with the same upright posture as always. I didn't blame him for packing it in early – he had every good reason for needing a breath of fresh air. Between us, we had shifted the backlog of the past weeks, and by now, Felix and Siobhán were able for the telephone without dragging us into disrepute among the nations. I was only sorry Du Moulin and I had to share a room for his remaining days. I would go easy on him. I felt myself at last in a position of strength. I was consolidating.

'I've a piece of good news,' I said.

'Don't tell me,' Sharkey smiled, putting his hand on my arm again. 'When is it due?'

'Next May.'

'Brian,' he said, 'I couldn't be more delighted if it was one of my own. Go away somewhere, the pair of you, before it arrives. Believe me, it'll be the last bit of freedom you'll ever have.'

Back behind my desk, I surveyed the section. For the first time in months, I liked what I saw. Batches of applications ranked in order of priority, not of urgency. The undesirables I was referring to Justice. The flash restaurateurs the country couldn't afford to lose, if only because the Minister ate there, we would give the benefit of the doubt to. There was no Du Moulin around now to create problems. Then there were the circus performers, the asylum seekers and the lovers whose love knew no border. Felix and Siobhán could apply their schooled intelligences to these. I had taken Felix aside on the subject of his socks, and more especially, to clear the air, his murderous farts, which we no longer lived in dread of. The ancient telephone by the window had finally been disconnected. If I looked out the window all I saw, instead of contortionists and illusionists, was the ordinary drift of Irish men and women along Baggot Street. We had turned the corner. I had reason to feel pleased, as a man does who is set irreversibly on a course of life in which he is beginning to reap rewards. Du Moulin too was set on his course. He had made his choices. Let him abide by them.

Before he left, though, I felt I owed myself one last glance at his inner life. I crossed to his desk and there they still were, the journals, where they had always been. It was both stupid and heroic, the more so as he knew now that I read them. Was there something in the man that cried out, in spite of the deep privacy of his life, for revelation? Was he desperate to bring some kind of submerged chaos to light, to the light of everyday consideration? For chaos it certainly was, in anyone's language. And Du Moulin's chaos I had had enough of, as my own life settled into its new pattern. Imagine my surprise then, as I looked into the journal one last time, that breezy afternoon at the end of summer, to find not turmoil there, but light, happiness, peace.

15

June 6

Now, at last, there is no one. Light alone, changing all day in my room. Suspension of dust motes, weightless, in summer air. I lose nothing by the absence of what for others is essential – the social dimension. A table, a chair are enough. Mattress on the floor, in a wooden frame. Books on the shelf, cold water in a washbasin in the corner. Silence upstairs, now that Tadhg is gone. Silence everywhere. Eastlight floods the room from four in the morning. I rise with it, in the utter silence while the world is asleep, climb the iron steps from basement to ground level, and look over the bay to Howth. Fantastic clarity. Numinous stillness. Windows, twenty miles away, gleaming like silica chips. Sutton, Fairview, Clontarf. Rourke, over there, is sleeping the sleep of the dead. Further in, at Mountjoy Square, A. is asleep, her limbs entwined with her new lover's. Blue depth, deeper than the blue of Dublin bay over which lighters, tugs and fishing smacks chug and drift in early light, spreads between me and them. Blue depth I have sought in myself, deeper than sea or sky, in which I have learned to float effortlessly now, not to drown.

Then it was a void, now it is fullness. All those years I carried it inside me, a blue void out of nowhere, expanding and contracting like an ache. Tried to fill it, in so many ways. Years of sexual frenzy, when any woman would have done. Went out into the night and found what I needed, like the time with R., when all else was a lie. Warmed my hands at the impersonal fires of the State, in a love affair with ordinariness. That pretence of identity, where has it gone? And the loneliness behind it, where has that gone? I have come from nowhere, I am going nowhere. But I exist, for the moment, in a kind of heaven.

Those Who Stand and Wait

June 18

On the sill of my basement window, in the glasshouse by the kitchen entrance, cracked earthenware pots full of old clay. Tendrils and green leaves have been creeping upwards from them all Spring. Now they cling to the railings at ground level. Every day, footsteps pass to and from work, at the same hour. Down here, in my kingdom of roots, I see it all differently – filters of air and water, growth points in the damp smell of mould, a screen through which green light fills the room I sit alone in, watching.

June 25

Hot, hot days. I wait on the platform of Seapoint station for the green suburban train that rattles its way around the bay to Howth. In no hurry, going nowhere special. It is the journey itself I want. To sit and think – no, not think, dream, imagine – while movement accomplishes itself beneath me. Passive inside, all eye. Sloblands of Booterstown slide by, thick with tidal grasses. Beyond the sea-wall, flocks of oystercatchers shift and resettle, facing the same direction, on the flat sands clear to the power station. All this clean on the eye, cinematic, untroubled by depths of feeling. Cricket ground at Sydney Parade, white figures stooping and standing as one. Plotted back gardens of Sandymount. Shadow of the west stand at Lansdowne Road, then Boland's Mills, its waters green and scummed with summer growth, its rotting hulks at anchor. Glimpse of the Liffey and city centre through railway bridge trestles. And the automatic doors opening at Connolly Station. South city crowds goodbye, north city crowds hello. Emergences, vanishings, seen from the calm side of the glass. The cutting at Killester, banks of waving grass. Suburbanites enter, with children and beachgear. Sky widening, as the blue horizon opens at Kilbarrack. Miles of estates, and beyond them sea.

[167]

Howth. They vanish, my fellow passengers, to tan their white bodies in the short Irish summer. By the harbour wall, a brass band plays. Ripples of applause, like the rhythmic collapsing of waves. Light north-easterly, feathering the sea surface as I climb towards Howth Head. Idling fleets of fishing boats out there, a rowboat cutting a slow wake towards Ireland's Eye. Blue openness, distances looking back from the Head to the smudge of inner Dublin, lost in its heathaze. The way I have come. No loneliness now. A calm contentment, at the heart of immensity.

July 12

What it means to be orphaned. No patrimony. You see things in a clear, unsentimental light, with the haze of family and tradition removed. For this, you are called amoral. Hysterical fools, upholders of social order, rage at you. They are protecting the lie by which they live. You embody something – what it is you cannot put a name on even yet – which brings their house of cards crashing down around them.

They live by continuity. Your life, like this journal, is a series of instants.

July 20

The back entrance, through the garden and down stone steps to the basement. A suntrap. Simon and his wife are taking the sun as I enter. Her breasts are bare. Two bronzed orbs she massages with whitish cream, out towards the nipples. I realise how completely in possession of this place they now are, how totally alien influences have been weeded out over the last twelve months. They smile at me from behind their dark glasses, they ask me how I am doing. I am leaving at the end of August, so there is no awkwardness. For now, they have no plans for the basement.

Eventually, they might rent it out to a painter. A painter with money, of course, for it would not come cheap. Already, they are beginning to miss the bohemian past of this house a little bit, the warren of rooms in which weird and wonderful characters lived through the sixties and seventies. Simon still remembers it, as a boy and an adolescent, before the responsibilities of ownership fell upon him. A great house, a great atmosphere. But they have cleaned it up now, in line with realer needs. Conscientiously, they send on post to whichever of their friends, as they call them, has left a forwarding address. And me, what am I up to? Leaving work, am I? To discover myself, I suppose. We have spent years discovering ourselves, they say, and look where it has got us. I share a laugh with them, at such folly. And it is genuinely amusing, seen in a certain light. Once, Simon frightened me. Now, I just see him as different. I am insulated from him by a wall of inner security. Against all reason and prudence, I have entered into, I seem to inhabit just now, an expanded world of happiness, where there is room for magnanimity.

July 22

A letter from A., with a cheque for the money I lent her. A happy letter, postmarked Galway. So she has really taken up with him, the middle-aged man who followed her all through winter so unsuccessfully. Wants a child quickly, she says, to fill the void she is still getting over.

Cheque, made out in her hand, to be paid from his account.

August 4

Alone for the first time in this huge house, as the year I have lived here comes full circle. Once again the breeze deepens and cools, there are early windfalls in the garden. Simon and his family have gone to France for six long weeks, leaving me house-keys and an account number to pay my last rent instalment into. By the time they return, I will have gone. For the moment, though, I am master of the house. I climb to the top floor and look out a back window at the neighbouring gardens. Mature like ours, with walls of fruited stone and mews at the back, shadowed by slate roofs and drainpipes. In those gardens, children play. Spoken for, their innocence leavened with privilege, a world I have never known. I look down on it with interest. I do not aspire to it, neither do I reject it. I am simply directed elsewhere.

Tadhg, Germaine and the others. It is as if they never lived here, so completely have their traces been erased from this bourgeois idyll. Their hysterias and crying fits, their drunkenness and cooking fumes, the sound of their lovemaking. In short, their humanity. A hushed tastefulness has replaced them, and I walk through it now like a ghost. The last of the ghosts.

August 7
R. has resumed her walking habits. Out along the seafront to the west pier and back in all weathers. Muttering to herself, her chopped hair and fine gaunt cheekbones radiating intelligence and quiet despair. Always alone. Where is the husband? When we meet, we don't allude to what happened in the past – that stupid adventure – but there is a terrible brightness in her eye as she speaks, only half-remembering me. Any news, she asks. No news, I answer as usual. Ah well, she says as me moves off, no news is good news.

August 16
What am I trying to become? Someone who insists on his own reality, on seeing the world through his own eyes, in the teeth of

every philosophy that is urged upon him to the contrary. That is the reason for his poverty and his marginal place in society, but it is also the reason why he is not required, from within himself, to satisfy the criteria of domestic stability, commerciality, success. He is a success merely if he manages, through his work or his existential stance, to hold to his own centre, and not be sucked into the vortices boiling around him at any given time.

August 25
Movement of a beetle across the floor of my basement kitchen. It strayed in from the clay bed outside the door. I watch it inching over the old tiles Simon has left untouched. It is unaware of the weight of consciousness pressing down on it, of the degree of its exposure, its total vulnerability at this moment. It could be stamped out in an instant, but it blindly feels its way forward, living on instinct. Half an hour passes like this, with the light of August flooding the kitchen through the greenhouse panes. Dim sounds of traffic outside, lost urgencies. I pick it up gently and place it outside again, in its bed of clay and greenery.

August 26
I grow smaller and smaller, realer and realer.

August 28
As I knew she would, Germaine emerges out of the crowd on a Dublin street. There is a room in her new house, if I need it. Together we will winter there, out of the storm, and let Spring take care of itself.

August 29
Any day now they will call me in, the colleagues and contempor-

---

aries, to pass their verdict on me. They will be polite, I will be polite. For what is there to be angry about? I will leave and stroll, for the last time, around the leaf-shadowed banks of the green canal, past the lovers, the walkers with dogs, the businessmen, the reeds and water-lilies, the dirty blast of water at Leeson Street lock. I will ask blessing and protection for the future from the unbelonging spirit that rests a moment on everything, possessing nothing, in lightness only, and transfiguration.

August 31

> *And saying goodbye once more*
> *I see myself, a spore*
> *Adrift from the family tree.*
> *Let the wind carry me.*

16

Thousands of Irish are over, for the Twickenham game. Not that we stand a chance of course, but they are in holiday mood. On the way home last night, as I hung from a strap in the tube, they filtered in among us with their green scarves and headgear. I was glad, for it brought back to me the times when I too had given myself the freedom of other cities, myself and a few of the lads, in fast-food joints and pubs, and later on, in the nightclubs. But that is Fergus's life now, Fergus who is with us for the weekend, who sleeps off his Friday night drunk in the front room, on the sofa bed made up for him.

'Poor Fergus,' I say, drinking Saturday morning coffee in bed.

'Don't waste your sympathy,' says Breffni. 'I heard him puking twice last night.'

Breffni is always up first on Saturday. Bar the kids of course, who are somewhere around. As she pulls on her underthings, I avert my eyes. When it is my turn, she does the same. There is not a lot of glamour left in our relationship, not that there was much to begin with. And time has not been kind to us. It is too painful for either to see what the years have done to the other. So, between us, there is a kind of tact in that area – not to mention the thing, just to get on with it when it has to be, and to hope someday for enough rest from the unceasing round of necessity to make it good again, good as it was once only, in that far-off summer before Brian Junior arrived and life became a hard, practical business. But grey as it is, it is better than poor Fergus's.

'What I meant about poor Fergus was his life in general.'

'What's wrong with his life?' Breffni says, dragging brown worsted tights up her shanks. 'He has money, a house. Is he missing out on something?'

There is something crushingly realistic about Breffni, as realistic as the dirt in the London air that blackens our windowpanes and she so regularly brushes off. What am I to say? Sexual pleasure? The life of the spirit? But I have stopped defending the indefensible long ago. I keep my mouth shut.

As she goes to make breakfast, I tune into the morning sports programme for the news of the international. They are running through the great days of the Ireland-England confrontation. Jacky Kyle. Mike Gibson in the legendary 18-3 Irish victory at Twickenham. Amateurism and fair play. When was it ever fair play? What about the refusal of England to play in Dublin in 1972, when we had the championship all but won? Where was the fair play in that? No, life is not fair play, Breffni is right about that. It is a matter of forces, dark forces that get the better of you. Unless you protect yourself, unless you are ruthless.

'Fergus!' I yell into the front room. 'Time to get up!'

'I know, Brian, I know.'

I hear him shuffling about in there, putting everything back as he found it, terribly embarrassed about the wastebasket he was sick into, which he hurries into the bathroom to scour. Terribly grateful and terribly frightened of Breffni at the same time. It is difficult for him, I suppose. He is always at the receiving end of our hospitality, poor Fergus. Still, it was a good night last night. A break from the relentlessness of Father Paddy and his social concerns. I knew he was on duty in Whittington Hospital across the road, so we were safe in the Crown. Fergus got a bit overexcited. He'd had a few on the plane on the way over, and the free and easy banter of the women behind the counter over here was a revelation to him. After closing time, he had to be warned by our oriental newsagent to keep his hands off magazines he wasn't going to buy. I pretended not to know him. After all, I go in there every day.

'Are you ready?' Breffni shouts. 'This is on the table.'

Breakfast is rashers, eggs and sausages, banged down in front of us with her usual efficiency. Fergus has brought over some good Irish bread. He is terribly polite, a man of the old school, unless drunk. A bit liverish this morning. But I warn him to fill his belly – it'll be evening before we eat properly again. Twickenham is away to the south-west, on the other side of the city. The kids look at him carefully, though it is not the first time they have seen him at our table. They need not worry. He is more harmless than they are.

'We're going to the park,' Brian Junior pipes up.

'Are you?' Fergus beams at him. He hasn't been spoken to by a child for twenty-five years.

'And what else are we doing?' Breffni asks him.

'We're going swimming,' he sighs. 'And we're going to the library.'

'The park!' Fergus beams. 'Which park?'

'Why have you got such big eyes?' Brian Junior moves in for the kill.

'You're going to Waterlow Park, aren't you Brian?' I put in quickly.

'Why have you got such big eyes?' he asks again.

The Northern line rattles us through ghost stations and deserted weekend platforms. Fergus reverts to his usual obsession – the geography of London, with special reference to red-light areas. I would like to help him, but my knowledge of London is a nine-to-fiver's. King's Cross station. Oxford Street. A coffee shop or two. When was the last time Breffni and I even went to our local Odeon? Apart from official receptions and church socials, we are too exhausted. Soho, I tell Fergus, you could take a stroll around there. He sits beside me in his green Irish headgear, flicking through risqué tat he bought last night, wondering will some representative of law or morality rise from nowhere to confiscate it. I have to remind him that things have changed, even in Ireland. That over here, the couple at the far end of the carriage might just as well be having it off as hugging, that the sudden stop in the middle of blackness means, for all we know, the removal of a body somewhere ahead on the system. That life here is naked, horribly without pretence. That a family man learns to keep his distance, to fall back on clean linen if he is to keep his dignity here and not go under.

'Any word of Du Moulin?'

'In and out of the God's,' Fergus says. 'They have him stable now, on drugs.'

'I heard he'd gone horribly downhill.'

'Horribly,' he says, going back to his reading.

'If you'd like at hour or two about town after the match, I'll leave you to it.'

'Brian,' he says, 'I was just going to suggest it. Where are we now by the way?'

'Leicester Square. If you get off here on your way back, you'll find everything you need.'

He elbows me in the ribs and gives his trademark belly-laugh, the one I have shared in, ever more half-heartedly, over the years. Poor bastard. If it comes to that, though, the whores themselves have probably read the match attendance figures more avidly than any of us.

'Don't worry,' I tell him. 'They'll be expecting you.'

We hurtle under the Thames, into Waterloo Station. Crowds of Irish are swarming onto a suburban train. You wouldn't want to linger here, we agree. A queer place full of queer people, walking around like zombies, their flies undone, the women aboriginal, with bare feet, staring into space. The dregs of society. Still, as Father Paddy says, we are all part of the same Christian family.

'There, but for the grace of God, go you and I.'

Green rugby vests and scarves flutter through the windows as the train shuttles west over the tidal flats at Chiswick to the suburbs. I might as well be in the suburbs of Dublin. The same lines of pebbledashed semis, the same rugby songs I listened to twenty years ago and join in now that there are no women around to be offended. When have I ever left the suburbs? What age am I? Have I ever grown up? I will live and die a suburbanite. I am on the same train I have been on all my life, with the same bunch of roaring, singing, blind drunk alickadoos.

They herd us like cattle through the cordoned-off streets, past the hot-dog stands. Mounted police, clad in yellow oilskins. This way, Mick, if you please. That way, Paddy, like a good man. They filter us through checkpoints, in the shadow of the stands. One by one we are bodysearched and our tickets are vetted. What do they think we are, Fergus asks in exasperation. Terrorists? We climb the concrete stairs at the back of the stands. Our seats, obtained through London Irish, are at the very top, near the halfway line. Far below us the corner-flags ripple, and a military band cuts its caper on the laundered green of the pitch. In front of us, all pipesmoke and plaid blankets, two clergymen pass each other an ornamented pocket flask of brandy.

'We've come a long way,' says Fergus.

'In what way?'

'In the old days,' he says, 'we'd be down in the enclosure. The whole group of us.'

'Now there's only you,' I say. 'That's progress, I suppose.'

He looks at me as the penny drops. Just then, in a V of green and white, the two teams explode out of the changing-rooms, and the whole place erupts.

Two hours later, we are on our way home. What did we expect? Did we seriously imagine a couple of early penalties were going to stem the tide? Through the deflation of late afternoon the train slips back into central London. Fergus has already forgotten the game. His face has taken on that tense, obsessive look I remember from that night he got us into trouble on Fitzwilliam Square a few months ago. God, what a glutton for punishment. Not that I have much to look forward to myself. A blizzard of statistics. The aftermath of all the games played anywhere. In the old days I would have trudged back to Sandymount, to be met by Gearoid asking Why did you bother?

'Do you ever see that brother of mine?'

'He's around. It's through him I get news of Du Moulin.'

'I wouldn't wish him on anyone. Not even Du Moulin.'

'Du Moulin's no different.'

'Oh, yes,' I say. 'Du Moulin is different.'

But Fergus's mind is elsewhere. He is counting the stations. Waterloo. Embankment. Charing Cross. His eyes, through pebble glasses, bulge with fear and expectation. Why spoil the agony of his disappointment, the ecstasy of discovering, in front of a real, available woman, how terrified he is? Off he heads, then, into the crowds at Leicester Square station, as the train slides north.

Tottenham Court Road. Goodge Street. King's Cross. I could climb out at any of them and find myself a free man in an unknown city. Instead, inert, depressed, I move between the same two points. Is it that I lack imagination? Or am I simply getting older? Mother, at home, is facing the sea and dying. Gearoid is going to seed. In front of his television, Old Man Murray is slumped. I will go back there soon, London having passed away like a last chance of life. I will move on and up, with the dark shadow of Sharkey one step ahead. In cowardice, in defeat, I will be welcomed back.

At Archway, a merciless crosswind funnels through the black-tiled entrance, rams itself down my throat. Dan Prunty, a crushed Tennants in one hand, is shouting at nothing in particular. A line of spittle trails astern of him as he rages, breaks into a snatch of romantic vibrato, and rages again. Father Paddy keeps an eye on him these days. They say he was once a talented man. They said that about Du Moulin too, I remember.

'Father Paddy called,' Breffni shouts, when she hears me in the hall.

'What does he want this time?'

'He'll be in the Crown tonight. He wants to see you there.'

'Does he think I exist at his beck and call?'

'Brian,' she goes on, 'while you still have your coat on will you cross the road for a pint of milk?'

'I said, does he think I exist at his beck and call?'

'And half a pound of marg,' she says.

I can feel the clogged sensation at the back of my nose again. Sinusitis? Blood pressure? Incipient haemorrhage? Brian Junior is watching me silently. If I break into a rage now, it will affect him for life. So Breffni says. So the psychologists say.

'Go inside now,' I tell him quietly, 'and play your games till Mammy calls you.'

London, at this hour of the February dusk, is a pearl grey flecked with the lights of empty offices. The watery blossoms of a false spring are everywhere. Across the road, the grocery shutters are halfway down, and I slip under them. They are that desperate for a sale they would unlock the place for me. At least I have the luxury of choice, which is more than they do. But choice depresses me now, and I drive it out of my mind. Better to be that girl in the lit cube of the Chinese takeaway next door – betrothed at fifteen, works six days and nights a week. Maybe we turned her away once at Aliens. Maybe she came here instead. She looks happy enough, with no choice.

'Fergus called,' Breffni shouts as I enter. 'He's on his way back.'

'That didn't take long.'

'Are you ready to eat?'

'I've got sweaty feet,' I tell her. 'I need to change my socks.'

'Put them in with the coloured wash. It's beside the bag with the white wash.'

The two bags are by the bedroom window facing east at the back of the house. Bits of Hornsey and Stroud Green flicker in the dark. A strip of neon, a square of light that is someone's bathroom, a couple silently shouting each other down in a kitchen. The backyards are choked with old wood and iron, wardrobe doors and derelict fridges. The fallout of old marriages. I press my brow gently against the windowpane to cool it. I do not open the window, for the London air would contaminate the immaculate counterpane of our marriage bed. Increasingly, I need moments like this, away from everyone, if I am not to get angry or depressed. I need to remind myself how good things are, in spite of everything.

'Are you coming down?'

'Yes, yes, I'm on my way.'

'Do you want to use the bathroom? Because I'll allow ten minutes if you want to use the bathroom.'

'No, no, I don't want to use the bathroom.'

Stealthily, from a folder in my bedside table, I take Du Moulin's journal, the entries I have flipped through in moments of distraction. Do I need it anymore? I could throw it away, but it would only come flapping to the window again, like a banshee. As soon cut off your own shadow. I put it back again and pad downstairs. My wife, son and daughter are eating, in front of the television. Ireland's defeat is being re-enacted, in slow motion. Silently, I slide in beside them and take the plate that is handed to me, at the head of the table.

Berkeley's Telephone

How many times have I rushed up these stairs, hearing my own phone in the depths of the building, feeding my key into the door on the first-floor landing while imagination ran ahead of me into the realms of wish-fulfilment – surely this is she, surely this is it – only to have it ring off just as I reached for it! To have it ring off, and the silence I live in now come back on me like a blow from a boomerang, and slowly, oh so slowly, to hang up my coat in the old absence of urgency, half-wondering, perhaps, would it ever blurt into life again and challenge me as in the past. And an evening ahead of me like this one, alone in my own head.

In the distance, trills, obligatos. A piano, a cello, somewhere in the building. The faint yelling of an infant, just woken for its evening feed. A man swearing, who has just dropped something. Tones of voice, reproachful, consolatory. Outside, the blazing klaxon of an ambulance passing away. That at least, by the way of a future. Or do I imagine it too? And as for Anna, who will not be coming back, was she anything more than a figment of imagination also? Yet I still feel her as a lack, and not simply because she brought in money. God knows how she stood my hysterical demands, on several planes of existence, as long as she did, across half the continent of Europe, unless I invented her myself in the first place. Anyway, she is no longer a reality, and life must go on. I understand. That is the way things happen. I understand, because I am a philosopher.

'An ansafone,' she said to me, on the day she finally snapped. 'That would solve all your problems, the abstract as well as the practical. Not to mention the imaginary.'

It was her parting shot, and it remains a strong argument even yet, though I have done nothing about it. Efforts of will are beyond me altogether now, as my inner attentiveness strengthens. Unquestionably, though, it would have quelled my terrible rush up the stairs on evenings in the past, though rarer and rarer now as fewer and fewer try to get through. How many of us are hiding from each other, I wonder, in this city of cities? For that is what Paris has become for me now – a paradigm out of Plato, a city of cities. But as to Anna's suggestion, an ansafone, though satisfactory in some respects, would carry snags. How many, for instance, confronted by that disembodied voice at the other end, that bleep and then the toneless darkness that is and is not a listening silence, hang back, and in the last analysis hang up? How many at the listening end, terrified by the bleeping otherness of that contraption, hang back under threat of an unwelcome voice, before picking up or leaving the receiver? Here we all are, in a vast electromagnetic field called Paris, playing cat and mouse with each other. Can any of us ever be sure who has hovered out there, on the brink of an ultimate communication with us?

'I will have to think about it some more,' I remember answering at the time.

'Well, don't hurry,' she muttered, bundling her stuff into a suitcase. 'Another two thousand years of European thought should sort it out. After six rented apartments, at least I will leave you with a telephone. That's progress.'

As I said, I am a philosopher. But let me qualify that at once. I qualified in philosophy, a long time ago, in the city of Dublin, among spoiled priests, a diplomat's daughter in jodhpurs, two would-be businessmen and the son of a drunken commissioner of oaths. And, of course, the gorgeous Anna. For three years we listened, an ever-diminishing audience, to the history of ideas. Little enough rubbed off on the others, for they have all been roaring successes. As for Anna and myself, having jettisoned all but our precious Berkeley in a secondhand store on the quays, we set off to piece together the conceptual map of Europe. Where haven't we pitched our tent, over the past ten years, attempting, at the back of our minds, to unite the ideal with the real? I am the ideal, Anna is clearly the real – which is why, unfortunately, we have parted. And now, so long after saying goodbye to all but my Berkeley, back the books have come to haunt me. Womanless, jobless, alone in a strange, strange city, I have at last become a philosopher.

'I'll go mad if I don't telephone someone,' I remember her saying one day, at the start of our wanderings. We were then, I think, in Italy.

'Remember Joyce,' I said from behind my desk. 'Sending a letter, getting a reply the same day. Keep faith in the written word.'

'In this place?' she shot back. 'It's worse than Tibet. Lend me some change for the callbox across the road.'

I watched her shapely figure, through the window of our studio, crossing the hot asphalt in the lamplit darkness, to hover with the others at the callbox. Like her, they were believers in communication. Every day, they waited in line to have a word with mothers, brothers and cousins twice removed. She would wait there a long time.

'What do we need all this distance for?' she asked when she finally came back. Sweating, beginning to undress.

'It gives us perspective,' I said, watching her body unsheathe itself. 'On our false society, our empirical selves.'

In fairness to Anna, I too was beginning to lose faith in the great Idea we had come there to seek. For the spread of pre-Socratic consciousness up from the Aegean was not all that it might have been, when seen through the cheap glass portals of a joint called the Academy of Learning, where we earned our keep through evening classes. If you see men in green, ignore them, the myrmidon who ran the place told us – it's only the police. If you see men in white, shut up shop fast – it's the tax inspectors. For the Academy of Learning ran on transient intellect, and a clientele with a short memory for where its money went. At a stretch, Heraclitus might have understood it. You never stepped in the same classroom twice, though you always got your feet wet. Men off the night-shifts, on the run from domesticity. Middle-aged women dressed like panthers, twiddling silver pens. Local cuckolds tapping at the windowpane, asking after their absent wives. Spumante bottles popped, dolci broken open. Cars coming and going, discharging the dissolute of the region. All who were fleeing reality, including ourselves, fetched up at the Academy. At night, when I locked up, cars were still rocking in the parking lot.

'Philosophy my eye,' said Anna, down to bra and panties. 'They're at it like rabbits around here.'

'When in Rome,' I said, rising from my desk and melting with her into the bedroom. For she could still get through to me then.

Berkeley's Telephone

*

My watch sweats, a fine fuzz of condensation under the glass. What time it is I cannot now make out, but thank God, it is getting late. The sounds are changing, diminishing, here inside the building where a great quietness reigns, and out in the rain-drenched street I came in from ages ago. The only other clock, the one on the wall, has registered ten minutes to two for the past week and a half, its pendulum hanging, a black metallic drip, under a dead mechanism. If I had an ounce of energy, I would get up on a chair and set it going again with a simple flick of the finger. But I have better things to consider. For instance, the esse est percipi of Berkeley. Here I am, in the depths of a building, no one to know if I am alive or dead. Well might it be said of me, then, that since nobody sees me I don't exist. I haven't existed since I was kicked off that homecoming bus an eternity ago. Lights, the sea of faces looking at me, the brief altercation over non-payment of fares, which God knows I have stopped doing forever since money became scarce. I have it all in my head, like an abiding vision. One minute zooming along in the social bandwagon, the next booted unceremoniously into nothingness. And the rest of them, solid citizens, barrelling on to their eventual destinations, suspending their terrors and disbeliefs – getting on with their lives, as the saying goes. But where do they go, or what do they dissolve into, these solid citizens, when the door closes behind them and they are alone in the night?

'If you had an ounce of faith in that machine,' Anna advised me one day, 'and stayed on the line, someone might amaze you by coming up with a job.'

'It's the Fantasias,' I confessed. 'They frighten the living daylights out of me. Five minutes in musical limbo while others are in there somewhere, considering my fate.'

'I'm fond of them myself,' she said. 'Especially the embassy one, when we ring for bail-out funds. If it wasn't for the coins running out, I could listen to them forever.'

'Watch out,' I warned her. 'Greater philosophers than you or I have vanished down that particular black hole.'

'Personally,' she said, 'I know the difference between a machine and a human being.'

I forget, now, which telephone box that particular conversation took place in. As it was all about employment, it must have been after we moved to the north of Europe again. A succession of images, as on a moving train, opens up instantly. Glimpses of winterbound border stations in the small hours, the train stalled between states and time-zones, the passengers pouring out to use the phones. Shouting into the mouthpieces, fishing in their pockets for loose change, stealing a march on the hours. A flurry of night-time snow under sodium light, with the crows hopping upwind, feeding on scraps, from tie to railroad tie. And myself watching, contented for a moment in that suspension of everything. For only upon entry to a given city did my frenzy begin again, my telephone hang-up, as Anna bargained for some job in a pharmacy we could actually see across the road. A slushy sub-zero street at dusk, our sense of exclusion deepening, in Munich I seem to remember. Or London in summer, the Bank Holiday coming up, the offices shutting, and the one public telephone occupied by a man telling his life story. And getting through eventually, but too late. A chain of telephone calls and missed connections, of falling through to the darkness in between, the darkness I am sitting in now, with the clock stopped and the dogs of the neighbourhood barking, territorial, making more sense to each other than the pair of us ever did, to each other or anyone else.

'Do you know what this is called?' she would say to me in despair. 'This is called falling through the net.'

True, the telephone on the street had by now become our operational base. Smashed kiosks with the wind whistling through them in winter, burgled coinboxes, boiling plexiglass ovens in summer, where we waited for return calls that never came, or were swallowed up in traffic-noise. Only today, zig-zagging aimlessly through the streets of Paris, I came upon one ringing and ringing unanswered in a void, and watched it in a trance, as all those years came back to me. Yes indeed, we had taken the open-plan concept of office-work to its logical conclusion and still things weren't moving. But I obstinately refused to have a telephone in any flat we then inhabited. Misapprehension was for the street. Indoors, we would exist only for one another.

'You're going mad,' she said to me gently, stroking my hair as we lay together in bed. 'Either that or you're the purest Cartesian who ever lived. Even Descartes would have found a way out of his own head by now.'

'We'll just have to go to France then,' I gasped out, choking back sobs. 'The home of Rational Enlightenment. Will we give it one last try?'

'Fine,' she replied, kindly but firmly. 'This time, though, I insist on a telephone.'

Mind you, the telephone we ended up with is nothing to write home about. A piece of white plastic, modern design, already quite obsolete. Nothing to the cordless wonders people in the streets and apartments around here bark into. A world of digital interconnectedness had already outstripped us, solipsists that we were. The phone purred, I left it alone in sheer terror. Anna picked it up and listened, there was nothing on the other end, and she hung up. Again and again it rang – the same listening silence and the click when she yelled into it.

'The boundlessness of the infinite,' I said. My worst fears were being confirmed.

'No,' she said, 'the dirty old man on the metro. He follows me home most evenings.'

By day, to keep us in rent and square meals, Anna went to work in a tourist agency. It was her looks that had gotten her the job, they told her quite frankly. That, and her telephone manner. Every afternoon at exactly three o'clock, she got in touch with me at the flat. Exactly three o'clock, for anything either side of that would have had me in the usual anguish as to whether to lift the receiver, leave it off the hook, or go out altogether and miss the one call that might solve everything once and for all. The only way I could calm myself was by imagining that everything, as Berkeley had said, was cancelled behind me when I went out – null and void, a blank. There was nothing there for anyone to get through to anymore. I was carrying it all in my head.

'That much at least is true,' Anna sighed, tapping my skull at the end of another day.

The last straw, I am afraid, was the destruction of our love-life. For if there was one thing, up until then, that could bring me down from my mental stratosphere, it was Anna in the flesh. Diogenes himself would have crawled to the entrance of his tub to get a better look if Anna's legs, instead of Alexander's, had blocked out his light. I remember with gratitude our vast *matrimoniale* in Italy, not to mention the calisthenic beds of Bavaria, and even at a stretch the one-and-a-half-person numbers in London, designed for the prevention of pleasure between the tenantry of whatever welfare hotel or rented room we ended up in. No, the rocket of philosophy, threatening burn-out, had a point of touchdown on a warm mattress. Until, that is, the calls started getting through to me – the wrong numbers, the ringings off, the shrill interruptions in the middle of lovemaking, destructive of what little instinctual life was still left to me after ten years' head-banging against the ever-receding wall of philosophical scepticism. For whether or not the telephone actually rang, I was now in a permanent panic, trapped between waiting for it, answering it or unhooking it and losing the critical call that would pull us through. Thrown back on ourselves we lay there in a hag-sweat, desperate. It was then, as a last resort, that Anna magicked up the Deus Ex Machina of the ansafone.

'That way,' she clutched at my throat, her eyes bulging, 'we lose nothing. We make love and the calls come through and all are recorded. Alright?'

'But philosophically …' I began.

'Philosophically, too!' she shrieked. 'Can't you see the genius of the thing? No more wondering, while you're away from it, whether this flaming hole-in-the-wall actually exists or not. For if a call is logged in our absence, surely to Christ that is a sign, when we come back to it, that the whole building hasn't evaporated in the meantime. An ansafone, you imbecile, is the true and absolute refutation of Berkeley everyone has been waiting for.'

I was taken aback. Imaginatively, I could see it all in a flash. Someone putting a call through to what Berkeley would describe as a void. No human answer, but a message left, and therefore, when the tenants of that space came back, the trace of something actually having happened in what otherwise might be pure absence. And then, by deduction, the whole place coming together again, solid and real and to be leaned on – the bed where we slept and made love, the tiled kitchen where we ate, the clock on the wall that whirred automatically every ten minutes, and yes, even the telephone.

'What if someone called,' I asked her, 'and left no message?'

'It would register anyway,' she said. 'You would hear a click. You would know if someone had been there.'

'But what if no one called?' I persisted. 'Wouldn't our place only exist then, if somebody tried to get through on the phone?'

'You don't want to believe me, do you,' she said bitterly, getting up from bed and starting to dress. 'It's not only your mind, it's your will that's diseased. Philosophy has ruined you.'

But I was thinking. If we left this room, this cell of a flat, this building, and went around the corner, not only would everything be blotted out, as Berkeley had said, but the ansafone too, with its disembodied voices speaking into a void, would be gone as well. There was, in fact, no elsewhere for the voices to come from or arrive at and be recorded. They were all there already, jabbering away in the depths of my own head. The voices that would rescue me or condemn me forever. How could I ever come back to an ansafone when there was no leaving or coming back in the first place? And this woman with the lovely face, who now was shouting at me from what seemed a great way off, had I not created her also?

'I will have to think about it some more,' I heard myself saying.

It was then, I remember, she threw the two thousand years of European philosophy at me like a piece of domestic china, and began to recede forever from my life, into a small, tearful figure bunched over whatever bundle of transient possessions was left after ten years in search of absolute truth. In philosophy, I knew then, there can be no real dialogue.

'I'm headed for Ireland,' she spat at me, slamming the door behind her. 'I believe it still exists, at least on the map.'

Maybe. Maybe not. But one thing is true. Between the mind and the body, the self and the other, the state and the individual, there is a dark well to trip and fall into, like Thales of Miletus with his head in the clouds, while Thracian maids like Anna, all health and realism, have a laugh at his expense. I am at the bottom of one such well. All around me, in this darkened building at the edge of the city, others sit at the bottom of theirs, all of us staring heavenwards at the same star, or the same lights of the same passing car. A hundred-year-old woman, deaf to everything, who lives behind the wall. A long-dead man who is still receiving letters. I will not be answering the telephone anymore, let alone installing an ansafone. But the voices inside me, twenty-five centuries of them, grow stronger all the time. And what they say to me is this. Keep faith with the written word, and leave the telephone be, whether it rings or not. I tell you, whoever you are out there, we are all in this together.

A Bigger Splash

I write this by the blue of an indoor pool, in north Germany. Outside, it is spring, but still cold. Inside, by the Hockney blue of the pool, the air quivers at body temperature above the mighty splashes of divers he froze on canvas. I could, if I wished, name the district, the nearby towns. The arabesques of vapour from the jets above the last American airbase, the rattling of military trains across the moors, would surely give away my whereabouts. But none of this matters. Nor is this a story, or an allegory of anything in particular, just a note about a man before I forget him, and the world forgets him. I am not a writer, I am a painter as he is. Maybe not even a painter since, unlike him, I am subject to the contemporary doubt about everything that has to do with form and expression. I have neither his arrogant self-belief nor his stupidity. If I make one concession to the formal distancing they call Art it would be to change his name. Or perhaps it is just politeness, since much of what I have to say about him is unpleasant. As he is Jewish, let me call him Benjamin.

'To defeat death, that is the great object,' he said to me once. 'Raise a family, raise several families, as I have done. Do great work, like me, on canvas, in celluloid. But defeat death, whatever you do.'

It is the only recorded comment of his that I have, squashed in my notebook between the addresses of German galleries and dealers in art materials. It dates from last September, and the first days of my stay here, when I had just moved into the white-washed artists' colony on the edge of the moors. He had been there for months already, through the grey rainy summer. He complained of it bitterly, for the way it afflicted his old bones. At the time, he was the only other person there, so my notebook entry reflects the exaggerated impression he made on me then. Reading it now, after the endless months of the northern winter, it gives me the essence of the man as I came to know it later, and the rain-sodden melancholy of those early autumn days.

'I have contacts here,' I remember him saying, as we sipped green tea in his studio and the rain slid down the big window. 'I may live in Israel now, but you know, I was born in Hanover. They still remember me as a wunderkind there, from before the War. They still honour me, you know, when I go back there.'

He went on about how loved he was by the young women at the local bakery, who vied with each other to cut his leonine hair, and how the local bank wanted samples of his work for their lobby, as a prestige exhibit. I listened vaguely, and watched the horses outside. They stood stock-still, fetlock-deep in water, manes plastered over their eyes, under sheets of rain crossing the bare land. Since the day of my arrival, it had been raining like this. I was depressed, in need of company. Any company.

'There are people who come here,' he said, 'and instead of

working, they stay in bed for months on end. Sheer depression. When they leave, having accomplished nothing at state expense, no one asks why, no one cares. That's how it is for people like us, in a rich society.'

There was one other artist, he said, a woman named Margit, in the third studio. She had gone back to her home town, near Essen, for dental treatment.

'But that was two weeks ago,' he smiled cynically, 'so maybe it's just an excuse.'

'At your age,' I asked him, 'wouldn't you be better off in Israel?'

'My wife,' he said, 'my fourth wife, you know, she wants me out of the way. She's a television producer, a busy woman. I talk to our daughter on the phone every other day.'

For company, he had bought himself a huge colour television. It blared away in the background while we spoke. Sometimes, he said, the noise of it bothered Margit in the neighbouring studio, and she asked him to turn it down. Sometimes he did, sometimes he didn't. His easels and tables were littered with half-completed work. He was in a storm of creativity, he told me. On the walls were a series of female nudes, erotically posed, flexing canes and chains. But the series on the easels and tables was what he was working on now, studies of flaming planets, incandescent in oranges and yellows, with futuristic machines swarming through the dark between them.

'It's my intergalactic series,' he said. 'Man has never before explored the artistic resources of outer space to this extent. My American dealers snap them up, for good money. I have hordes of admirers in America. I lived there for years, you know.'

I noticed, on the wall beside the nudes, a series of photographic self-portraits entitled 'The Many Faces of Benjamin'. He was a handsome man, even in old age, with a white mane of hair.

'People tell me I have wasted my talent painting,' he said at once, noticing I had noticed them, 'that my real talent is for photography.'

Crumpled against the skirting-board by our feet was a magazine open at a reproduction of a work, an installation, in the Museum of Modern Art in New York. He gave it a kick with the side of his foot.

'Bullshit,' he said contemptuously. 'Two pieces of wood coming together at an angle on the floor. That's not art, that's bullshit. Why can't I get *my* work into the Museum of Modern Art?'

I said I had to go.

'As you're not able to work at the moment,' he said as I was leaving, 'you could be useful to me. Come around in the morning.'

It was true. I was paralysed, intellectually, by the space and freedom accorded to me. So I filled those first weeks with routine errands, bumping on my borrowed bike along flooded tracks through woodland to the village, visiting local galleries, full of kitsch landscapes, and lending the old man a hand. He was working, simultaneously, in many media and he needed carriers for the blocks of stone or wood that were the raw material of his creations. I found myself, on dripping mornings, carrying these in and out of his house while the television blared in the background and he discoursed on stone as the first medium for representation. I could see, soon enough, that he was used to having people around who could be useful to him.

'Your materials have arrived', he said to me one day, 'with the stuff I ordered for myself from Dusseldorf. Now there is no excuse for you not to work.'

That was the beginning of my first good spell there. Maybe it was the fine October skies that set in over the moors, or my becoming used to the flat infinity of the landscape, or the return of Margit to the adjacent studio, but my heart lightened and I got down to work. Instead of bothering me, Benjamin turned his attention to Margit, whose washing-powder he stole for his own machine, who drove him into the village to do his endless shopping and banking, or left him at the bus-stop for his weekly trip to the city, from where he returned each time with new electric gadgets that littered his workspace. Sometimes, as I worked by the light of my big studio window, I saw him out on the moors, a tiny figure under a wide sky, being pushed along, on the rickety bike he had decided, in old age, he wanted to master again. And it was Margit who was doing the pushing.

I was working towards an exhibition, to be held the following spring in the local Rathaus. People would come, at least for the free drinks, and whether or not I sold anything it would add another line to my curriculum vitae. Over the years, I had worked towards many such exhibitions, and I had no illusions. I began with some coloured abstracts, then did a mixed-media piece with ball and chain protruding from canvas, on an environmental theme. Meanwhile, I photographed the landscape constantly, in all its changes of watery light, for another series. Then I went back to the coloured abstracts – dozens of them, several a day, on crinkled watercolour sheets that littered my floors and tables. Later on, I would decide which, if any, were worth framing. I didn't need to be told I was a blind man groping in the chaos of a time without definitions or values. I had heard it all before. Now, I cultivated a proper modesty, and simply got on with satisfying whatever urge it was in me that issued in these expressions, quietly thankful, under the fine skies of October, for the peace and freedom to do so. But Benjamin brought me up short again.

'There are too many ideas in your work,' he told me. 'Too much torture, too much confusion. Art, like everything else, is a matter of survival, of adaptation. Look at me. I am a brilliant artist, a Michelangelo of my time, because I respond to whatever demands and commissions are in the air. Because I am humble, I conquer everything.'

He was leaving for Hanover the following week. The urban council of his old home town was honouring him, with a commission to paint the animals in its zoo. Then he would continue south to Switzerland, where a ghostwriter was waiting to collaborate with him on his life story. He was glad to be going away, for a while, from this godforsaken moorland. He hadn't enough people to talk to, and he was getting stale.

'And yet,' he sighed, 'I used to have connections around here. Family connections. Out there, on the Friesian Islands, is where my third wife came from. A most wonderful woman, gifted in writing, in singing, in painting. But I wanted a child, and she died having it, at forty-one.'

In the halflight of an evening at the end of October, I watched as the cattle were shunted into barns for the winter. From then on, only the horses were left, cropping the hard ground that bristled white with frost in the mornings. I worked until late afternoon, while the light was good, and then went walking, under the wide cold sky. High above me, wedges of geese honked faintly, on their long migrations. A jet screamed past, from the nearby airbase. I had heard the trains at night, moving war material out of the East. America was leaving, after half a century in this corner of the world. The War, then the Cold War, the tensions that were Europe, had given way to an emptiness, a giant pause, the wide cold sky I was walking in, that Benjamin and Margit walked in, suspended between past and future.

'He wrecks my day,' she said bitterly one day. 'He steals my powder for his laundry, I lose my temper, and he walks away whistling, to buy his own. For the rest of the day, I am choked inside with anger.'

During those early winter weeks, she and I worked in our adjacent studios, not seeing each other, as is the German way, for days on end. At times, to break the isolation, I asked her in for a drink or an evening meal. She always accepted, but never returned the invitation. Behind her politeness, a hysteria manifested itself in the febrile designs that cluttered her studio walls. She had broken long ago with her own mother and father, with everything that represented the past, or even the present, of her own abhorred society. In Essen she lived alone, in a free flat overlooking waste ground by a factory, in return for tending the factory-owner's sheep that grazed there. She tried, with scant success, to sell her designs at textile fairs in north Germany, or to persuade company executives to sponsor an exhibition. Neither of us were under any illusion as to our commodity value. If we were allowed to exist, and to keep our hands clean, that was enough. And to keep our hands clean, in the exhibition we had now decided to collaborate on, we would have to exclude Benjamin.

'Have you seen his paintings of women?' she demanded. 'Have you see how he degrades us? Slaves and sex objects. And his attitude in real life is no different.'

As it happened, I bumped into Benjamin few days later, returning from his travels. It was a cold, grey morning in early December. I had come into town to escape, for a few hours at least, the isolation of the moors. There he was outside the railway station, among buses and trams, with his travelling bags. In early evening when I came back to take the bus out again, he was still there.

'I missed it this morning,' he said, settling beside me as we sped through the dark. 'But you know the saying – when you meet someone twice on the same day, they must invite you for a third meeting.'

'Come around at eight,' I told him.

When he came, he brought with him slides and a hand projector. His African series, as he called this one. Woodcuts of nude women, faces like primitive masks. Hardly original, even by his standards. They were motifs, he told me, for the Palace of Culture he had decorated in Dakar. The Senegalese had kept him there a whole year, on expense account, in the finest hotel in town. Eventually his wife had tired of the adventure and gone back to Israel. That was when he had moved in the woman who was the model for the woodcuts.

'Comfort,' he said benignly. 'That was her name. Comfort. Isn't that a beautiful name? I'd have brought her back with me to Israel, if I could have squeezed her through border controls.'

He was expecting a call from his wife and daughter. They always phoned around ten at night. He had run up a huge telephone bill, he said. He had even hired a cleaning lady. God knew how the stipend we were receiving would cover it. That could wait, though. Everything to do with money was fantasy.

'But an old man like you,' I asked him again, 'why spend Christmas in a place like this?'

'When I lived in America,' he went on, pretending not to hear me, 'I drew 25,000 dollars a day from my bank account. Once, in New York, I decided I needed a haircut. So I flew to Tel Aviv, to my favourite barber. When I showed up, he pushed all the other customers aside, and sat me straight in the chair.'

I didn't ask where the money had gone. Or the American years. There were wives there, children. Extraordinary exploits.

He had learned English in six weeks, to address an architects' conference in Houston. Afterwards, they had given him a standing ovation. And they would always want the Intergalactic Series there, if he needed money. Always.

'My life,' he said caressingly, in a half-dream. 'What an adventure. Money means nothing. Only images count.'

I saw him off, down the icy path. The night above was black, subzero, brilliant with remote galaxies. The moor was a sea of blackness, a silence broken only by the hoofbeats of invisible horses on the frozen ground out there. Between his place and mine, in the third studio, a square of yellow light glowed through a front window.

'Margit,' he said with satisfaction. 'She's staying here for Christmas too. We can have a party!'

And that is what we did, in a manner of speaking, three people at a loose end, in the darkest depths of winter, in that lonely corner of north Europe. By midday on Christmas Eve, Germany was shutting down. Our local supermarket and bakery closed at one. By four, with the light already fading, there was nowhere to get a drink. Even the railway tavern was closed, and the inn on the bridge that led to the moors was dark and silent. For lack of anything else to do, Margit and I walked on towards the horizon, into an icy wind and grey overcast broken only by bird cries.

'Nature!' she said contemptuously, pointing out the signs. 'In Germany everything is legislated for. Every bird, every insect is on file in some office.'

A man walking a dog came towards us on the path. Before I could greet him, she stopped me. Don't bother, she said. He is German. He would be too shocked at the idea of a stranger saying hello. The only other person we came upon out there was an angler huddled in the reeds, with his canvas chair, his baitbox and keepnet beside him, and his long rod suspended over a stretch of icy water.

'Not only do you need a licence to fish in this country,' she sneered, 'but you have to go to school to learn how to kill fish properly. It's because we're such a *humane* society.'

The following evening, in my studio, she served us pieces of badly cooked supermarket goose by way of a Christmas dinner. None of us believed much in anything, but I had a traditional Advent wreath of candles in my studio, given to me by the German administrator. *Gemutlicht*, she smiled coldly. I was on my guard, knowing the severity of her attitudes. But Benjamin, it seemed, could get away with anything.

'She does my washing up, don't you, dear?' he said, taunting her. 'At least I'm buying my own washing-powder now. You taught me that.'

Maybe it was age, or the generation he belonged to. Maybe he was the father she never had, since she had turned her back on her own one. But whatever her anger afterwards, she caved in to him at the time. And the old manipulator took full advantage.

'I'm going to Amsterdam', he said, 'for the New Year. Can you leave me at the bus-stop first thing tomorrow morning?'

'Yes.'

'And another thing. I have packages for dealers and clients. They must go out in the next few days. Can you deal with them at the Post Office?'

'I'm going away myself ...'

'Take them with you,' he insisted. 'But deal with them somewhere. Do you know Amsterdam?' he asked me.

I had been there twice, I told him. I preferred the Rijksmuseum, with its huge, dark Rembrandts, to the overcrowded and badly displayed Van Gogh collection.

'Never mind the art,' he cut in, 'what about the bars, the clubs in the canal district? Some of the most beautiful women in those clubs are friends of mine, did you know that? The owner of Sex Universe is one of my oldest friends, a wonderful man. That's where I'll be, on New Year's Eve. Surrounded by those who love me.'

'It's painful for me to say this,' Margit looked at him, 'but I'll say it. You remind me of the worst caricatures of the Jew in Streicher's *Der Stürmer*. I hate my own society. I try to be on your side. And yet, you disgust me.'

'Well, you know,' he said with savage satisfaction, 'Hitler was not the worst. He stuck to his big vision, even in the face of death and destruction. I like that in Hitler. Who is like him in this boring country today? Who has that vision, that imagination? And I say this, mind you, knowing what happened to my own neighbours in Hanover after I left them.'

We ate the rest of the meal in silence. By then, I knew enough about his past to fill in the missing links. How the wunderkind of Hanover, able to draw classically at three, had gone on to study art in Hamburg, and left for Palestine on the eve of the outbreak of the war. How women always looked after him, how his brilliant techniques adapted themselves to every medium, every situation, how he had made and lost fortunes. Now here he was, eating away between the two of us, indifferent to the impression he was making.

'Were you an only child? I asked him, as we said goodnight. 'An only child!' he echoed me. 'The only survivor! A disgrace to my kind. Is that what you want me to say?' Then he turned deathly pale. 'You will never know what the atmosphere was like, in those last hot days before the war broke out. It was eerie, like sleepwalking. Everything was already fated ...'

In the weeks and months that followed, between bouts of working towards the exhibition, I took trains through that Germany he had escaped from so many years ago, when it was still an intact system of marketplaces, the domes and spires of Protestant churches, and old rathskellers dozing beneath heavy stone arches. I saw ruin and reconstruction, the ersatz glitter of shopping streets raised on rubble and powdered bones. I was looking for a future to be part of, to take shelter in, in the money and drizzle of Köln and Berlin, in the half-built optimism of Leipzig, in the heartless wealth of the Ruhr. Surely there was space for my small dream in the minds of art dealers, in the vast foyers of banks, in the plush interiors of commercial galleries?

I returned from these sales trips to my silent studio on the edge of the moors. In the light off their bleak, snowy flatness, I looked again at what I had done, at what I was trying to do. Vision without technique, unsaleable subjectivity. I felt, not for the first time, my lack of formal training. Even the vision looked borrowed, derivative of a hundred others. I was a cold wraith, given shelter a while in the warm room of the German economy, its radiators on full all day and all night through the long winter, rich enough, indifferent enough to accommodate even zeroes like Margit and me, obsessed as we were with our harmless swirls of colour. Benjamin, whatever his cynicism, at least had technique.

'I'm engaged on a new series,' he phoned me up one day, from his studio. 'Saddles of the Wild West' – for a Bavarian who's paying thousands of deutschmarks. But that isn't what I wanted to say.'

'What, then?'

'It's the exhibition,' he said. 'I want my Intergalactic Series to be part of it. I've found someone who can compose space music to go with the pictures.'

'It's too late,' I said, cutting him off as if by accident.

It was the end of winter when he left. In recent months, I had distanced myself from him. In other words, I had disentangled myself from the web of his complications, which drew in everyone who came near him. His charlady, a middle-aged woman in a housecoat, who I met pinning out his underwear, filled me in on the chaos surrounding him, the lorries that would be needed to take away his unsold artwork, the nightmare of his unpaid bills.

'I'm doing horse portraits for local people,' he buttonholed me on his last day, 'to cover the telephone costs. Could you use a colour TV? You'd have to take on the rental too, of course, but think of the company it would provide while you work!'

'I bought an old black and white,' I told him, 'for fifty marks. It'll see me through.'

He wasn't going back to his wife and daughter in Israel. Eventually, of course, but not yet. He would finish the Hanover zoo series, then shuttle between his commission in Bavaria and his ghostwriter in Switzerland. His network of friends throughout Germany would provide for him.

After five long months, spring finally broke. The rivers unfroze, the birch trees came into leaf and the cattle were set free from their barns to chew the rough grass outside my studio window. The air thickened with insect life over standing water. The isolation, the bleak silence of the dark months gave way to swarms of cyclists out on the roads, to lines of speeding Volvos. The moors had come into their brief season as vacationing space for half of north Germany.

'Sunday painters,' Margit snapped. 'They own better easels than you or I ever will.'

On a warm evening at the start of May, our exhibition

opened. I stood, a glass of Mosel in hand, in the same suit I had worn for the past five openings. A local politician spoke about the continuing commitment of the northern Lander to art and artists. Cognescenti in silk scarves, painters unknown to me who arrived in Mercedes, drank at the good wines on the table. We even sold a piece or two each. To be precise, I sold two and Margit three, though hers were miniatures. A Hamburg dealer I had been phoning all winter agreed to consider a possible exhibition. He thought he might do a good line in the coloured swirls. Between one thing and another it was, if not a successful occasion – for what is success? – at least a useful one.

I had forgotten Benjamin when he phoned out of the blue one day. He wanted to know how the exhibition had gone, but I could hear, behind his voice, the need for company. And the sound of passing trucks. Amazingly, he was phoning from twenty kilometres away. A tiny hamlet, just off the Hamburg autobahn. He hadn't gone to Hanover, let alone Bavaria or Switzerland, or even Israel for that matter. No, he was living with his cleaning lady. She had taken him in, she was looking after him, catering to his latest visions, his schemes.

'The important thing', he told me yet again, 'is to have lived in a big way. To leave some trace of yourself before you die.'

That was two weeks ago. Since then, I have heard no more from him. Margit is back in Essen, applying for another studio somewhere this autumn. I go from one to the other, she told me as she said goodbye.

Since the exhibition, I have stopped trying to work. I spend my days here, by the indoor swimming-pool. I am alone, now, in the studios at the edge of the moor. No German artist wants to spend time so far from the business centres of Berlin and the Ruhr, where reputations are made. I have been told I can stay on, at least through the summer, and who knows, into the autumn too. My horizons, as always, are open-ended.

I don't fear the return of Benjamin. He will never come back, and anyway, like the man in the Hockney painting, he has made a big enough splash already. I sit by the blue pool, with its Schwimmeister in white shorts, with the tanned, lazing bodies of men and women given over to the physical, with the crash of divers through the glassy surface – and I hold him in my mind for the last time, before he vanishes into the dark depths on the other side of existence, that other side he fears so much, where he will meet the rejected ghosts of family and race, all the dead women he is accountable to. Or more terribly perhaps, nothing at all.

The Rembrandt Series

We have our own Rembrandt. A small one, to be sure, of doubtful attribution, but this is Dublin. An old man with a flowing white beard. I often used to visit it with McGrane, in the days before he was persuaded into early retirement. I never shared his lifelong obsession with the great painter, but I admired how he could relate to that bearded old man to other bearded old men in galleries throughout Europe, in the cities where he passed his holidays. For the civil service he was an intellectual, which is why, I suppose, he never got farther than Assistant Principal, and why the delicate balance of his nerves forced him out by the time he was fifty.

I have his notebook in front of me, with its jottings on art and other matters, from here, there and everywhere. It is all I kept of him after we emptied out his flat near Leeson Street bridge. It was the cleaning lady who found him, a day dead. I involved myself, as an old friend and former colleague. He had been an only child, and there was little family left to come up from Sligo.

I doubt if he had ever considered marriage, not because he was unattractive to women or they to him, but for his own reasons. There was, besides, the sweetness of his nature, as if something childlike had never been overcome in him by the rough and tumble of life the rest of us were accustomed to. He was, as they used to say around our corridors, one of nature's gentlemen.

The notebook. It has a hard, blue cover and yellow pages, unlined. The handwriting, recognizably by the same person, transforms itself over the years from the uncertain scrawl of the first pages to the devil-may-care lostness, the near illegibility of the last entries. In between, in varicoloured inks, are the steady and the shaky, the bits written in the silence of a hotel bedroom somewhere in Europe, and the unsteady jottings made in more public places. Trains, cafés. I know this for a fact, since I was sitting opposite him in a compartment on the night express from Amsterdam to Berlin, in September 1961, when the earliest entry was made. I had just annihilated him in a chess game in which my own aggression had surprised me, and the flat landscape was darkening as we barrelled east towards Hanover, two students on the long summer break, acquainting ourselves with Europe. The blue cover, the yellow pages, are what connect me now with that moment long ago, that landscape. But the mental horizon of the notebook entry itself is another matter.

18 September 1961
The Hague. Mauritshuis. Rembrandt self-portrait as a young man. Buttoned up in white collar, waiting to be unbuttoned by life. Energy, sensuality, in the full lips, the redgold hair.

20 September 1961
Amsterdam. Rijksmuseum. Rembrandt 'Jewish Bride'. Two betrothed,

in ceremonial cloth of gold. His hand on her breast. Proprietorial, but with grace, gentleness. A study in chastity.

Her. Him. The wedding photo on our mantelpiece in Sligo, that I grew up with. And later the Other One, brought so brazenly in to join us for supper. A foursome, painfully eating in silence. My childhood.

Later, T. and I along the canals, the chill streets. Women in the windows, tapping for attention. Acres of images, there on the shelves. Girls copulating with dogs on drawing-room floors. Horses in stables, being fellated. Man with a light mustache and artificial tan asking me, as a fellow friend of liberty, do I wish to see the harder stuff at the back of the shop? As if the bottom had dropped out of my mind, and something dark had risen to unbalance me …

Listen, T. laughs at me later, over soup with an egg floating in it, if you lived where I live, you'd see it every night of the week. It's just that you're not used to it.

Strange years. The Berlin Wall had just gone up, while in Ireland, for the first time in decades, barriers were collapsing that had kept us from the rest of the world, in the claustrophobia of our extended childhood – mine, McGrane's and the nation's in general. I was able, for the first time, to drain a long glass with the girl who later became my wife, in the smoke of public bars, though she still had to resign her job in the civil service when she married me. A few years later, with new money and freedoms flowing into the country under Lemass, and we might not have bothered with the civil service at all. I might have gone into business, McGrane become something in the Fine Arts. But we were the last of the cautious generations. Old hungers and deprivations, or the memory of them transmitted through our parents, still pushed us into the safety of state offices.

Five years later, just before I got married, McGrane and I

went to Paris for our last holiday together. Actually, there were three of us. Meagher, my deskmate in Finance, had decided to join us. We found ourselves in a cheap three-bedded room in a hotel in the Arab quarter, near Gare du Nord. Half my reason for coming had been to scout Paris as a possible honeymoon desti- nation, but I still remember that Easter as a time of constant rain which kept us off the streets, sprawled on our beds, getting on each other's nerves. As always when there are three, someone becomes the butt of the others' moods. That, as it turned out, was McGrane. I still regret some of the things I said to him then, considering his state of mind at the time, if I infer it correctly from entries like these.

27 April 1966
Paris, The Louvre. In the Rembrandt room Hendrickje Stoffels, his mistress, the dominant presence. High breasts, strong legs, mature folds of the stomach – a nude Bathsheba, having her feet washed. Watched by Saskia, the dead wife, from the opposite wall, with the aged painter himself, all bulbous nose (overdrinking?) and incandescent skullcap, in his framed self-portrait, at a safe, artistic remove.

The doomed triangle. Mother. Her endurance, back then. And the Other One, brought into our house, making free in front of me, with her big, white body.

Later, the women behind Les Halles. Leaning in doorways, out of the rain. Aged faces, fat bodies in openwork tackle. Anguish. I cannot go through with it. Trapped on a wooden stairs, in frozen, emotion- less space. Later, at the hotel, it is recognized in my eyes, McGrane, sneers T., you've got a problem. Not to worry, Meagher adds, at least you've avoided the Pox.

I admit it. Early marriage, as is so often said, brings on a kind of smugness. Is it the freedom to indulge, as often as one likes, in socially acceptable sex? Perhaps. But in a sense, those were smug years for everyone in the country. There was money around, a sense of optimism, infinite possibility. McGrane and I, in our different areas, moved steadily up through middle management, at times even refusing promotion because it seemed to lead in the wrong direction, and because there was the certainty of something better around the corner. We bought property, I out in Dalkey, a house for when the first of our three came along, and he the flat at Leeson Street bridge where he lived to the end of his days, his Old Master reproductions on the walls, his shelves full of art books.

At the time, however, I regarded him as a somewhat pathetic figure. I made remarks at the dinner table which my wife – my then wife – sharply corrected. I see it all differently now, of course. But good times make you blind. Only misfortune opens your eyes. For a while, McGrane dropped out of the picture altogether. I had other friends, politicals leaning to the left, espousing a nationalism I now feel embarrassed by. Our high point, I suppose, was marching with the crowd through Dublin, on that day of driving rain in January 1972, to chant outside the burning façade of the British embassy. We looked at ourselves in the mirror of the times. Our hair had curled and grown longer. McGrane, on a rare occasion our paths crossed, said I reminded him of a Rembrandt from the middle period – curlicued and complacent, as he put it, amid the trappings of prosperity.

It didn't last, for me or the country. Suddenly everything froze into the beginnings of that long disillusionment, that depression that has stayed with us, on and off, to this day. I got stuck at the same grade for over a decade, in a monotonous section, under an ill-disposed superior. My sense of myself began to buckle.

Trapped, I womanized. At night, my car joined those streams of lonely lights cruising the leafy precincts of Leeson Street, seeking a fleeting moment of escape. All this might have passed had I not, one night, out of what recklessness or desperation I don't know, brought home the woman I am still with now. I didn't need the horrible scene with my wife, or the hellish weeks of moving out that followed, to lay bare the truth of things. One look at my children's eyes was enough to tell me the marriage was over.

In this, my blackest hour, McGrane reappeared like an angel of mercy. For six months I lived with him in the flat at Leeson Street bridge, in that terrible interim between the collapse of my old life and what, if anything, was still to come. I got to know his art books well, the bachelor quiet of his rooms, his sweet nature. I got to know the stretch of canal above the bridge, and my face reflected in its weedy waters, the ripples merging with the new deepset lines, the etchings of experience, of middle age. We lived together like two bachelors, not intruding on one another, forging the basis for that newer, later friendship, so full of warm unspokenness, that lasted until his death. And was it delicacy that took him off for two weeks towards the end of our time together, and left me and my lover the freedom of the flat at that so important time for our subsequent life? I will never know, and his jottings in the blue notebook around that time cast no clearer light.

9 April 1981
London, National Gallery. Late Rembrandt self-portrait, dated 1669, and portrait of Hendrickje wrapped in white furs, strings of pearls. In both, maturity touched with the prospect of death. They stare at each other, from opposite walls, the 1669 painting a clear variant on its Paris counterpart. Her plunging neckline, inch of cleavage. She came into his life with a full cargo of experience.

Two months ago, turned forty. Visit Her often in Sligo now, with Him and The Other One long gone. I know it clearly now – the types I seek are Her in disguise. In first-floor rooms off Drury Lane, in backstairs cubbyholes in Hammersmith and Bayswater.

Honesty that comes with middle age. Compassion, towards myself as well. The loneliness replaced by self-sufficiency. Is it work that saves me?

Rembrandts. It is the selves, the wife, the lover that matter to me. Crises of sex and death, in those reds and golds, those dark oils.

My logjam finally cleared, in the early eighties. I moved out, at last, from under the shadow of my superior, into the grade of Principal Officer. I started to travel more. I can't say things in the country got any better, but by then I had stopped thinking of myself as in any way political, other than in the matter of pragmatic advice, the text of a reply to a parliamentary question. I was a man doing a job, and trying to keep the rest of himself on the rails.

Bit by bit, my private life resolved itself. After a spell when financial ruin stared me in the face, my ex-wife and I came to an arrangement, cold to be sure but manageable, that allowed me to set up in a two-room flat in Monkstown with my woman friend, as she prefers to be described. I had access, again, to my own children, and the younger two forgave me. But the eldest boy, Patrick, took the whole thing to heart, and though we see each other from time to time and our conversations are always civil, his nervous depressions, his problems at school and then at university, and his tendency now to solitude and introspection must be laid at my door.

Patrick was lost to me, but McGrane restored. Once a week we met for lunch at Merrion Square, in the restaurant of the National Gallery. I got to know a little of our own painters – Jack Yeats, whose wild colours put me off, the Roderic O'Conor nudes, which I fancied discreetly, and the Walter Osbornes, which I could imagine on our walls out in Monkstown. Upstairs were the Dutch, their winter scenes and spicy tavern interiors, and that old, old man of Rembrandt's. Only recently had I developed the patience to look and to contemplate, though with nothing of McGrane's practised eye. Sometimes, instead of looking at the paintings, I looked at McGrane looking at them. His hair was greyer than mine, and his face was lined. His gentleness, his lack of ambition, had got him no higher than Assistant Principal. It was as clear to his superiors as it was to me that his real life was elsewhere.

When the Berlin Wall came down, he was on the phone to me from his office. It was thirty years, almost, since we had been there, and the lid was off again. He was excited, for his own reasons. Art reasons. He was already planning a trip east. The Dresden Rembrandts were ones he had wanted to see, to get the complete picture. Not that Dresden had ever really been off-limits, but like many of our priest-ridden generation, he had held aloof, almost superstitiously, from entering what we had been told was enemy territory. The following autumn, when the fuss and euphoria had died down a little, he flew to Dresden, stopping over for a couple of days in Berlin. It is all there – what little there is – in the notebook, which still, despite all those years of odds and ends, has a third of its pages unused. The pages of unlived life, if life is measured by some natural span of seventy years instead of a self-completed entity, as some say it is.

2 November 1990
Berlin, Gemaldgalerie. Rembrandt self-portrait as a young man, 1634. Society fop in feathered tricorn. Thirty years back, I didn't notice. But why should I have?

A Hendrickje, leaning in a window. Chaste presence. Heavy folds of red and gold, on a dark background. Companionship, not sex. A woman to turn to, after the end of marriage, before the last aloneness. With time, understanding. With understanding, forgiveness.

4 November 1990
Dresden, Staatlich Kunstsammlungen Gemaldgalerie. Tricorned fop again, this time the young, married, successful Rembrandt. Self-portrait with his wife, Saskia, turned pertly round as she sits on his lap in what appears to be brothel or public house. Laughs, in complacent superiority, raising his long-stemmed glass to us, as if in answer to our toast to the happiness and success of his life, its sex that is both licentious and licensed by society. Young marriage.

And that other Saskia, two frames away, dated 1641. Probably the last before her death. All life withdrawn to the eyes, and the hand extending, as if from beyond the grave, a flower. To Him who will continue, in another life.

Outside, freezing dusk of Middle Europe. City of stopped time. Trams clang past, through the gloom of Hapsburg streets. A solitary meal, to the tunes of a jazz band from fifty years ago. Innocent society, like our own, about to be thrown open to the big, bad world.

No nightlife. But I need no distractions now.

Freedoms began to blow our way too, at the edge of Europe. It was as if, after decades of dirt, the sandblasting of our public life was at last under way, even as the public buildings of the city were being blasted clean. New forces were gaining the upper hand. I was too old to be marked by them, other than the hope I might some day divorce properly, but I saw them at work in my children, as they moved unafraid through open worlds charged with energies no one could predict the future of. The younger two passed out of university into good jobs in the private sector. Patrick, after much hesitation, followed me into the civil service, where he remains, clever, enigmatic, inert, on a lower rung of the ladder, showing no ambition but covering the cost of his independence in the small flat he rents on Anglesea Road, living alone, as far as I can determine, and only in touch with his mother.

Overnight, McGrane aged terribly. It was the death of the only person who really mattered to him that brought it on. The benign remoteness at work, the dress-sense slipping, the inability to get things done. I had seen it all before, a thousand times over. The father, I knew by now, had been out of the picture for many years. I said what I could, given the reserve and discretion that governed our friendship, and what I said amounted to the suggestion that he take the lump sum and get out early, that his stint was done. I knew by the way he allowed me to pay the bill for lunch, something he almost never did, that he agreed with me the time had come to let go.

The last entry is no different from the others, a casual jotting breaking off into nothingness. But was it any different for Rembrandt? I hold these written scraps to myself for the same reason, their sense of a life with its central tensions, through time and experience. What else has anyone to leave? Here it is, then, scribbled somewhere in the Rhineland, where he had gone two months after retirement, against the advice of his cardiologist, to chase down one more Rembrandt.

16 May 1994
Cologne, Wallraf-Rickartz Museum. A half-lit face, vanishing into the earth-brown night of its own background. Old, stooped, beaten, cowled in a gold wrap. On the face a half-smile, looking back at me. Asking for what? Forgiveness?

Reconciliation with the father (as in the Leningrad 'Prodigal

Son'). Alright then I forgive Him, wherever He has got to, on this side of the grave or the other.

Humid night over Cologne. But the fresh breeze down by the Rhine. Wide water, threaded with river traffic, slipping past in the darkness. Trains coming in, glow-worms of light, across the trestle bridge to the station. Alone, but not lonely. At peace.

We all vanish.

He must have got the gas-ring lit, for it was still going when they found him. If he had got his saucepan of soup onto it before the attack came, the smell of burning would have brought someone sooner. But he was sitting on the kitchen chair, emptying the tin into the saucepan when it hit him, according to the inquest. Massive, instantaneous, fatal. He knew nothing, and he was still in the chair, head slumped over, when the cleaning lady let herself in the next day.

One more thing. The tickets. Bus tickets, metro tickets, train tickets, from all over Europe and Ireland too. Stuffed in the back of the notebook, interleaved among its pages. He collected them, and one or two of them I recognize. The faded rectangle of a Dutch Railways ticket to Berlin. The yellow stubs of Paris Metro tickets. And this one, Córas Iompair Éireann, fifteen years back, before our friendship resumed. It was Easter. We had bumped into each other at Connolly Station, exchanged politenesses. He was carrying a large, gift-wrapped cake. He was going home, to Sligo. To his mother.

Debriefing

It was somewhere across town, on the other side of the river.
The Thonburi side, that ebbed away south towards Malaya, a
wilderness of shanties in the blood-smell of the abattoir, of weedy
klongs and lanes flooded under seasonal rain, so that the whole
place became a floating world in her mind, in her memory as she
drove, where children dived and soaped themselves in the brown
water, where houseboats rocked and women waded and the broken trunks of trees from the interior drifted seaward. Somewhere
in there, in that floating world, herself and Harkin had made love
for the last time. A hole in the wall, an hour of anonymity, their
naked feet, tormented by mosquitoes, twitching in the dirty
sheets. That was an age ago and the waters had closed over the
streets again. She would never again find that place, even if she
wanted to.

Tonight she was driving to Anders' place, on the good side of
the river. There would be other doctors there, specialists like herself. Diplomats and company men, the cutting edge of Western

interests. And a scattering of Thais, of course, from the upper echelons. Young men with exquisite manners and high, effeminate voices who giggled, irritatingly, whenever they were spoken to. No danger there, to a woman of forty. No danger anywhere, with Harkin back in Dublin, trying to dry himself out. No hope either of even adopting a child. They had killed that one off, the church committee, when the state of her marriage became an open secret. So what did that leave? Work, the dry satisfactions of ethical fulfilment, in the dust of refugee camps up-country.

Anders lived in a quiet, leafy *soi* at the wealthier end of Bangkok, on the fifth floor of a modern apartment block. Outside his door there were piles of shoes already. She liked that custom of leaving the streets behind and easing your feet on the polished hardwood floors of domestic space. Anders had found a nice place for himself, but he was pulling out now, like the rest of the Swedish medical team. He was going home, after two years in the camps. Everyone was going home, or moving on. This was his farewell party. He was taking with him his Lao batiks and his Khmer woodcarvings. And he was taking a lovely Thai woman who had moved in with him, who smiled and said nothing. If he had been good to the country, it had been good to him in return.

'You forgot your Impressionist prints,' she reminded him as he greeted her.

'They were never ours,' he smiled. 'The French team left them there.'

The prints hung on the bamboo wall of an operating theatre in Nong Khai field hospital in the far north of the country. She had sometimes wondered what impression they must make on the gunshot victims coming out of anaesthetic, unluckily caught in the searchlights on the Lao shore as they swam towards something called freedom. Did they think they had died and gone to heaven, that they were wandering now with Renoir's bonnetted women through the grassy meadows of a French summer, picnic basket in hand? For that, after all, was where they wanted to get to. France, America. The chocolate-box cover of the West, with nothing inside.

'It was Chet Vira who reminded me to ask you,' she said.

'I'm sorry about Chet Vira,' he answered gently. 'That was a pity.'

For they all knew what had happened. She was not going to be given Chet Vira. Another sponsor, a tall man called Clement Thompson who ran a TV repair business in Jacksonville, Florida, had been given an option on her. She had watched Clement Thompson, a greying widower, trawling the orphaned girlhood of the camps from Nong Khai to Mairut in the far south. He knew exactly what he wanted. Twelve to fifteen years old, long black hair like hers. And they would allow him more than one, the church committee. He had the paper credentials, she did not.

'They haven't moved her out yet,' she said to Anders. 'Any day now.'

For the moment, Chet Vira would go on with her old work. She would scrub the yellow lino floor of the operating theatre with other young Laos who aspired to medicine, whose studies had been cut short in 1975. She would read English books in the camp library she ran, its crude tables waterproofed with red plastic, in the dripping silence of the rains. She would incubate a future for herself, and the weeks would pass. The gates would open, a military bus would take her away with others to the transit camp at Panatnikom. Then there would be the Philippines, then Japan. After that, the tender mercies of Clement Thompson.

She mixed herself a drink and moved to the balcony, through the music and the chatter, the medical shop-talk she fended off

with a joke or a sarcasm. Humane deterrence. The Depo-Provera
issue. The under-5 clinics. All that was for another day, when she
would sit in his office with the camp commander and some college boy seconded into the United Nations, shivering, out of his
depth. She would fight, then, for the rights of the women to have
their babies, not to abort for political reasons or submit to preventive injection. She was a good fighter, but not now, not tonight.

She looked over the balcony. Far below, a child's air mattress
floated on the lit blue of a swimming-pool. In the distance,
through the trees, were the red and blue lights of Bangkok. Its
steady thrumming reached her, the lorries barrelling in from the
hinterlands twenty-four hours a day. Tomorrow, she would go
north again. Her driver would call for her at six, and they would
be out of the city while the sun was still gilding the klongs and
the monks in loose orange robes stood at corners with their cop-
per bowls, for the daily gift of rice. They would be through the
wet blue paddies and into the central hills by noon. They would
sit out the hot hours under a corrugated shelter, eating pork and
rice. By evening they would be in the far north, on the Mekong
banks, in the deep silence again. There she would stay for weeks,
working and sleeping, her only diversion an ice-cream in Lopburi
on Saturday afternoons, when she went for her post. Lopburi,
where the overgrown aerodrome was, the grasses hissing on the
tarmac that had launched American bombers over Vietnam.
Lopburi, where history and crisis had passed, leaving in their
wake an ice-cream parlour and a clutch of crossbred orphans on
the dusty streets.

Up there, two years ago, she had met Harkin. He was out of
his religious phase, but still driven, ethical. He worked for a tiny
aid programme, making artificial limbs. She had taught him to
drive in the evenings, on the hot grass-grown asphalt behind the

military base. Things had gone on from there, in the accelerated way they did in those days of high crisis, when work and relaxation were equally intense. He had insisted, almost instantly, on marriage. Only afterwards did she discover the hold the bottle had over him, and his wild insecurities. Within weeks, he was laying siege to the operating theatre. They were working her too hard, he insisted. She was his, she should be at home. As he fell apart, he started to live in Bangkok, on the wrong side of the river. Blaming everyone for everything. It was there, in the shadow of the abattoir, that the last act of their marriage had played itself out.

'It could have been worse,' Anders said to her afterwards. 'Remember that Australian woman who married the Hmong tribesman in Nong Khai? As soon as he had his Australian citizenship, he left her.'

Others drifted onto the balcony, drinks in hand. Babs, the wife of the Reuters correspondent. Kevin, the engineer from Dublin whose sense of humour kept them all going when the bamboo camps were first going up out of mud morass and the misery two years ago, at the time of the big influx. Anders himself. In a few months, they would all be gone. To other troublespots. Somalia maybe. El Salvador. Or off the merry-go-round altogether, debriefed at home. They would all be gone, except for her.

'I have a theory,' Anders said. 'Those who come out here to work in the camps are over-compensating for some inadequacy at home. Do you agree?'

There was the usual explosive reaction. Anders smiled, having achieved his aim. He liked to provoke. She had seen him do it over weak tea on hot afternoons in camps up and down the country, with medics, agriculturalists and social workers. Even the alternative types, the workers in natural medicine, put aside their massages and cauterizings to have it out with him. But she knew him too well to rise to the bait.

'Shut up, the lot of you!' Kevin shouted. 'This is my favourite song.'

Someone had turned the sound system up. A heavy Western beat, to which people were dancing. The young Thai women begged off, giggling. Jumping around, they called it, not dancing. And that was what it was, as she watched it from the balcony. A lot of Westerners jumping around on a hardwood floor, while their Thai hosts watched in embarrassment. All because they owned the world, or thought they did.

'Kevin!' a beautiful Eurasian woman was chased onto the balcony. 'Defend me, Kevin!'

He made a grimace of mock terror. She collapsed, laughing, into the seat beside him.

'Kevin,' she became serious, 'there's an excellent French restaurant I want to introduce you to. It's called La Grenouille. On Soi Kasemsan …'

She had seen this woman before, breezing in and out of camps in UN vehicles. Collecting material, she had said, for an article for the United Nations newspaper. What had brought her here in the first place no one knew. Was it the attraction of the rootless for the uprooted? Anyway, that is what they had given her to do.

'And do you know,' she was telling Kevin, 'Geneva have *finally* acknowledged my existence. After nine months, I'm on their payroll at last.'

She was the last of her kind out here. Sensation-seekers. The others had already left, up the Asia Trail or back to their Ivy League studies. The string-and-chewing-gum paramedics and nutritionists. The grow-your-own enthusiasts. That pretty Bostonian woman who slept with everyone from Nong Khai to Ko Samet. The funnyman who made the camp children laugh with his giant cardboard toothbrush and set of teeth, his Lao jingle for dental hygiene, and who later killed himself. Vague do-gooders from everywhere and nowhere, mixing vanity with compassion, disappearing once the glamour had gone, the world headlines. Anders of course was right. They needed the situation more than it needed them.

And her? For ten years now she had been on the circuit. First it had been Africa, a medical station at the end of a dirt road. Two black nuns – she had forgotten which order but their faces remained – dealing, on the spot, with bush emergencies. A scrubbed little theatre, at its centre an operating table. That strange articulated brokenness, like the shape of a deposed Christ, to accommodate the slippages and weird angles of the human body under surgery. It had stayed in her mind, that metal shape, like the touchstone of actual suffering. That, and the faces of the sisters over dinner at their tiny mission out there, in the hot insectivorous night. How their eyes burned when they spoke of Paul. Not Saint Paul, but Paul. They were beautiful young women, they had taken orders and they loved Paul. It was as near as she had come to a sense of holiness, of true vocation, the impossible blend of beauty and goodness that is tested by real suffering and not found wanting. Everything afterwards had been a falling-away, a complex of mixed motives, duty mixed with pride.

'I'm in line for a consultancy', Anders told her, 'in a Stockholm hospital. But we'll come out again to be married Thai-style.'

They shared the same specialism, epidemiology. They had worked together for two years with equal conscientiousness. So why had everything worked out so well for him and not for her?

Beauty and goodness had combined for him alright, but not in the way she had felt it ten years ago in Africa. *Verily ye have had your reward.* Yes, it was a good moment for Anders. Duty done, a beautiful woman to marry. He was holding, for a bright instant, the unimaginably high ground she knew from experience comes only once in a lifetime.

'Congratulations,' she said, raising her glass to him.

She had passed the point of no return. No children now, her own or anyone else's. No home either. She had tried to go home, twice. To fit in again to the narrow world of delegated duties that was hospital life in Dublin. The women she knew as a student had abandoned their medical careers to have families, the men had hidden their complexities behind the supernormal exteriors required for professional advancement. Houses, wives, rugby and golf. It was a place to retire to, Ireland, but not to live one's life in.

'What will you do about Sirilak?' she asked him.

Sirilak, Most Beautiful One, was the housekeeper he had brought south from Nong Khai when he opened up the Bangkok apartment. She had cooked in the American embassy in Vientiane before fleeing across the Mekong when Laos fell to the communists. She was a troubled woman, Anders said, a bit of a witch. Jealous of any other woman he brought into the apartment. Banging the food down wordlessly in front of them. Weeping in the kitchen, always sewing little dolls. Maybe she needed a child. But the same men she went with, always younger than she was, ran around with car-girls and bar-girls. Bangkok was no place for her.

'Yes,' he said, 'biology is hard on women. At forty it's over.'

'Do you know,' she said, 'I might have a place for her.'

'Because you're staying?'

'Because I'm staying. And not in Bangkok.'

She had taken a house in a village near Nong Khai, where the Mekong made a border with Laos. In the far north, in the total silence. There was an outreach programme she wanted to devise, against women's sicknesses. Preventive, not emergency medicine. It would take months, but the time was there, now that the crisis was past. She would drive each morning to the camp in a shroud of grey fog off the Mekong, past banana groves and cycling soldiers, through a slowed time in which elephants trundled, with logs chained to their feet. Everyone stilled in the dawn, as the morning prayer came over the public speakers. She would need someone there, to polish her huge teak floors, to cook and clean, to hover between the English that would keep her company and the local dialect that she would buy her vegetables in.

'I should warn you,' he smiled, 'she cooks only Western food now.'

The others had gone back in. Kevin and the Eurasian lady were dancing, while the Thai women looked at their feet. Couples from the aid agencies were necking openly while Anders' Thai fiancée sat alone. But he hesitated a moment before going back in himself.

'Your friend,' he said. 'Is he back in Dublin now?'

'In detox,' she answered. She had visited Harkin once, in the drying-out unit at Jervis Street hospital. She had brought him reading matter. They were still on speaking terms.

'What will he do next?'

'He has to make up his mind,' she said. 'We all do.'

That had been a sordid time, before he had left. Not only with her, in the short-time hotels across the river, but with others too, local women he brought home at night to his cubbyhole by the abattoir. He had had to be pulled out and sent home, bitter and disillusioned like so many others who had lost their way in the weird atmosphere of privilege and corruption that was the camps. What had she fallen for? Unhinged religious instinct, tipping over into mania? No, it was the common terror of anyone at forty – not of God, or of atrocity, but of simply being alone.

'I don't know what will become of him,' she told Anders.

But for her, there was always work. That was the good thing about work. It redirected consciousness outward, away from the self and its insoluble dilemmas, into the objective realm. There, she had been lucky. A profession which authenticated her, whose results were measurable and whose individual ministrations brought her the gratitude of the sick. She could walk away from what had happened, into the work that was waiting for her, but he would have to find some other way of going on, of feeling himself real and useful. His order wouldn't want him back. He would have to find salvation, like everyone else, in the secular world. In the everyday.

'Won't you be bored,' Anders said, 'or lonely?'

'I'll get more work done,' she laughed, 'with you out of the way.'

No, there was nothing much up there. She was under no illusions. Lopburi province was no more than the map of her own internal void at forty, dotted, here and there, with ice-cream parlours and ethical consolations. But at least there were the women at the feeding-centres, the wetnurses chatting like philosophers, their loose breasts heavy under their shifts. At least there was the kingdom of values. They would think of her as far away, Anders and the others, impossibly remote up there in her cloud-hung valley, with the brown shallows of the Mekong feeling their way, quotidian, through ages of striated rock. Bathing alone in cold pools full of fish that bit your ankles when you swam. Sharing a house with a half-mad cook. She would get their letters at Lop-buri post office and know that it was no stranger there than in their own lives, when they had woken after the crisis, and daily life flowed on.

Bird of Passage

I remember a bright clinic.

The noise and sunlight of the Hong Kong streets comes through the window. Beyond is the blue of a harbour riddled with sampans. The examination, brief as it is, is complete. The blue flame of a Bunsen burner, over which slides and instruments have been passed, is extinguished. The doctor, a cheerful Australian, is saying It's our Old Friend I'm afraid, and calling to his laboratory aide for a shot of strep. Picked up something in the nightclubs have you, he says as the point goes in. I don't even need to reply, but think of Yokohama we sailed out of three weeks ago – I was on deck with the officers since I alone knew that channel well. Or Taipei, with its giggling girls speaking Americanese. Or Manila, where the women are Catholic, guilt-ridden. Was it the blind boat? he asks me, referring to that sad place in the harbour where women blind since childhood are kept, for their heightened sense of touch. I wouldn't go near it, I tell him. I hate the exchange of money for sexual favours. He's the first to have spoken to me like a human being for any length of time. He plays piano in his off-hours, at the honky-tonks. That's how I was referred to him. Do you catch colds yourself, I can't help asking. Oh no not me, he laughs, I always wear an Overcoat.

If I could talk to him now …

But I did take his advice. I'm not a fool. I knew I had burned out the best years of my life already. I needed to rest a while and think the future out. My thirty-fifth birthday had come and gone. The shipping company was decent. They saw the state I was in and flew me back to Europe in the spring, with an option to sign on again this autumn if I felt up to it. I have always liked working with the North European shipping lines. They respect us men. You don't have to spend your days saluting officers. And they fly you home too, at the end of your contract. Home? For once I came back to Ireland, instead of cooling out in Hamburg as I normally would between voyages. It was early June. The weather in Dublin was blue and warm as we taxied to the terminal. I felt at once the homelessness the soul avoids all its life, but sooner or later must come back to. At the end of the corridor, an old man who seemed to have dropped like a disillusioned angel into his crumpled black uniform held open a door. If I was you, he muttered, I'd go back where I came from.

Me? I came from nowhere. And I am going nowhere. Of this city I remember only orphanages, a backstreet childhood where the word Diphtheria was on everyone's lips and old men followed the coffins of their own children to the grave. What else? Brown thruppences gleaned from smashed telephone booths. The hard green baize of pool tables I spent the night on. And running away from it all at twelve – in the wrong direction. To Belfast of all places, through Amiens Street station where the lazy officials took me at my word and let me on the train. No one cared, either way. It was the Fifties. I wandered through a maze of redbrick streets that was Belfast. Some political murder had happened. By nightfall I was in the police station, sitting across a table from a man who was smoking and looking at me. How's the Republic these days, he said to me coolly. Then he took out a packet of sweets and gave me one. Then he took a revolver from his desk and placed it on the table between us. Go on, he said, pick it up and aim it at me. I did, but with difficulty, because the bloody thing was almost too heavy for me to hold with two hands. Now pull the trigger, he said. I squeezed as hard as I could but nothing happened. Good, he said, and took it away again.

The next day, they had me back in the Republic. When I left again, it was in the direction of the high seas, and it was for good.

Seamen's Missions ... I never could stand them for more than a day or two. Lonely souls tread water there, shoaling into the net of Christendom. The religious bring in women to dance with you, until the stroke of midnight. Then you thank them for so graciously offering you their society, as they disappear forever from your life.

It was early summer then, and the city was full of abandoned rooms. I took a cheap one south of the Liffey, at a tenner a week. The landlady, a woman with bleached hair, dark glasses and an English accent, pulled stacks of empties out from under the sink. The last one here was a divorcee, she said. Just passing through, on her way to London. I'm the same ma'am, I told her. Obviously it didn't bother her, for she started on about the state of the lampshade – as though someone had made love while hanging from it was the expression she used. Some stupid, tantalizing remark, the stock-in-trade of these people everywhere. She dusted it down anyway and left with a week's rent in her hand, promising to send someone in to give the place a lick of paint. I put a few books up on the shelf, lay down on the bed and watched a square of afternoon sunlight moving along the wall.

For most of the next week, I slept. By the time I felt ready to start moving around again, I knew what kind of place I was in the middle of. During the day, dead silence. After dark, the sound of people rousing themselves. Mutterings first, then shouts and curses, the crash of furniture. Small piteous weepings, voices crying Kitty Kitty here Kitty Kitty Kitty. In the hall, the payphone ringing. Footfalls pounding down the stairs, followed by brogue shouted down the line to Limerick or Roscommon – no jobs, no money, no jobs, no money. Through the walls and floorboards smells drifted – sharp and spicy, the smell of vegetables cooking in the small hours, or the sweetness of perfume from below stairs where a penniless drunk started in on his wife's cosmetics. In the hallway people passed. I began to connect the voices with the names, the sounds with the forces that produced them. Dark forces they were, the forces of frustration, wreaking havoc after dark, while the Republic slept.

I am not a lonely man. I prefer my own company, but I like to feel there are people around me too. When I think of heaven, I see myself circulating endlessly in a city crowded with people who I know without asking are of the same mind as I am. The man who did me the greatest favour in life was the man who introduced me to reading. He was a mate on one of the early ships I worked on. Every so often he would be released for courses of special study. He used to pass the stuff along to me, and together we would gut it. In a sense, books saved my life. They structured my mind at a time when it was nothing but a confusion of people and circumstances, without religion or political belief to hold it together. Now I am rarely without a book of some sort – any sort, provided it corresponds to what a man in possession of his senses can imagine or come across as he goes through life. Otherwise, I would do with it what the soldiers who guarded me through two long months in an African jail used to do – tear out its pages and smoke them, philosophically, as cigarettes.

In the room next to me, a teacher was living. Every morning, a smell of bacon and eggs wafted through the thin partition between us, and the voice of a radio newsreader. After he left, there was silence for an hour or so. Then the creak of someone bestirring himself in another bed – his unemployed brother. Then the door slamming as he went out, and silence for the rest of the day. In the evening, one returning after the other, and the sound of an argument in rising tones of recrimination. Did you even *look* for work? a voice would begin. There's nothing here, I'm going to England, the answer would come. You think England is going to support you the way the rest of us look after you over here? You think I'm going to carry your dead weight for the rest of my life? And what about the money you already owe me? Ah stuff it for once can't you, the answer coming again. Then the door slamming, and again the silence. Hours later back in they would come when the bars had closed, the voices mollified now, conciliatory. Do you know what, one voice would say – if I were to bet successfully three times a week, I'd make as much as the Minister for Finance. If the politicians paid more attention to the betting system the economy would be up and running in no time, the other would reply. And on they would go into the night, the small voices of the Republic talking to itself, consoling itself, singing itself to sleep.

One night I had to force the lock for him, this teacher. He had left his keys inside. After that, he was my friend for life. I discovered he was going to get married later that summer, which may have helped his attitude to me a little, but he fell over back-wards to be kind to me, even offering me the use of his car, a battered old Anglia, if I ever needed it.

Shortly afterwards, an old problem recurred.

People I meet sometimes say to me You should marry and settle down, you'd make a good husband for someone. But it doesn't happen like that, unless you belong on one of the levels that make up society anywhere. I belong on none of them. The women I sleep with are classless like myself, the daughters of everyone and no one, coming in cold out of the north European night, or met by chance in an African transit lounge. There they are, spontaneous as the moment of need that creates them, giving and taking freely, equally, emerging and disappearing in that dark underworld where they thrive off you and you off them, the carriers and transmitters of intensity and the price of intensity – flesh, beauty and the seed of experience they have in them.

And so do I.

She was quiet, this one. Beautiful too, with intelligence and grace, occupying a barstool in a Camden Street licensed premises I happened into. Attracted by the book I was reading – both of us freefalling, in our own way, through the dark hours. Her place was one of those Corporation flatlets at the back of the main streets, where bicycles clutter the hall and other tenants sleep unaware of anything in their midst. I could kill you, she said to me with a smile. I had a fair idea what she meant, even then, but if you weigh every risk and yield to no impulse, you might as well not exist. Afterwards, I smoked a cigarette and watched her feeding a scatter of goldfish in a long tank on the mantelpiece. They took away my children, she said, and put them in custody. I suppose my life is ruined, but I'm not afraid and I don't feel guilty. I just don't care anymore.

She too turned out to be a carrier.

One hot afternoon at the end of June, I sat across the table from a young doctor in white coat and sandals. Tell me a little about yourself, he said nervously, trying to sound like a man of the world. As gently as I could, I laid my 'history' before him, while his pen travelled across blue and yellow medical forms. Fresh from his world of anatomy charts and rugby club dances, he was doing his best. The place was awkwardly silent, with that cleansed, almost religious silence peculiar to hospital clinics at the end of the day. Wait a moment, he said, and went to fetch his senior man. They laid me out in a sexless calm, while their fingers probed and pressured. They withdrew, two priests in white coats, talking the Latin of their profession. The older one came across briskly and said Of course what you have is Neutral probably, not Malignant at all, but we'll perform an excision anyhow. Samples to the laboratory please, and see the nurse at reception for a date. A while later I was walking east again, through the complex of streets that was Dublin on a summer evening. Women were packing vegetables in boxes, stowing away their weighing-scales. Shops were closing, lovers drinking out on the pavements. I, in my strange state, drifted unnoticed through it all – neither better nor worse than any of it, just somehow realer.

Two weeks later, I was wheeled down a disinfected corridor, my doped body in hospital shift and skullcap, tagged like a corpse with a name but no fixed address and no religion. Ceilings passed. There was a descent in a liftshaft. I was strapped to a table. The kind face of the porter gave way to a circle of faces in masks, grey as death. Then they had the pentathol going through me, but I wasn't going under quickly enough for them. The worried girlish voices behind the masks were saying Sister Sister he's not responding. A voice from behind my head said Check his name on the tag and talk to him by name into sleep. I'm perfectly alright, I heard myself booming at them with the reassurance of a god, from the preternatural calm at the centre of myself. I'm *already* gone …

Hours must have passed. They were waking me up again, the anxious hands of nurses and student doctors. I was back in the rinsed antiseptic light of the public ward. If pain is felt, morphine may be given, a voice was reading from a chart at the end of the bed. No thank you, I interrupted. Pain or no pain, I was discharging myself at the end of the day and I wanted my consciousness back intact.

Propped in their beds, middle-aged men with hangdog expressions stared over at me. Bladder and prostate cases, up from the depths of Ireland for a day or two, grateful for the institutional peace. In their faces defeat was written, an immemorial dependency. They had guessed what I was in for. For Religion I had None, on the tag around my wrist. I was an alien, with blood on my thighs, and the yellow ash of cauterization.

The weeks of summer passed. Halcyon weeks, with a Mediterranean light over the blue of Dublin bay, and the white dust in the vacant heart of the city. The awnings were out, the tables were set on the pavements. In the purple shadows of Stephen's Green, young couples walked with their prams and children. Life was suspended in the blue of an eternal moment. On the rocks of Sandycove, in the noontide haze of the South Wall, old men sat naked as the days of Greece, reading newspapers, talking sport and politics. For days on end I sat and swam out there, still as a migrant bird between past and future. I was coming from

nowhere, on my way nowhere. In between, there was bitterness
or magnanimity. I chose magnanimity.

My body was healing. My mind was at peace. For the first and
last time, I looked at the city of my birth, to which I would never
return. Beggars were on the streets, and the hysteria of wealth
based on nothing. Drunkards outside churches sang the national
sadness. In the patches of waste ground at the edge of the city,
the fires of gypsy encampments burned. Through it all I moved,
half an outcast, half a god, in the hot light that for a few summer
weeks bathes the streets of Dublin in a Greek strangeness.

Warm nights … the sexes were seeking each other out, in
dancehalls thrown open to the streets, guarded by thickset men
in dinnerjackets. Strobelights picked out couples on the dance-
floor. I too waited there, drink in had, for someone to material-
ize out of the darkness. A nurse dreaming of house and children.
A hardvoiced Arnotts sales manager, with plans for her own bou-
tique. A beautiful stray from the university circuit, whom I could
talk up to with my smattering of booklore. Who are you? What
do you do? they all eventually asked. I am what you want me to
be, I always answered, and left it at that.

And suddenly it's autumn.

Already I can feel a change coming over the streets and parks.
I don't mean that sudden deepening of the breeze that sets in
around the middle of August, littering pavements with the first
dead leaves. Or the early wasp in my room, nudging me awake at
first light on a September morning, softly beating at the windowpane to be gone. No, I mean the people – how they seem to
be drawing together imperceptibly, out of some hidden instinct,
sensing the cold that is somewhere ahead of them. There they all
are, in shops and cafeterias, the families more completely family
than before, and the university students, back from wherever the

summer months have taken them, comparing odysseys over end-less cups of coffee, waiting for Michaelmas.

Only last week, the landlady knocked on my door and said I have two nice Nigerian gentlemen who would like to look at your room if you're thinking of leaving. The way she said nice Niger-ian gentlemen, with her English accent, I knew she thought them the scum of the earth. As far as I was concerned, it wasn't the same house once the teacher moved out to marry and begin his new life. Even his brother had moved on, to try his fortune in England, I suppose, or crawl back with his tail between his legs to the family kitchen in Roscommon. That was the kind of house it was – weekly visits from a fake aristocrat talking endlessly about her husband Captain something or other who owns a whole chain of such houses and sends her around to collect rent from riffraff like us.

Today at the clinic the line of outpatients moves slowly along the wooden bench of the waiting-room, beneath a statue of the Virgin Mary and a blackboard chalked with the words of hymns for the invalided and dying who take mass here. One by one, our names are called by a nurse, and we are directed to this or that examination room.

The doctor who confronts me is a foreign intern – small, portly and cheerful, with a shock of black hair and a loud floral shirt under his housecoat. He shuffles through a pile of blue and yellow forms with typewritten inserts that represents the history of my tissues in this institution. Climb up on the daybed there, he says, and let's have a look at you. In the middle distance a stonefaced nurse hovers, disassociating herself from both of us. I have good news for you, the doctor says eventually. You are a nor-mal man. I've been normal all my life, I feel like shouting at him. Abnormally normal. That's my tragedy.

Now we are at his desk, and the talking continues. Something happened to me once, he says, with someone I met in a Glasgow cinema. I tell him of the boredom of life below deck, the whole backbreaking business of painting a ship from end to end that has to be started again as soon as it's finished. All experience is good experience, he says, not hearing me, as long as we learn from it. Now he is talking about someone he met in a lift-shaft in Geneva. All of a sudden, the essence of my life is flooding this senseless conversation. Take it easy, he says, aware that something has broken in me. I am talking ecstatically, uncontrollably, while the white, ghostly presence of the nurse hovers between us, waiting for instructions. She can wait forever, as far as I am concerned. For time is suspended now. We are in the realm where events conflate themselves and intensity is all that matters. The jungle heat of the docks after we had waited a week in the breezes off Port Harcourt to put our goods ashore, the women who came out to meet us in the estuary and stayed on board for days while the officers turned a blind eye. Or that place on the Klong Toey waterfront, on the other side of the world, where the currency of understanding passes between those like myself in transit – at this very moment, I see what is happening there. A woman does a slow dance, her body reflected to infinity by cheap mirrors. A man in a turban is quietly drinking. A customs official sleeps with his head on the table. Snatches of spontaneity and laughter, a breathing-space of souls, a beat that goes on and on. Outside, the flash of harbour lights, the blaze of phenomena in a world closed in by the steady drip of monsoon rain, with the horizon somewhere beyond, and the prospect of a death no more terrible there than here or anywhere else.